Blood
and Grits

Books by Harry Crews

GOSPEL SINGER

NAKED IN GARDEN HILLS

THIS THING DON'T LEAD TO HEAVEN

KARATE IS A THING OF THE SPIRIT

CAR

THE HAWK IS DYING

THE GYPSY'S CURSE

A FEAST OF SNAKES

A CHILDHOOD

BLOOD AND GRITS

Blood
and Grits

Harry Crews

HARPER & ROW, PUBLISHERS
New York, Hagerstown, San Francisco, London

"A Walk in the Country," "Charles Bronson Ain't No Pussycat," "Going Down in Valdeez," "The Knuckles of Saint Bronson," and "Carny" originally appeared in *Playboy*.

"L. L. Bean Has Your Number, America!," "The Most Kindest Cut of All: Vasectomy," "Tuesday Night with Cody, Jimbo and a Fish of Some Proportion," "The Car," "The Hawk Is Flying," "Television's Junkyard Dog," "The Wonderful World of Winnebagos," "Running Fox," "Leaving Pasadena—Resume Safe Speed," "The Trucker Militant," and "Climbing the Tower" originally appeared in *Esquire*.

"Tip on a Live Jockey" originally appeared in *Sport*.

FIRST EDITION

Designed by Janice Stern

Library of Congress Cataloging in Publication Data

Crews, Harry, 1935-
  Blood and grits.
    I. Title.PS3553.R46B5   814'.5'4   78-54605
  ISBN 0-06-010933-5

79 80 81 82 83 10 9 8 7 6 5 4 3 2 1

Contents

A Walk in the Country 1

L. L. Bean Has Your Number, America! 24

A Night at a Waterfall 31

The Most Kindest Cut of All: Vasectomy 45

Going Down in Valdeez 51

Tip on a Live Jockey 79

Tuesday Night with Cody, Jimbo
and a Fish of Some Proportion 88

The Car 96

The Knuckles of Saint Bronson 101

The Hawk Is Flying 127

Television's Junkyard Dog 134

The Wonderful World of Winnebagos 152

Carny 158

Running Fox 182

Leaving Pasadena—Resume Safe Speed   190

The Trucker Militant   195

Climbing the Tower   208

For Harvey Heller,
without whose kindness and generosity
it all would have been more difficult

"I can't believe that," said Alice. "Can't you?" the Queen said in a pitying tone. "Try again; draw a long breath, and shut your eyes."

—Lewis Carroll,
Through the Looking-Glass

A Walk in the Country

We came out of Johnson City, Tennessee, three of us in the cab of a pickup truck with an enormously fat mountain girl who worked in a Frosty-Freeze ice-cream parlor. She had on her Frosty-Freeze uniform, and a vague but insistent odor of sour milk floated out of the deep creases of her body. She lived in Erwin, Tennessee, which practically straddles the Appalachian Trail, and drove the pickup into Johnson City five times a week to the Frosty-Freeze, a distance of some fourteen miles.

What we were doing fourteen miles off the trail in Johnson City is boring and need not be related. Enough to say that Dog and I wanted to get drunk, and more than that, we wanted a decent-sized city to do it in. Dog and I were good and drunk. Charné was disgusted. She didn't mind the drinking particularly, even drank some herself, but she thought a sixteen-hour bout from one bar to the next was tacky and middle-class, showed—she said—poor taste. We kept our packs on while we hiked around Johnson City, getting drunker and drunker. It's a God's wonder some Grit didn't kill us. Grits don't take to long-haired freaks wearing packs in their bars.

We were squeezed tight inside the cab of the pickup. The girl, whose name was Franny—it was stitched over the pocket of her Frosty-Freeze uniform—took up half the seat by herself. Charné had to sit in my lap. Dog sat squeezed into Franny, his entire body imprinted and half-buried in her fat. He didn't seem to mind it.

He'd been licking the side of her neck. She didn't seem to mind

1

it, or even notice it, for that matter. I wondered if maybe there was an old residue of Frosty-Freeze ice cream slathered up on the side of her neck. It was July, and I was sweating pure vodka into the little space between our steaming bodies and the windshield. The smell of sweat, vodka, and sour milk had made me incredibly thirsty. I was beginning to sober up and longed desperately for a beer.

"You reckon we could stop and get us a beer, Franny?" I said.

"I could use a beer myself," Charné said. "It stinks in here."

"I ain't familiar with beer joints," said Franny.

"Ah, come on, Fanny," Dog said, taking a long lick at her neck. He'd called her Fanny ever since we got into the truck. She didn't seem to mind. I noticed the place he'd been licking on her neck had changed colors. It was now considerably lighter than the rest of her neck. Dog's tongue, when he ran it out, was kind of pink. I thought he might have a little pancake makeup on it.

"We nearly to Erwin," she said.

Dog licked her again.

I said: "I don't want to go to Erwin. I don't care if I ever get to Erwin. I want a beer."

"It *is* one li'l ole place up here not far they say sells real cold draffs," she said.

"I believe that's the place we been looking for," I said.

"Fanny," Dog said, "damn if I don't think I'm in love with you."

She stared grimly through the windshield at the highway. "I been divorced oncet already and got two younguns."

"Hell," Dog said, "I don't mind. I don't give *one* shit."

"I could never care for a man that cussed," she said.

"I could quit," Dog said. "I got iron willpower. I quit smoking before."

She turned to look at him, her face a mask, as if she were considering some grim alternative, as if maybe he was a doctor and had just told her she had cancer but that he could take care of it for her.

"All right," she said. "All right, then."

She looked back toward the highway, and as she did, she raised her huge arm and drew Dog in. His head disappeared between the wall of her arm and the massive lump of tittie.

With Dog's head clamped under her arm, Franny let the old Dodge pickup have the rest of the gas pedal, and we shot down the highway for another couple of miles, where she swung into a red-dirt parking lot beside a wooden building. There were only two other cars parked there.

She slid to a stop and looked over at us. "It don't seem like much," she said, "but they got good cold draffs."

A cloud of red dust sifted over the truck and came to hang in the air between us. Dog fought his way from under her arm, a mashed look on his sweated face.

"We here?" he said. "This it?"

Charné was already out of the truck. I slid down behind her.

"Me 'n' him's gone talk a minute," said Franny.

"Go on and order us a beer," said Dog. "We'll be right in."

"Don't order us no beer," said Franny. "We'll be there torectly."

She looked like she was going in for that cancer operation and Dog looked like he wasn't real sure what the hell was going on. We left them sitting there, her arm still weighted around Dog's neck, and went on into the bar. After the bright sunlight, it was dark inside. Plain wooden floor, unpainted walls, about ten bare tables with chairs, a long unpainted bar with pickled pigs' feet floating in jars and pickled eggs and potato chips on a dented rack.

One man sat at the bar, wearing a neatly pressed blue suit and a snap-brim hat with a red feather in it. He was slender and dark and gave the impression of tension, although I didn't know why, because he didn't move, didn't even glance at us. A bald man in a T-shirt read a newspaper behind the bar.

We went to a table by a window and sat down. I was watching the bartender. He looked up at us and then back at his paper. He didn't move off his stool. I had thought there might be some breeze by the window, but there wasn't. Through the screen we could look directly into the cab of the truck, which sat baking in the hard sunlight no more than fifteen feet away.

Charné glanced at the truck and said: "We ought to move away from this window."

"It's all right," I said. Only Franny's head was visible in the cab of the truck.

"It's embarrassing," she said.

"They're just talking," I said.

I wasn't about to take another table. I wanted to see. That's the way I am.

The bartender still had not moved, except occasionally to turn a page of his newspaper. The man in the blue suit had not moved at all, and I realized that's what made him seem tight as sprung steel. He didn't turn his head, hadn't touched the full glass of beer in front of him, didn't seem even to be breathing.

"That's a strange one up there in the suit," I said.

"This godforsaken place'd make anybody strange," said Charné. "I'll flip you to see who wakes up the bartender and gets us a beer."

I lost and went up for a big pitcher and four glasses. When I got back to the table, Charné said: "I told you it'd be embarrassing."

I poured myself a glass and looked through the screen. Damned if they hadn't rolled up the windows to the truck. The windshield had steamed over, and that old Dodge truck was rocking like a cradle. While I watched, an enormous flat foot rose foggily into view and pressed itself slowly but with tremendous strength against the glass directly below the rearview mirror.

"This is better than a movie," I said.

"Pervert," Charné said.

"You from around here?"

We both jerked around at the same time to see the man in the blue suit sit down across from us. He placed his glass of beer carefully on the table. His movements were strangely angular and precise, as though his body moved through space proscribed and exactly calibrated. His eyes were the color and texture of the screen wire. He asked us again if we were from around here.

"No," I said.

He had plopped down at my table without being asked, and I didn't like his manner, but there was something about him made me feel I ought not to cross him. I didn't get this old by being a fool.

"What y'all watching out there?" he asked.

"Nothing," I said.

He leaned forward and stared through the screen wire, watching the truck endlessly rocking in the distorted air rising out of the clay parking lot.

"Somebody in that truck, is it?" he asked. His voice was as careful as his movements. "What they doing in there?"

"What my friends do is their business," I said.

"Good way to be," he said.

We watched the Dodge truck. It seemed to rock with a life of its own. I emptied the pitcher, and Charné went for another one.

Just as she sat down at the table again, he said: "This is where they hung Alice, you know."

I drank off a quick glass and didn't answer. I have quite enough craziness in my own head without borrowing any from somebody else.

"I usually drink vodka," I said, thinking to change the subject, whatever the subject was.

"I got some if you want it," he said.

"You have?" I said.

It seemed fate. Who would be foolish enough to contest with fate?

"It's in the car," he said. "I'll just get it."

He got up and cat-danced out of the bar. When he was gone, Charné said: "He scares me."

"I think he'll be all right," I said.

"You have to be crazy to mess with a crazy person," she said.

"I admit he's a little scary," I said. "But we'll just have a drink with him and go. People sometimes get freaky if you refuse to drink with them."

He suddenly appeared in the parking lot outside the window. He went right to the truck and stood looking in the window. The rhythm of the truck had grown erratic. After he'd had a good long look, he walked over to his car, a baby-blue Corvair.

"What was that about Alice being hung?" I said. "Did you hear that?"

"Of course, I heard it," she said.

"I thought maybe I misunderstood," I said.

Directly he came back with the vodka. He had a hit out of the bottle and chased it with beer. I was relieved to have a drink. It settled me down, and things didn't seem so melancholy.

"You know," he said, "we've got the Nolichucky River here."

"We crossed it," I said.

He considered that for a moment. "When?" he said.

"Three days ago, best I can make it," I said. I didn't know why I was answering these questions. Something about the man made it impossible to consider doing otherwise. He kept staring at me, so I said: "See, we're hiking."

"Hiking?" he said.

"With backpacks," I said. "You know, on the Appalachian Trail."

I thought he would know about the trail because Erwin wasn't two miles from where the trail crossed a mountain. But he didn't. Had never heard of it. There didn't seem to be anything to do but explain the whole thing: that I was a writer walking the trail, that the girl was a photographer I hired to come along, and that the other guy walking with us was still out in the truck.

"And that's the other one out there in the truck?" he said.

"Yes," I said.

The three of us watched the truck baking in the sun for a moment. It wasn't rocking anymore. The windows had been rolled down. No heads were showing, though. I tried to imagine how Franny and Dog could accomplish anything in so small and stifling a space.

"Hard by the Nolichucky River is the Clinchfield Railroad," he said.

"I remember seeing a trestle," I said, only because he seemed to be waiting for me to say something. "I always liked trestles when I was a boy."

"Hadn't been for that damn railroad, they couldn't have hung Alice."

Charné said: "Back to that, are we?"

"Ma'am?"

"Why don't you get us another pitcher, Charné?" I said. She was capable of saying anything. I was afraid it would make him mad. And I didn't want him mad. I just wanted to drink a couple of more beers, maybe another shot or two, and get back in the woods.

When Charné came with the beer, he said: "It's ruined my life."

"What ruined your life?" she asked.

"The hanging of Alice."

At that moment the door of the pickup opened and we watched Dog stagger into the sun. His thin corn-colored hair was plastered to his forehead. Then Franny came out of the same door behind him. She looked kind of mean, like she might just want to slap the shit out of somebody. She did reach out and give Dog a cuff behind the head, but it was affectionate and full of goodwill, just the sort of lick, it seemed to me, one football player gives another when he's made an impossible score. She spent a minute or two twisting her Frosty-Freeze uniform, adjusting whatever was under it. They walked toward the bar holding hands.

"Perversity has ruined more than one man," he said. I think both Charné and I thought he was talking about Dog and Franny rocking in the truck. They came through the door behind where we sat at the table and I expected him to turn and say something to them, but instead, he said: "It was my birthday, my fifth birthday, when it happened. That was a long time ago, but I never got over it."

"Never got over what?" said Dog. He stood beside the table, holding Franny's hand.

He got up with great formality and removed his snap-brimmed blue hat. "You are the other member of the team," he said.

"Team?" said Dog.

"The wilderness team," he said.

Dog said, "Oh, yeah, sure, walking with the packs. I'm with them. The other member of the team." He licked his lips. The words seemed to please him.

"I was speaking of Alice and I forgot myself. I often do when I remember her. I've not introduced myself. I'm Jake Leach, a lawyer by avocation."

"I'm Ronnie." He looked out the window. "They call me Dog cause when I drink I sometimes commence to howl. It's a little joke they got, Dog is."

"But it's really Donniger," said Franny, "Ronald Donniger."

"It is my great pleasure, Mr. Dog."

He held out his hand. I had not realized before how drunk Jake Leach was. He was carrying an enormous load, and for the first time I realized that was why his movements seemed so careful and deliberate. He was one of those drunks who would just go on and on, never slurring a word or staggering, until finally he closed his eyes and collapsed, his clothes as unwrinkled and carefully brushed as they had been that morning when he put them on.

I had always held such men in great admiration, being as I am one of the all-time sloppy, disgusting drunks, the kind mothers can point out to their children as an example of the final evil of alcohol. Not so with Jake Leach. He would never be pointed out as anything except everything a man ought to be, even when he was stunned with whiskey, which is what he was now.

After we had all introduced ourselves several times, managed to get everybody seated, and Franny had knocked the dust off the session in the pickup by sucking down a glass of cold draft, Dog said, "Now, sir, I believe you was talking about Alice."

If a Grit meets another Grit who is formal and courteous in his speech, he immediately begins to trade formality for formality. They call it manners, and it's quite a lovely thing to see. Jake had fallen into the cadences that mark the gentleman (or so a Grit who uses them thinks) the moment he saw Ronnie Dog. He had not done so with me because I think he knew me for a bogus Southerner.

"The hanging of Alice marked me, sir, *marked me.*"

Jake handed the bottle of vodka to Dog, who took a pull and passed it to Franny, who did not hesitate but daintily wiped the mouth of the bottle on her Frosty-Freeze uniform and sucked down some herself, careful not to make the bottle gurgle in an unseemly way.

"Well, now my daddy, sir," said Ronnie, "he seen a man hung oncet. A nigger. Rape is what it was he done, so they taken a pertater and pushed it in his mouth tight where he couldn't holler and hung him. It was some small children there and they didn't want his hollerin scarin'm, you see."

Jake Leach was waving his hand, not discourteously but with some show of impatience, while Ronnie talked. "Alice was not a man, Mr. Dog."

While Jake paused for a controlled sip of vodka, Franny said: "Donniger. It's Donniger, not Dog."

Dog smiled at her. "It's all right, honey."

"I don't get in the pickup with nobody named Dog."

"All right," said Dog. "It ain't nothing but a joke."

"Alice was not a woman, either," said Jake Leach.

Charné had been over taking photographs of the bartender, who sat like a rock with his newspaper. She came back just in time to hear Jake.

"If it wasn't a man or a woman, what was it they hung?"

Jake made a little motion with his head indicating he meant to get to that in good time. "One is forced to the conclusion that hanging the nigger could have been justice."

Charné said something that made Jake Leach blush.

"Now wait, ma'am, hear me out. Not justice because it was legal. But what does justice care for legality? Very little it seems to me. If the nigger was truly guilty of rape and the community decided to hang him, that can only be justice, or so it seems to me. Even to the potato in his mouth. It might have been emotionally detrimental to the children to hear him scream but morally instructive to see him hanged."

He had spoken all of this in an impartial voice. It was a problem, theoretical, academic, something that could never touch him, and therefore, it was interesting for precisely the reason that it had nothing to do with him.

Then for the first time he became agitated; his fingers trembled. His face flushed scarlet. "But Alice was an elephant." He struck the table with his fist. "She was a goddamn *elephant*, Alice was, and they hung her!"

"They hung an elephant?" said Dog.

"Everybody knows that old story," said Franny.

Jake squinted at her. "You from Erwin?"

"Unaka Mountain," said Franny.

"*That* is not Erwin, Tennessee, lady," Jake said.

"It's still everybody heard that old story," she said. "Ma told me about hanging Alice when I weren't no more than a yearling girl."

Jake dropped his head back and his voice was a lament. "Yes, yes, dear God. It has become a favorite story with children." When he looked at me, he had tears in his eyes.

"Listen," Charné said, "listen. People do strange things. They think it's all so goddamn simple and funny."

She touched his arm, and I could tell she was genuinely moved. Not by what he was telling but by how much pain it was giving him to tell it.

Jake grabbed the vodka bottle and leaped up from the table. "Come on," he said.

I sat where I was. "Where are we going?" I said.

"Come on, goddammit," he shouted.

There was that jagged madness showing again, like the outcropping of a rock. I was drunk enough by now that he no longer seemed very strange and threatening. But I wasn't so drunk that I didn't hear the hysteria in his voice. In a calm, relaxed way I knew he was capable of killing me, and I remember wondering vaguely if he might have a gun or knife.

"I don't want to go outside," I said, "it's hot."

There was an abrupt hitch in his throat, and his voice came out soft, persuasive. "I know it's hot. It's very hot out there. But I want to show you something—to show—all of you this thing—I can't help it. It's just something I want to do. Christ, didn't I get the vodka for you?"

"Yes," I said, dispirited now by the way the conversation was going. "You got the vodka."

"You wanted vodka," he said, "and I got it." He was still standing, and he carefully adjusted his smart snap-brim hat. "I'm going to get three six-packs of beer to take along in my car. See that little Corvair out there? That's mine. And it's air-conditioned." He stopped and looked at me, but I could tell he was prepared to go on if it looked like he needed to.

"You serious about them beers?" I said.

He turned his head and called: "Tommy, sack up eighteen of them beers. Good cold ones. No, make it twenty of them good cold ones."

Tommy, who had not moved since we had been there, was immediately off his ass and packing up the beer.

"We got some time," I said. "Let's go."

"I got to feed them younguns of mine sometime," Franny said.

Actually, I hadn't thought of her coming. I'd supposed she would roar away in the old Dodge. But she didn't. When we got to that air-conditioned baby-blue Corvair car, she was the first one in it. Dog was the second. She just reached out and took him like he'd been a doll and drew him in to her. I could hear his stifled breathing, and she was making a sound like a dog eating raw meat. Charné and I got up front with Jake.

Jake didn't say a word. Nobody else seemed to feel like talking, either. We opened the beers. Jake's air conditioning was not worth much.

We went maybe three miles down the highway, when, without any warning at all, Jake drove his incredible baby-blue Corvair right across a ditch. A deep ditch. I thought we were having an accident. I was screaming and clawing at everybody, and it was embarrassing as hell when I realized that nobody else was screaming and Jake was driving (calmly and deliberately and competently as ever) right across a meadow. There were lots of jeeps in the world that could not have taken us where that Corvair took us. Finally, he stopped the car and we got out. Everybody except Franny and Dog.

"I just cain't bear weeds and scratchy things in this heat," Franny said.

There was no use to ask Dog if he was coming. Franny had him, and it was clear he was about to be tested again right there in the back of the car Ralph Nader had grave doubts about. We got out of the car, Charné doing me a huge favor by carrying some of the beer that she didn't want to drink but that I didn't feel I could do without in that heat and jungle of weeds as we walked up toward the stony roadbed of a railroad.

Jake went straight along the railroad and stopped finally on the crossties. "Here is where it happened," he said.

"What happened?" I said, but I already knew.

"The hanging of Alice," he said.

"Yes," I said.

I sat down on one of the steel rails to watch him. It was too hot, and finally, I ended sitting on the side of the ditch with Charné beside me. She had opened a beer, too. Jake looked truly crazy, or I guess crazy is the wrong word, *majestic* rather.

He stood between the iron rails of the steaming roadbed with his arms outstretched. Who knows when the king is mad? And who is brave enough to say when a king's vision becomes a delusion?

And by God, Jake—since he'd gained the prominence of the roadbed—Jake was a king when he walked up there, spread his arms and looked up at the sun. Then he lay down on his back. Really, right on his back, still staring up at the sun. The blue suit was as pressed and as neat and clean and handsome as it had ever been. Charné and I were drinking beer with both hands and had broke out a couple of downers and eaten those because this was a performance you've waited all your life to see and now that it's here, you know you could have done without it.

"Alice was an elephant." Jake spoke not looking at us but still straight up into the sun. "And this is where they hung her. On this very spot. Here, nowhere else. I told you I watched it when I was five years old."

He lifted his head up off the stones of the railroad and looked at us briefly. "When I was a boy, circuses used to come through." He was staring again at the sun. "They came through in wagons. They brought Alice the year I was five. She had a wagon of her own. Such a beautiful . . . beautiful. . . . She was gentle and she smelled like something your mother had made for you. I remember that. She was gentle and she smelled like something your mother made for you.

"She killed a little girl. The little girl tried to feed her something in her pen. I don't remember. I wish I could remember. But it was something about feeding Alice and Alice took the child with her trunk and beat her on the ground like a bundle of weeds and walked on her and it was awful and I didn't see it, but I heard it all, they told me all, everything and put out the little girl's body for everybody to see.

"That's not the horrible part. That's horrible, but that's not the horrible part. The town decided to kill Alice. Eye for an eye.

Except by now, Alice was sweet and gentle and dust-smelling as she ever was, but there was nothing to do but to kill her.

"They didn't have a gun big enough to kill her. They thought and thought. Shoot her in the eye with a shotgun, they said. They said all kinds of things, but they could never be sure it would kill the elephant and she might run crazy with the pain and mash the life out of somebody else. Poison, of course, came up. But that wouldn't do. It had to be quick. It had to hurt and be quick. It had to be an execution. Alice had to know.

"The Clinchfield Railroad had a derrick in those days. I don't know, maybe it's not called a derrick, a winch maybe, but anyway, it was this huge thing that runs on the tracks and lifts a section of rail into place by drawing it up with steel cables.

"They brought it out. They put it where I'm lying. Right here. They put a logging chain around Alice's neck. The whole town watched. I was there. And they hitched Alice to the derrick by the logging chain around her neck. And started pulling her up. I was there.

"She didn't understand. She started shitting. She stood on her back legs and kept shitting when she saw what was going to happen, and then it did. They pulled her right up in the air and then she stopped screaming, because she was screaming before, but she kept shitting until she was dead. I don't remember anybody cheering or saying it was good or wonderful or anything; they just stood there staring at Alice hanging off the derrick and then went home."

We sat in the ditch drinking the beer and trying to think that this was a madman and that if anything we ought to laugh because. . . . But we didn't, and Jake kept lying on his back between the steel rails. I wanted to say something, but I didn't know what to say.

"I went to law school. You'd be amazed where I went to law school. But I don't practice law. Oh, I do something now and then. My brother has a law office. It was our daddy's office. I'm a partner. But I don't do anything much. Mostly I come out here and remember Alice straining on her back feet, shitting until she was dead, and my brother stays in town and keeps the law office going."

He stopped talking and turned to look at us again.

"Why do you suppose that is?" he asked. "My brother was at the hanging of Alice, too."

"I don't know," I said, "I don't know anything about that. We're out of beer."

He looked not at us but straight up into the sun. "You can go get some more back there."

We weren't really out of beer, but I wanted to leave, wanted to leave bad. "OK," I said. "I think we better do that."

He just lay where he was and didn't move. Finally, he said, "I'm going to stay here awhile. Take the car and go back."

"You can't do that," I said. "It's hot and it's too far to walk."

"Tell Tommy to come git me after a while," he said. "He'll know where I am."

I stood up. "It's been good knowing you, Jake," I said. "You keep yourself together."

"It'll be all right," he said.

We started across the ditch alongside the Clinchfield Railroad.

"Hey," he called. We turned to look at him. "That little girl and Alice were the same age. I went to some trouble to find out, and they were the same age. That's what gets me."

Suddenly, bitterly, Charné said: "You ought to get out of this goddamn sun."

Jake said: "When I found out they were the same age, that's what ruined my career." We walked on through the weeds toward the car. "It's what ruined my life!" he called after us. Later, as were getting in the car, I thought I heard him yell something else. But I didn't wait. I didn't look back.

If anybody's interested in such things, Erwin, Tennessee, is in the Cherokee segment of the Appalachian Trail. That part of the trail goes through both the Cherokee National Forest and the Pisgah National Forest. We were headed for the top of Unaka (pronounced "You-nake-a" with the accent on the *nake* by the folks thereabouts) Mountain, to a place called, unfortunately I think, Beauty Spot, which was supposed to have a great place to camp, water and, according to the guidebook, one of the longest, most open views on the entire trail.

When Franny found out which way we were going, she said: "When you git up on Unaka Mountain and it starts raining, why, you just look and see which way the water is running on the ground. Run one way, you in Tennessee; run the other way, you in North Carolina."

Dog said: "Run *one* way? Which way, Fanny?"

"Which way?" she said.

"Which way to North Carolina and which way to Tennessee?"

"You can tell," she said. "Oh, you can always tell."

He watched her blankly. "You know you're a sweet thing?" he asked. "You know how sweet you are?"

"I still got to feed them younguns," she said. "Them two younguns of mine don't even know where I am." We were still at the Blue Pines Bar and Tommy had gone after Jake Leach and I didn't want to be around when they got back. "Y'all might as well come and sleep at my place, tonight." Franny was looking at Dog. "Might as well come on and git a early start in the morning."

Dog didn't hesitate. "Cain't. Got to go. We already been thrown behind by all this like it is."

Dog wouldn't even take a ride in her pickup, and we walked down the highway with our packs and camped behind the Erwin city dump because I figured that's the only place where we would be safe from the local police. If we could have made it to the mountains and the trail, we would have been safe there, but you start camping along the highway or sleeping under a bridge or in an open field and you're apt to wake up looking at a cop.

I have nothing against cops if they're home-grown. But if you're not from around there—no matter where *there* happens to be—and you run into a cop and you look like you're outside what is called the "economic and political mainstream" of the country, then you're just apt to get hurt. And hurt for nothing, hurt because you're not from around *there*. That's only a judgment, and it's only based on five years on the road, not being from around *there*, and not looking as though I was in the "economic and political mainstream." Understand that I don't condemn cops for that, either. It's the job they're paid to do. They do it well. To condemn it would be to condemn the country.

So anyway, we spent the night at the dump, and when we were getting our tents together the next morning, I stood watching Dog slam his stuff around in a particularly vicious way. We had hardly said a word the night before. We were sobering up and hung-over but mainly thinking about Jake lying between the rails of the Clinchfield Railroad. But the next morning I was feeling better, and I said to Dog: "Why the hell didn't we sleep at Franny's last night?"

He didn't even look at me when he spoke. "I'd a slept oncet at Miss Fanny's, I'd a never left." He saddled his pack and started slogging over the dump toward the mountains, leaving Charné and me standing there looking after him.

So I don't think any of us much gave a rat's ass that we were on the Cherokee segment of the Appalachian Trail when we left Erwin. It was probably the quietest day I remember on the trail. Charné carried the guidebook as she always did, telling us where water was—or where water was *supposed* to be—what the mileage was like, what the names of the shelters we passed were called, things like that. But mostly we were quiet.

We walked out of Erwin down to the Nolichucky River and along the north bank to a trestle of the Clinchfield Railroad. The Nolichucky's not much of a river at that point—I don't know what it may be elsewhere—but where we left it east of Erwin, it was maybe 200 yards wide, 10 or 12 feet deep, or so it seemed to me, with a lot of rocks and easy rapids. It was also extremely yellow with what I hope were minerals but might have been your ordinary piss and shit from the local folk, most rivers being as they are these days worse than raw sewage.

I bent down once to drink from a stream high in the mountains on the trail, and just as I was about to, as they say, *slake* my thirst, I saw a little sign put up by the Forestry Service or somebody that said: "DO NOT DRINK. CONTAMINATED WITH UN-TREATED WASTE." I always love that: *untreated* waste. As though I might enjoy—perhaps really like—to drink *treated* waste. But, alas, why dwell upon it? The planet is tired and dying. I understand, though, that even the most pessimistic predictions give us (or at least a few of us) another million years or so.

There was a crazy man who used to wander the roads of Bacon

County, Georgia, sleeping where he could, living how he could, who used to say: "Them that shit can eat what they shit." He, of course, was speaking about ultimate alternatives. I have always thought it eminently fair.

I'll never forget that walk out of Erwin, Tennessee. We'd been on the trail so long and steadily we were lean and mean enough to eat rocks. I think because we were all melancholy and sad— Charné and I about old Jake Leach, and Dog about old Franny —we took it out on ourselves physically. Nobody said anything about it; there was no planning; that's just the way it happened. In paroxysms of guilt, my greatest workouts have consistently come after my greatest drunks.

Four miles up from the Clinchfield Railroad, we caught up with five members of a hiking club. Or the patches on their little green matching uniforms said they were a hiking club. They looked authentic enough, smelling vaguely of sweat, red of face, booted, bedrolled, and canteened.

"If you like," one of them said, "we can hike along together. Where you from?"

Charné pointed to the direction we'd just come from. "Back there," she said, and then deliberately turned what they'd said around. "Sure, you can walk with us if you'd like. It could be fun."

The trail at that place was narrow, and we were tandem behind the five boys, who all looked to be about eighteen and very sturdy, soccer types. But the trail from the Nolichucky to the top of Unaka Mountain crossed fields and meadows, and the first field we got to, Charné swung out of the line and walked around the boys. Once she was in the lead, nobody was ever to head her.

In less than a mile, she was about 200 yards out front, and Dog and I had passed the boys, too. Maybe the boys just thought we were unfriendly or they didn't like the pace, or any number of other things. But I think what happened is that Charné simply walked their young asses off. Later we saw them once from a ridge, way back and still coming, their heads bent earnestly under their little green hiking caps. Then we never saw them again. At the pace we were holding, we were drinking a lot of water and the first place the guidebook said we'd find water, there was no water, which truly we had not expected there would be, since we had come to distrust the *guide*book in almost every detail. It didn't worry us much because Franny had told us what a wonderful spring was at Beauty Spot on Unaka Mountain. She knew because there was a little mountain road that would take a truck and she had been up there often. She said a lot of people drove up there for picnics and—here her voice dropped—*other things.*

So we went more than seven hours dry. I discovered while hiking that summer that I need six quarts of water a day. That's just to drink and doesn't count what water I get in the reconstituted dehydrated food. I'm a nonstop sweater, one of the world's great sweaters, and consequently, I have to drink water almost constantly. If I don't get the water, it ruins my disposition. I think it affects most people that way. Certainly, by the time we got to Beauty Spot—which incidentally is an incredible place; there must be 200 acres of open, treeless meadow right on top of the mountain—but by the time we got there, we were pretty bitter about the whole trip, even the world. Our swollen, dry tongues made us talk like we had cleft palates.

We carefully followed the guidebook's instructions to find the spring, because they sounded just like the instructions Franny had given us. We followed the crest; we found the boulder shaped like a heart; we turned left down the incline. No spring. We read more carefully. This wasn't funny. Then we did the whole thing over again. No spring.

"Listen," said Dog.

We were sitting on the heart-shaped rock. Charné and I had heard it, too.

"Somebody's whistling," I said.

It was the kind of whistle somebody whistles *at* you, so we stood up on the rock, and there across the meadow was a car where, if we had been looking, we would have seen it already. It was a '58 Chevrolet, and even from this distance one could see it had mag wheels, about thirty coats of paint, and no doubt a supercharged engine. Three men were sitting on the hood. We could see somebody else inside. They were waving us over.

I said, as we neared them: "Are they drinking beer?"

"Christ," said Charné, "we'll never get out of Tennessee."

I thought to myself at that moment that we may not, but it wouldn't be because of drinking. I instantly recognized the guys on the hood of the modified Chevy as Good Old Drinking Boys who were capable of anything, including castration. It occurred to me that this was Friday—late Friday—and they'd come up here from some factory or construction site to sip a few cool ones and get a little meaner preparing for the last savage few hours at midnight down in town at some bar named The Wagon Wheel or The Dew Drop Inn. I also knew they would have some poor hapless and helpless girl in the backseat or on a comey blanket in the weeds behind the car, down on her back, rooting around in her.

They didn't smile at all as we walked up, and when I looked at Dog, I saw that he had seen what I saw, knew what I knew. His face was tight and actually looked meaner than the guys sitting on the hood of the car, who were wearing pointed, hand-carved boots and some kind of fake cowboy shirts. There was another man—about the same age as the others, twenty-five or so—in the back seat, and while I watched, a woman's sweaty head rose into view only to have the man clamp his hand on the back of her skull and push her back down again.

The one sitting straddle of the hood ornament waved his can of Bud at me and said: "Well, friend, damn if it don't look like you lost."

"We ain't lost," I said. "But we thirsty."

"Well," he said, showing us the mean smile he no doubt practiced in the mirror, "we didn't bring no water up here."

"It's supposed to be a spring," Dog said.

The guy whose boots looked to be outlined in aluminum paint studied Dog a minute and then said with an exaggerated Grit voice: "What you doing playing boy scout with a long-haired freak?" His smile as he looked at Dog seemed almost good-natured, but I knew better. "You almost look normal, but this other'n here look like he'd suck a dick."

Two things leaped immediately to mind. One was Big Jim Dickey's novel *Deliverance,* and with that thought, a tightening of the asshole. The other was a scene out of Larry McMurtry's novel *All of My Friends Are Going to Be Strangers,* in which two Texas

Rangers catch a longhair out at night on a highway and proceed to have a long humorless conversation with him, the basis of which was that since he had long hair, he'd surely suck a dick. The Rangers ended by throwing the kid over a ditch by his hair.

It only took a second for all that to flash on me, and while it did, Charné threw down her pack and said: "You gutless Grit sonofabitches, do you know where water is or not?"

Obviously, what Charné said scared the shit out of me but didn't seem to bother the guys sitting on the hood of the car at all. It reminded me a little of the time in the summer of 1972, when I was arrested at the Slipped Disk Discotheque in St. Augustine Beach, Florida. When the cop threw me in the back seat of his cruiser, one of the people I was with, who happened to be a lady, turned and knocked the piss out of the cop and said: "You sonofabitch, you can't do that to him."

All the while I was yelling from the back seat: "Yes, he can. Yes, he can."

The cop threw her in with me. I expected at least a beating back at the station, but we got nothing. They even let us bail ourselves out. I here salute the police of St. Augustine, Florida, as among the fairest and finest of my experience.

But those weren't cops sitting on the hood of that car. Cops, among other things—unless you've done something very personal to them—almost always leave you living. I mean, after all, if they don't, they've got all those forms to fill out. But those cowboys on the Chevy didn't have any forms to fill out.

"Look," I said, "this has all gone off in the wrong direction. We just looking for some water."

One of the cowboys sitting on the hood of the car said: "I don't know what you looking for, and I don't give a shit. But I know what you found."

The door opened, and the girl got out of the backseat. She came to lean on the fender. She wasn't an ugly girl, but she was terribly thin, with light-yellow skin and what looked to be cold sores on her mouth.

"What's gone happen?" the girl said.

The boy who had been in the backseat with her and was wearing cowboy clothes, too, came to stand beside her. "Shut up," he said. "When I want you to know something, I'll tell you."

Dog, who had stood without saying anything, slipped the straps on his pack and eased it to the ground. Almost nonchalantly he said: "Back home, we always figure people that keep on talking about sucking a dick would."

I think it stunned them as much as it did me, and it stunned me a lot.

The girl leaning on the fender said: "You gone let that skinny fart talk to you like that, Edsel?"

Edsel, sitting straddle of the hood ornament, didn't even look at her but slapped her over sideways with the back of his hand.

"You prick," said Charné. "You dumb Grit prick."

"Now we just gone have us some goddamn fun," Edsel said, drawing his leg up to get over the hood ornament.

When he did, Dog shot the hood ornament off. Edsel froze with his leg in the air and turned yellower than the girl. My bowels felt very loose. Dog had a snub-nosed .38 Special in his hand. I knew it because my stepfather has one that he keeps in a drawer beside his bed. It is a very blue and blunt and nasty-looking little thing.

Dog spoke so softly and easily that we all unconsciously leaned to get the words. "I'm not really a good shot," he said. "I mighta shot your balls off, Edsel."

"Listen," said Edsel. "Listen, you don't under—"

Dog blew an empty beer can away where it sat on the hood beside another cowboy.

"You crazy?" asked the one who had got out of the backseat of the car. Then he made it a statement. "You a crazy man."

"I think I am," said Dog. "I think I just went crazy listenin to your goddamn mouth." He watched the boy who leaned on the fender where the girl had been. "How'd you like me to shoot your right eye?"

"Please," said the one sitting beside Edsel. "Please—"

"You ain't fitten to live," said Dog.

"Ronnie, wait a minute," I said. "You—"

Ronnie turned to look at me and his eyes seemed glazed and his mouth had a strange kind of droop to it. Or else I was so scared his face wasn't focusing.

"I think you better take Charné over yonder behind that rock," he said. "Just leave the packs here and go on over yonder behind that rock."

Edsel still had not put his leg down, and he was crying. He was a huge man, and he was crying soundlessly, his face twisted, tears running on his cheeks. He slowly and steadily shook his head.

"Ronnie," I said, "I'm not leaving you here with these guys."

"Yes, you are," he said. "This ain't none of your business."

"I'm not going to be part of this," I said. "We don't even know these guys."

"Don't let him hurt me," the girl said. She wasn't crying, though. Edsel was still the only one crying.

"You better step over there behind the rock," Dog said. "This don't look to be none of your business. Charné, you take him on over there."

There didn't seem to be anything we could do. I didn't want the guys killed. But much more than that, I didn't want to get killed. We walked across the meadow, leaving them there in the late-afternoon sunlight with Edsel still crying. Just as we stepped behind the rock, we heard two quick shots.

"Oh, Jesus, Jesus," said Charné, pressing her hands against her head. I don't know for sure, and I can't remember, but I think I was crying. I probably was crying, too.

There were two quick shots, and then we heard the Chevrolet engine roar into life and saw the car leap into view around the rock, the rear end fishtailing, gravel and grass spewing from under the wheels. Ronnie came walking across the meadow toward us, carrying a six-pack in one hand and the .38 in the other. He was smiling. It was the same old Ronnie we'd known and he was smiling and there were no bodies lying in the meadow and I was so happy I stood right still and thanked God, prayed, and made some promises I couldn't keep.

When he got to us, he lifted the six-pack to me. "Care for one of these Buds?"

I took the six-pack and held it in my hands, not taking one out of the package, but just standing there with it.

Ronnie waved the pistol off in the direction the car had gone. "I known we'd run into a sumbitch like that before this was over." He looked at the .38. "Probably should have shot him, too, if it weren't but just in the foot."

"But you didn't really—"

"Hell, no," he said. "I wouldn't shoot nobody."

"What if they come back?" said Charné.

"They ain't gone come back," Ronnie said. Looking at him, I believed him. He could say what he wanted to, but I knew all of this hadn't been entirely an act. Those guys had seen his face, too. Ronnie'd kill you if things got just right.

"You know it's against the law to carry a firearm in a national forest," I stupidly said because it was the only thing I could think of and I thought I'd better say something before I screamed.

"I know," he said. "Listen, you want to make camp? I'm gone come over here and—" He put his arm around my shoulder and turned me. It was getting dark. Lights were coming on down in the valley. Far there to the left, we could see Erwin. "Well, I think I can see Fanny's house. I figured it out, and see that little green-and-red light? That's the water tower. Now, if you look right up behind it and to the left, why, I think that's Fanny's house. I'm gone set over here and have me a beer and wonder what old Fanny's doing in there with them younguns of hers. I mean, if you'll make the camp, I think I will."

"Sure," I said. "I'll get everything set up and start some food."

"The spring's off behind that rise of ground." He pointed. "Just where the bushes start there." He smiled. "Edsel swore on his mother it was and aye, God, I bet it's right where he said it is."

"Right," I said.

I was just turning to go when he vaguely waved that pistol he was still carrying. "By the way," he said.

"Yeah?"

"I don't think I like that name Dog no more," he said. "I think that joke's got old."

"Right," I said. "Right, Ronnie."

"Ronald," he said.

"OK, Ronald," I said.

Charné and I walked away together to get the packs.

"God, he's something, isn't he?" she said.

Ronald didn't eat any supper that night. He sat in the grass watching that light behind the water tower until it went out.

L. L. Bean Has Your
Number, America!

It was two o'clock in the morning and I was standing in a parking lot in Freeport, Maine, a little town about six blocks long from start to finish. The building in front of me, the L. L. Bean store, was a miserable-looking structure. The whole thing might have been an afterthought in the mind of an apprentice carpenter. L-shaped and covered with beige asbestos shingles, it leaned tiredly in upon itself. For no good reason, I thought it looked like the kind of building that would house a third-rate plumbing company on the verge of bankruptcy.

But there was no bankruptcy here. Even in the dead hours of the morning, with a cold rain falling, the green smell of money was everywhere in the air. You had to step lively to keep the life from being mashed out of you in the parking lot, filled as it was with minibuses and Volkswagen campers and Winnebagos and Airstream trailers and cars of every sort. I'd already checked the tags, not quite believing what I'd heard about how far people drove to get to this place, but they were true, the stories I'd heard. The tags said Texas and Utah and California and Canada and most other places you could think of.

A steady line of men dressed in hunting caps, plaid shirts, heavy cord pants, and Maine hunting shoes (ah, that Maine hunting shoe on which this entire fortune had been founded) streamed across the lot toward a brightly lighted door. The door had sleigh bells hitched to the top, and they were ringing for all they were worth. And they never stopped. *Never.* The L. L. Bean bells ring twenty-four hours a day, every day of the year. What would cause people from all over the country to pour through a door like that is something a man wants to see with his own eyes.

The door opens onto two steep flights of stairs, and the stairs lead up to the L. L. Bean store, which at first seems a mistake. You think you must be in the wrong place. This is the salesroom of the company that's turning better than $20 million? a year? I step it off, just for the hell of it. Thirty-five paces wide, sixty-one long. This is the showplace for the merchant who sends out six million catalogues and circulars a year?

It was country tacky. An Army-Navy surplus store with an outdoor flavor. Stacks of heavy flannel shirts and cord trousers were thrown on a long counter against one wall. A rack of wide blue ties stood at the head of one aisle. Hammocks hung from the ceiling. Exposed pipes of a sprinkler system crooked in and among the hammocks. And the men—dressed to hunt but shopping their little hearts out just as though this was the basement of Macy's in the last mad hour of a sale—stumbled along the aisles, fingering and testing stoves and skillets and snowshoes and thermal underwear and sleeping bags and packs and hiking staffs and knives and fishing rods. All of the stock looked as if it had just been set down and would be moved in an hour or so to another building, perhaps to another sale.

I went to the back of the store to look at The Shoe, the product that started all this and in many ways made it possible. Every available chair was filled with men sitting cheek to jowl and looking very serious while they were fitted with the Maine hunting shoe, the legendary L. L. Bean's very own design, a shoe that L. L. himself had tramped the Maine woods in for over half a century. I picked one up and turned it in my hands. Undeniably a great shoe. It did what it was made to do better than any other shoe in the world. It was light, waterproof, durable beyond belief, and comfortable. It was also about as silly-looking as any shoe you're apt to come across. If I hadn't been told otherwise the first time I ever saw a pair, I would have thought they were used by guys who waded around in sewers under New York City. The shoe itself is rubber with a crepe sole vulcanized to it. The part that goes up around the ankle and lower calf is made from heavy cowhide and sewn right into the top of the rubber shoe. It is without question the most widely used sporting boot in the world, but it is still, to my mind anyway, an ugly little mother.

I had been taking some pretty good shots to the kidney from shoppers moving up behind me, so I decided to pack it in for the night. On the way out, I saw a place where you could sign up to have the famous L. L. Bean catalogue sent to you. I stopped and put down my name. While I was writing, I noticed a little red book on the table. It was called *You Alone in the Maine Woods: The Lost Hunter's Guide.* Just beyond the table that held the books, the solemn, solid face of L. L. Bean looked down from the wall, over the cash register, and out onto the men thrashing about in a shopping frenzy. It was hard to imagine L. L. needing a *Lost Hunter's Guide,* or ever holding one in his hands for that matter, but someone had obviously thought it was an item that would move well enough to be put here by the cash register in the place the old man had started sixty-three years ago. Before I left, I got myself an L. L. Bean Inc., Fall 1975, catalogue, thinking to do a little light fantasizing before I went to sleep.

I made one brief stop before I got back to the motel. A quarter of a mile away I pulled off the road and sat for a couple of minutes looking into a green field where two enormous brick buildings loomed against the morning sky. I've seen cotton fields smaller than either of the buildings, and there was not a single sign, not even a number, anywhere on them, nothing whatsoever to identify them, not on the buildings, not on the green field in front of them, not on the gate to keep unwanted people from entering, not on the highway. But I knew what they were. This was the *real* L. L. Bean. This was where it was all stored and shipped. Never mind that rinky-dink thing down the road. That was PR. This was where the heavy cheese was made. But it was a little eerie sitting out there in the dark with nothing to show what it was.

When I got back to the motel, I sat down with the catalogue, the one that goes to all fifty states and to seventy foreign countries. Coming as I do from a little farm in South Georgia, my experience with catalogues is long and profound. I've even proposed that the federal government strike a medal for the Sears company for bringing so much mystery and color and magic into the lives of people who would not otherwise have it. I now include L. L. Bean in my proposal. Men all over the world who will never get any closer to the outdoors than running over an occasional squirrel with their cars can sit bemused and dreaming on long winter nights, thumbing through 128 pages of everything anybody ever thought of to use in the woods. Except guns. Bean sells no guns. Most people don't know it, but there is hardly any markup on guns. But you don't miss them in a catalogue like L. L. Bean's. It has enough for everybody, a real page turner. I actually fell asleep sitting there imagining myself tricked out in a plaid shirt, cord britches, and The Shoe.

"This machine here opens the letters," the lady was saying. "Would you like to see it open some?" She slapped a handful down and they zipped away quicker than a blink, but I wasn't paying much attention. Those kinds of things never make a lot of sense to me anyway. Besides, I was looking dead in the eye of a computer that would have scared James Bond. The entire building—the first of the two unmarked enormous brick buildings sitting in the green field—was alive and throbbing with automation of every imaginable kind.

There was nothing country tacky about this. This was serious as only American business can be serious. L. L. Bean's funky, down-home Maine dream had been repackaged, automated, and computerized. I'm sure L. L. would have approved because first and last he was a businessman, even though throughout his long life he maintained he was really only a hunter who tolerated business to support his life in the woods. He started out with the hunting shoe he designed in 1912 and gradually added other items to the line, all of them of the finest quality and backed by a dead-solid-certain guarantee.

When L. L. passed on in 1967, at the age of ninety-four, the company went to his son, Carl, but unfortunately, Carl followed his daddy eight months later in the same year. Then came L. L.'s grandson and namesake, Leon Gorman, who took over at the age of thirty-two, and things have never been the same. Young Gorman automated everything, dressed up the catalogue, and the enterprise quadrupled its business in the first five years under his leadership.

I left the building full of computers and went next door into something that looked like it wanted to be a blimp hangar. It had a ceiling thirty feet high and was big enough to hold three football fields. Backed up to it, three U.S. Mail semis were being shoveled full of packages. I tried to imagine where in God's name all that stuff was going and what it would be used for. There're not a million men left in this country who could find their way out of a ten-acre woodlot, much less have any real use for the kind of high-grade, finely wrought outdoor gear carried by L. L. Bean. The only possible answer has to be that all across America men are squeegeeing around the local A & P supermarket in the Maine hunting shoe and wearing L. L. Bean's camouflage parka to the drive-in.

I'd been standing in the parking lot of L. L. Bean's for about two hours listening to little groups of people who said they were hunters talk, and I knew why thirty-five guys had been shot in the Maine woods last year. They were science-fiction good ole boys, turned out in the latest hunting clothes, and discussing the newest gadgetry with all the woodlore of dim-witted bird dogs. Every few minutes their talk would turn to L. L. Bean, the old man, the store, the world's best outdoor gear.

"I'll tell you something right now," one of them was saying. "When a Yankee craftsman makes something, it stays made. L. L. Bean's got pride in workmanship."

Of course, 80 percent of what L. L. Bean sells it does not make. The company simply orders it from outside manufacturers—in Europe—and resells it. The fact is apparent from the most casual glance at the catalogue. Intellectually all those men must have known that. But in their secret hearts I think they believed that everything was made there in the Maine woods in an ancient, collapsing store by the descendants of an old man who was an actual hunter. That was what kept them buying; that was what kept them making the pilgrimage to Freeport, Maine. The bottom line is that L. L. Bean sells something gone out of the world. It gives suburban America the slightest whiff of a blood spoor.

"How you?" said a pudgy guy in a hunting cap about two sizes too big.

"I'll be all right," I said.

"You come here much?" he said.

"Not much," I said.

"Come here every year," he said. "Great for the kids." He put a pinch of tobacco in his mouth, gagged a little on it, spit once, took it out, and discreetly dropped it behind him. "Night like this makes you wish you were in the woods."

Rainy, chilly, early October? It didn't make me wish I was in the woods. He was standing beside not a trailer or a camper but a *coach:* about forty feet long, tinted windows, double wheels all around, low, sleek, two enormous whiplash aerials coming off it. Just your basic $70,000 home-away-from-home. It had an Illinois tag. I tried to think what a man might hunt in Illinois. Couldn't.

"What do you hunt up that way?" I said, pointing to his tag.

"I'm from Chicago," he said.

Well, hell, that *was* Illinois.

"I don't actually hunt," he said. "The wife and I take the kids out camping, though." He turned and tapped gently against the side of the coach. "You know what this little baby's got in it?" Then he rattled off things like self-contained shitters and television sets. "We just pull up in a nice place in one of your national parks and. . . ." He shrugged and lifted his hands. "The wife and kids—we really enjoy that."

"You do much business here?" I said.

"A *lot* of business," he said. "Hell, I'm wearing my Beans."

He looked down and I looked down, and sure enough, he was standing in The Shoe. Its ugly little rubber nose poked out from under his cord britches.

"You ever seen a Chicago winter?"

"Never have," I said.

"Death," he said. "Just death. And what I love is knowing L. L. Bean's open up here, no matter the day or night, open and just like it's always been." He looked off at the brightly lighted windows of L. L. Bean's for a moment and then back at me. "Listen, you want a little drink before you go? Great night for a drink."

"I'd be obliged," I said.

"I have to be quiet," he said. "Wife and kids asleep." He went into the coach and came back with a bottle in a brown paper sack.

He took a pull at it, looked at the neck of the bottle sticking out of the sack, and said, "You know, I wish we could do this in the woods somewhere, sitting around a fire, maybe with a dog."

It was a sweet and vulnerable moment. It made me want to hug him. He handed me the bottle, and I took it, thinking there might be hope for this boy yet. I bubbled it pretty good before I got the full taste, and I'll be twice damned if he hadn't come all the way from Chicago in a double-wheeled coach with a self-contained shitter to hand me a bottle of sherry wine.

I swallowed it anyway because I did not want to seem impolite.

A Night at a Waterfall

We'd come up from U.S. 19E, just west of the Tennessee-North Carolina border along the crest of the White Rocks Mountains. For much of the day to the north we could see Holston and Iron Mountains; to the east Beech and Grandfather Mountains fell away into clouds. We were headed for the gorge of the Laurel Fork, which is supposed to be as rugged and spectacular as anything the trail crosses anywhere from Georgia to Maine. The gorge is almost at the bottom of a watershed that drains nearly 15,000 acres and something in excess of 26 million gallons of water a day pour through it.

From what I had read and heard about it, I expected a flock of tourists and hikers to be nesting on the banks at the bottom of the Laurel Falls. But when we got there, we were alone. It was early afternoon, and we'd walked hard to get there that early because we didn't know whether we were going to try to find a place nearby to camp, go on out to Tennessee Highway 67, a distance of another five miles or so, or risk Laurel Fork Gorge shelter, which we knew to be only about a half mile away from the actual falls.

I could understand once I got there why the spot didn't seem very popular with hikers. If you ever see Laurel Fork Gorge, you've got to *want* to see it pretty badly. And I'm not even sure it's worth the effort. But I've already admitted I have never really cared for the Great Outdoors and by the time I got down into the gorge I cared even less.

The fall itself is about three stories high, that is around thirty feet, and maybe twenty yards across at the place where the water starts to go over the edge and then narrower at the bottom. Charné and Ronald beat me down into the gorge by a half hour or more because the trip is straight down and the footing entirely on a trail of broken rock and very unsure. When the footing is secure, I can go pretty good, but when you have to be careful about ankles and knees—well, I don't have any ankles and knees, or rather, what I have is what is left after years of karate and motorcycles, and that's not much. So by the time I was down in the gorge I was in no mood to appreciate it or even to look at it for that matter. Ronald and Charné were soaking their feet in a little pool that eddied out from the main fall. I sat down beside them and took off my boots.

Just as I was easing my feet into the icy water, two black hats came out of the woods about fifty yards away downstream. I mean they both actually were wearing black hats, but if they had been in the movies, Sam Peckinpah would have had them wear black hats, too. They were young men, but their faces were drawn and lined and blank. I don't mean without expression; I mean you could tell that blankness was a deliberately chosen expression. It was not in the least hostile, but it wasn't friendly, either. They were looking right at us, but we might have been rocks. That might have been what they wished to convey, that we were rocks or something like rocks until we proved otherwise.

"Wow," said Charné, who was not given to saying such a word.

One of the black hats had a little boy on his shoulders. The little boy had yellow hair, and he had a face just like theirs, including the deep lines. They came straight on toward us, stepping on stones and sometimes up to their knees in the Laurel Fork River, the same one through which 26 million gallons of water poured a day. All they had to do was step wrong and all three of them would have been gone forever, their goddamn heads torn off in that torrent of water. But they didn't step wrong, and more than that, they never looked where they were stepping; not once that I saw did their eyes ever drop in the slippery trail of stones and gravel they were moving over. With great and careful unconcern their eyes stayed on us.

All three of them, including the little boy, were wearing boots

—the kind that laced—and Levi's and the sort of denim work shirt you can buy out of the Sears store.

"I'm a Boocum," said the one carrying the little boy.

"I'm a Crews," I said.

They had walked right up close enough to spit on us before either of them spoke. I won't try to reproduce their dialect because as long as we were with them, I could hardly make out what they said. With two or three brief exceptions, they had lived their entire lives in the mountains there above Hampton, Tennessee.

"Hiking?" one said.

"Trying to," said Ronald.

"Hot," said the other one.

"Fit don't rain," said Ronald.

"Most generally do, though," said the little boy.

He must have been seven or eight, but he was a runt, weighing no more than about fifty pounds. He was right about the rain, too. I remembered the guidebook saying the valley averaged fifty-four inches of rain a year. An inch a week is a lot of rain.

"You ever killed anybody?" asked the little boy suddenly.

"What?" said Charné. "What?"

"Killed," said the little boy.

"Shut up, Mayhugh," said the man who was carrying him. He looked off toward the sheer face of the cliff going up to the top of the falls. "You all Crewses?"

"No," I said.

"We all Boocums," he said. "Ain't but twenty-two Boocums in the whole world and they everyone on this mountain."

"I'm a Crews," I said, feeling a little like a fool. "Harry Crews. He's Ronald Donniger. Both of us from Georgia. Her name's Charné Porter."

"Me and him's brothers," said the one carrying Mayhugh. "This one up here ridin me is my sister's boy. Mayhugh ain't a Boocum. He's a Lardly. His daddy come from up north, Massatwosets. I'm Josh. My brother here's Pudd."

"They brung me up here to see Uncle Pudd do it again," said Mayhugh.

"What do you do?" said Charné.

Pudd looked up at the sheer wall of the cliff. "Go over the fall," he said.

"How you do that?" asked Ronald.

"I don't believe I understand you," Pudd said with that tremendous, and genuine, politeness a Grit can get in his voice.

Ronald said: "I mean when you git up there . . . how . . . I mean, what do you do?"

"When I git up there," he said, "I go over it." He smiled a slow, strange smile and made a little gliding motion with his hand. "Just like the water do. I let myself in the water and there I'm gone. Nothing to it."

"He was in Veet Name," said Mayhugh.

"Hush, Mayhugh," he said.

"Wounded twicet," said Mayhugh.

"Mayhugh's a talker," Josh said. "But he might grow out of it."

"Oncet in the back," said Mayhugh, "and oncet in the ast." He reached over and took off his uncle's hat and petted his thick, matted hair. "Take off your shirt and show'm."

Pudd smiled up at the boy with one of those beautifully indulgent smiles my Uncle Alton used to give me when I was a boy. "If you want me to go over the fall, I better git on to it."

He walked away without saying anything else and disappeared into the tangle of stunted trees and vines and bushes growing on bottom of the sheer face of the rock cliff going up toward the top of the falls. The man took Mayhugh off his shoulders.

"Set back down if you want to," he said, "it'll take him a minute to git up there."

We sat back down and put our feet in the water. Mayhugh found a small stone and sent it skipping across the pool. All three of them had been wet to the waist—belt, boots, everything—but they didn't seem to mind. Josh opened the pocket of his shirt and took out a Prince Albert can. "I have brought some marijuana" —he spoke the words very quietly and carefully—"if y'all care to smoke."

"I'd be pleased to smoke with you," I said.

He took out a joint rolled tightly in a paper that bore the emblem of the American flag. He lit the end that had the stars on it. "Feet bothering you?" he asked.

"Bothered me the whole way," I said, taking a hit and passing it to Ronald.

"This marijuana will help that," he said.

I liked to hear him call it marijuana instead of grass or hash or shit or tea. I liked to see him treat the mild little drug with some respect. I liked the ordinary respect in his voice. About what he might have had for aspirin if you'd had a headache.

His brother had appeared on the sheer face of the cliff now. He was still wearing his boots. They were wet and half unlaced. He hung splayed against the wall, slowly moving in the cracks, a finger here, the edge of the sole of his boot there. He moved slowly and carefully, and one had the sense that there was no showoff in any of this. It was just something he could do and that his little nephew liked to see him do and he had nothing better to do, so he was doing it.

It took him three joints to get to the top. Charné didn't smoke any. Once at the top of the falls, Pudd began to work his way from boulder to boulder, sometimes having to jump what looked as much as six feet, out to the center of the falls.

"He's going to get killed," I said.

"If he goes off there, he will," Ronald said.

We were all very calm now, as if we were talking about something happening in a movie.

"No," said Josh. "He ain't gone git hurt. We been coming over that fall since we weren't much biggern Mayhugh here."

"He'll drown if nothing else," I said. "How's he plan to get out?"

Josh pointed downstream maybe fifty yards. "He'll come out right yonder. It's a way to ride that water right up in that bend there. It's a trough, see, the water's cut right outen them rocks. All you got to do is find that trough and ride it, slick as owl shit, it is, and he'll pop up there like magic."

"What if he misses it?" I asked.

"He ain't gone miss it," said Josh. "He ain't missed it yet."

And I'm proud to say he didn't miss it this time. He stood for a long time on a high flat rock in the center of the falls, looking down into the roiling water, and then, feet first, he just slipped over the edge and disappeared. And even while he was gone and my heart was slamming around under my ribs and I couldn't see him, Josh was telling me in his quiet, steady monotone that this was the easy falls, that there was another one—I missed or can't remember the name—higher, rockier than this one that somebody sometimes got hurt shooting but that he and his brother had always been lucky with it and the worst that had ever happened was a little cut on the back of his head. And he was bending his head to show me a sawtooth scar at his hairline just as Pudd literally shot free of the river at the bend right where Josh had said he would. Mayhugh was clapping and shouting and saying that he'd try it dammit if they'd only help him up there to where he could jump off.

Pudd, smiling slightly, his soaked shirt sticking to his massive chest and back, came walking along the rocky shore to where we sat. He cuffed his nephew on the back of the head and told him if he ever decided to start growing, they might—just might—let him shoot the falls, too. The little boy handed Pudd his black hat, the only thing dry he had now, and Pudd squared it precisely on his head.

"Scared my pony," said Ronald.

"It ain't nothing much to it," said Pudd. "All you got to do is turn loose. Want to try it?"

"I'll let you know when I'm ready," Ronald said.

"Where yall camping?" asked Josh.

We stumbled around and finally admitted that we didn't know where we were going and hadn't thought about it any farther than this, and now that we were here we didn't know what the hell to do. It had darkened considerably in the deep gorge while we had sat there smoking. Pudd said they were camped about three-quarters of a mile back up there and they had a place we could set up if we wanted to. Mayhugh said his ma was up there and his daddy from Massatwosetts was there too and his grandma and everybody.

By the time we got to their camp it was black dark, which didn't seem to bother the Boocum boys a bit. They walked downriver, then up the side of a mountain that would have strained a goat, made a ninety-degree turn, and went through a solid black wall of second-growth timber, Pudd still carrying Mayhugh on his shoulders and the three of us following them by sound for the first half of the walk before I asked them to stop so I could get my flashlight out of the pack. I offered to let them use the light. They thanked me but said they really didn't need it. And they didn't. We eventually walked out of the woods into a clearing that was at the head of an old dim logging road. Coleman lanterns were hanging from the limbs of trees over three pickup trucks and a 1962 Thunderbird car. There wasn't a sign of a tent, but there were quilts and pillows strewn about over the leaves and a huge woman was working over a homemade barbecue cooker made out of a fifty-five-gallon drum that had been cut in half and had legs welded on it.

A pit had been dug at one end of the clearing, and it was full of white-hot oak coals. An animal was spitted over the coals. I recognized it immediately. It was a goat.

Josh took us over to his mother at the barbecue cooker and introduced us and then to his daddy, who was not so much tending the cooking goat as he was watching it. Josh's mother had hoecake cooking on a flat skillet and hamburgers and hotdogs and those store-bought buns that I used to love so much as a child and that I detested so much now warming on the back of the drum, and a gallon pot of coffee simmering on the side.

Mayhugh's mother and father were asleep in the Thunderbird. Josh went directly and got them up and brought them out to the fire where the goat was cooking to be introduced also. All the time I was protesting that we didn't want to bother them and that they had already done enough just giving us a fire and a flat place to camp. But say what we would, the lady brought us all coffee, and the boys, including Mayhugh, helped us set up our tents and string our packs, and they insisted we have the first hamburgers and then the first slice of goat.

I told them about the goats I'd owned as a boy and about our farm—when I talk to anybody I always speak of the *farm* rather than the *farms* out of my childhood because it simplifies everything—and finally about my mother, whom I always seem to get to talking about one way or another, and the lady smiled and the man smiled and Mayhugh's daddy from Massatwosetts, who had teeth missing, smiled and they told us how they came up here every year and camped for a weekend during their two-week vacation from the packing plant where they all worked, including the women, down in Hampton.

They reminded me exactly of my childhood, of the people out of my childhood, of how my mother would have insisted that we be served first if we had been strangers and come to visit her, of how she would have fussed around us, checking to see if we couldn't eat a little more of this or didn't want to try a little more of that.

All the men, with the exception of Mayhugh, were smoking marijuana. Josh and Pudd's daddy got to talking about how bad he used to be to drink until his son had come back from Veet Name. Since then he'd found he really preferred to smoke marijuana. One reason was that he had always suffered badly from hangovers and found that smoking got him like he needed to be and didn't seem to hurt him like alcohol did. I was feeling pretty good by then from the beer and the marijuana and started to confess my own problem with alcohol—I always confess after I get a little high, confess to everything, which is one of my worst character failings—and, during my confession, let slip that what I was actually fondest of was vodka, and I'll be damned if the daughter, whose name was Lillian, didn't send Mayhugh over to the 1962 Thunderbird and presently he came back with a Dixie cup filled right up to the brim with vodka. She said she liked some now and then herself.

"I really can't," I said. "I been trying to cut back and. . . ."

But there was nothing to do but to drink it. They sat watching me, smiling, and they would have been genuinely hurt if I hadn't. After all, Mayhugh had brought it brim-full without spilling a drop and the very least I could do was enjoy it.

I drank it off and chased with a beer. Josh's daddy watched me with some satisfaction. "I don't see why a man cain't have him a little something to help him along," he said. "Speaks well of a man to need a little something in this world. I wouldn't trust a man who could git through it cold sober."

"Pudd used to be bad to drink before he went to Veet Name," said Mayhugh's daddy. "He got us to smoking, though, when he come back and we all about quit drinking now." They turned to watch Pudd, who watched the fire stonily. "They given him a medal, you know?"

"Shore did," said Pudd's mother. "Given my boy a medal."

"He was wounded twicet," said Mayhugh. "Oncet in the back and oncet in the ast."

"I told you enough, Mayhugh," said his grandmother, "I'm gone jerk a knot in you about cussing."

"Yessum," said the boy. Then to me: "You want yourself some more of that vodka?"

I shook my head. It was about all I could do. You may have wondered why I haven't said anything about Charné and Ronald. I don't remember what they were doing. They were there; I remember that. I think Charné had done a pill because her legs had been bothering her. She was actually carrying far too much weight. I outweighed her by fifty pounds, and yet her pack was within a pound or two as heavy as mine. So I think she probably had a beer and a pill. Ronald, I know, was thinking pretty heavy about Franny, which would become obvious later on in the trip. He was probably lying back in the shadows, just honing on those lights up on the hill behind the water tower in Erwin, Tennessee.

A hand took my shoulder. It was Pudd. He had come up behind me. "You want to step over here?" he said.

I got up and followed him over by the Thunderbird. I thought he wanted to give me another drink. Instead, he held out his finger with something about the size of a pinhead on the end of it. "Swaller this," he said.

"What is it?" I said. But I already knew, or thought I did. I could see it in his eyes after he shot the falls earlier. But I hadn't wanted to believe it. I didn't want to think about it.

"Acid," he said.

"I don't want any, Pudd," I said.

"Ah, swaller it," he said. "I want to talk."

I don't know why people who drop acid are always trying to get everybody else to do it, too, but they are. The last I'd had was given me by the children of a writer. I was staying in the writer's house, and his children, whom I'm very fond of, insisted I eat some acid with them. I had not wanted to, but it had been a fine day up to that point and they said I'd ruin everything if I didn't go the rest of the way with them. So I did. And it scared me very badly. Every time I've ever done it, it has terrified me. I don't know why people do acid.

"Listen," I said, "that stuff's always full of strichnine and killing hits of speed, and it does bad things to me. Really, I'd like to, but it's always just such bad stuff."

"I want to talk," he said. "Can you understand? I want to talk about what all they—ma and them—said back there. But I cain't without this. I cain't if I don't and you don't. Can you understand? You gone in the morning. It don't matter. I ain't gone see you again. You me neither. What could it matter?"

I looked at his finger that he was pointing at me. It still had the hit of acid on it. "That stuff scares me, Pudd."

"Not this," he said. "Ain't no speed, strichnine, nothing in this. This ain't off the street. I know where it come from. God, believe me, man. Swaller it."

Well, I had two pounds of goat in me and about five slabs of hoecake. I thought it would go down easy, but I knew I was lying and that I'd probably end up in trouble, and if I hadn't been drinking, I might not have done it. But I probably would have, too. You would have had to be there. You would have had to hear his voice and see his face there by the Thunderbird car in the dim light from the fire. I liked him. More—I loved him. I said to myself: cheap at the price. And swallowed it.

We went back to sit by the campfire. I should have told Charné or Ronald. But I don't remember seeing them. Pudd lit another joint. His mother and I popped another Budweiser.

I've seen movies and read accounts of how acid affects people. Colors flare and swirl. Walls melt. They taste music. They hear hotdogs. They feel red. And so on. In my experience, nothing has ever melted. Lampposts have never run down into a puddle on the curbstone. My senses have never "switched." But things have tilted pretty badly on me. Walls stand at angles. I've found myself walking uphill in hallways I knew were flat. But mainly for me it has been anxiety, a crushing, sourceless, terror that things are not right and never will be right again. The feeling is not unlike the fear I've always known when I wake from sleepwalking. It is the knowledge that neither man nor God will forgive me for.

. . . For who knows what? Physically, my heartbeat has run up to about 170; my breath has been short; I've been unable to stop talking or moving sometimes for as long as an hour, all of which suggests that whatever I'd eaten was laced with a good lump of speed.

The dose Pudd gave me was much more mellow than anything I'd ever had. My heart didn't bounce around. I didn't sweat. I was calm. But the world was excessively vivid. Whatever was dark was darker; whatever was loud was louder; whatever had color was brighter. And one other thing: pieces of time and experience simply disappeared.

The next thing I clearly remember was Pudd saying we had to go back to the falls. It did not seem a particularly unreasonable thing to say, and I can clearly recall my only reaction was to point out that it was much too dark and that we'd lose our way. He said he never lost his way and that there was a full moon. Once we got through the woods to the river it would be just like day. It did not occur to me to ask him why he thought we had to go back to the falls, but I said even though I was sure he never lost his way and that the river would be just like day under the moon, I had no intention of going with him. I'd walked all I intended to walk. We sat staring at each other, and I have the clearest image of the pores in his face and how sweat was beading his cheeks and how like glycerine the sweat was, bright as quicksilver under his eyes that were brighter than any eyes could have been.

Then without transition the river roared under the moon with rapids and boulders snow-crested with foaming water, and the roar was so loud it shook the teeth in my mouth and the breaking water so bright I could only look at it for a little while before I had to glance away toward the black face of cliff rising to the top of the fall. We were sitting at the very eddying pool where Charné and Ronald and I had sat that afternoon.

Pudd said: "People talk about shit they don't know a thing about."

He was wearing his black hat, and the voice came out from under the black hat. It seemed the blackest hat and the blackest face I had ever seen and the most profound truth I had ever heard.

"You ready?" he said.

"Yes," I said.

I knew instantly that he meant for us to climb the face of the cliff, the same one I had seen him climb that afternoon. Something in me did not want to do it—not fear exactly—just some heavy stubborn resistance. But curiously, there seemed no alternative. I stood up and the world tilted. The falls went more than forty-five degrees to the left, and the water rushed so loudly that the noise was like nausea in my throat, like my stomach rising.

I thought: he means to kill me.

And curiously I did not care. I followed Pudd to the vertical wall of rock, which did not seem nearly so fearsome now because it had tilted some. It would be no more than walking up a slope.

There is no memory, though, of walking up the slope, no memory at all of the sharp rock face leading up to where the water dropped. I turned my head and we were there. The white water made the river shine like lace as it ran curving down the gorge between the dark wall of rock and trees. Pudd and I had gone out on the stones over the falls. I was nimble and sure as a goat. But that heavy resistance was still in me and I knew that I ought to be afraid, that part of me was afraid. But the part of me that was afraid didn't count. It had no will to act. It could know but not act. Perhaps the strangest part about the whole thing was that I knew I was zonked on acid, acid given me by this Grit whom I liked or maybe loved, but the love I knew or thought I knew was coming from Darvon and beer and self-pity. But mostly I knew I was being had.

"They give me that goddamn medal," Pudd said.

We were standing in the center of the fall on a wide flat rock.

"What medal was it?" I asked.

"Silver Star," he said. "They given it to me cause I was just so goddamn brave." His voice was sharp and bitter above the roar of the water. He looked at me, but I couldn't see his face under the hat. He put his arm around my shoulder. It was the gentle gesture of a comrade, but I felt the threat in it. "Mayhugh's right, you know. I did git hit in the back and the ass. You know how you git hit in the back and the ass?" I refused to say anything. I saw what was coming. "You got yourself turned the wrong way, that's how." His arm had tightened on my shoulder. He no longer seemed the boy I'd eaten goat with back at the camp, whom I'd seen look at Mayhugh with such patience and love.

"They don't give Silver Stars to people turned the wrong way," I said.

"You think that? Is that what you believe?"

Of course, I did not think that or believe that.

"When the shit starts flying," he said, "half the time you don't know who's with you or who's against you or which way's up or what the hell you're doing and it was night and I was crying and screaming. I didn't know a goddamn thing about nothing, just I wanted to stay alive, to git back to this mountain." He was quiet for a long time. I didn't know what to say. Then he said: "But they ruined everything when they given me that goddamn medal." He tilted his head back, and the moon fell full on his drawn, lined face. "Now I'm scared all the time. I'm never not scared."

"Ah, shit, Pudd," I said. "Come down. Everybody's scared. I never knew anybody that wasn't scared. Anybody that can be shot at and not be scared to death is a goddamn fool."

"That don't count for nothing. I don't give a damn how anybody else is." He looked over the falls. "Do you know this thing scares me to death? Shooting this goddamn thing makes me puke I'm so scared. I come up here and do it, though. I come up here and do it." He turned back to me. "You saw me do it."

"Yes," I said. "You went over it like a fucking fish. Listen, let's go. I want to go."

"Nobody's ever gone over this fall at night," he said. "Nobody I know of ever has."

I wasn't surprised. I'd seen all of this coming. But there had been no way to get off the rock. I knew if I tried, he would take me over the fall with him. He was no longer trying to prove his courage; he was trying to kill himself.

"You and me can do it," he said. "I can show you, and you and me can shoot this goddamn fall like nobody ever did."

The thing that had lain in me before as heavy stubborn resistance turned to fear as deep as I had ever know, but it was still as though that part of me belonged to somebody else. I was very calm. I knew exactly what I was going to do. And I knew that it was going to work exactly.

I once wrote a book called *Karate Is a Thing of the Spirit* and studied karate with a great master, a black belt karateka named Dirk Mosig, who never thought very much of me as a pupil for the reason that I was never any good. Karate takes among other things the balance of a ballet dancer. With my gimpy legs, I have no balance at all. I'd never been able to make an Okinawan reverse roundhouse kick work in my life. I knew what it was, I'd practiced it, but like most other karate techniques, it had remained sloppy and ineffective.

But I not only knew when I moved to the edge of the rock that the kick would work but also that it would hit him where I meant to hit him, over the heart, and more, I knew he would fall straight forward onto the rock.

I hate acid. I categorically condemn it. But it is passing strange. I remember a high jumper telling me about the first time he cleared seven feet. He'd been trying for months and his training had come to nothing. He was stale, frustrated, dying as a jumper. One day he dropped some acid with a friend, went out to the track, warmed up, stretched for about an hour, and the first time he approached the bar at seven feet he cleared it. He then did seven feet more than a dozen times in a row before he missed.

"Hell, yes," I said. "I'm with you. Show me that groove. Show me just where to jump."

The rock we were standing on was maybe six feet across. He took his arm off my shoulder and moved to the edge. He pointed. "See them two rocks there? When we go, put your feet right between them. You'll hit the groove and you're home free."

"Step back here," I said. "Let me look."

He moved to the back of the rock, and I moved to the edge and looked over the falls. When I knew he was as far away as he was going to get, I spun and went into an Okinawan reverse roundhouse kick that leads with the point of the heel. I caught him directly over the heart. He didn't make a sound, only a soft explosion of air from his mouth, and went straight down like he'd been struck in the head with a hammer.

That night on the rock in Tennessee, I stood over Pudd, the calm and perfect karate master I'm not and have never been.

The Most Kindest Cut
of All: Vasectomy

We were talking about rubbers, the doctor and I. You remember rubbers? Little round things rolled up in a circle, the kind you bought in a filling-station rest room and kept in your wallet until it caused a permanent ring in the leather and you never ended up using it. Adolescents in those days knew something about the true nature of hope and bone-deep longing, to say nothing of what it meant to live in a perpetual atmosphere of failure.

But despite the fact that I was not an adolescent and the wallet in my pocket had no ring in the leather, we were talking of rubbers. I was having my half-decade physical checkup, sitting naked on his examination table while he fooled around with a little K-Y jelly and a thin surgical glove, getting ready to inflict his final ignominious gesture upon me by probing my mellow, yellow, smellow farrow.

We were talking about rubbers because not only was he my doctor, he was also my friend, but even being my friend didn't mean we could live through the lifesaving indignities of a physical in absolute silence.

I was bent over the table and he went for me. I said: "You doctors knock me out. You really do. It's all right for us to go to a drugstore and spend a fortune on Four X's, but you won't take fifteen minutes to fix it so we won't ever have to go there again."

"Four X's," he said in a bemused voice, still probing.

"The best rubber on the market," I said. "A buck a shot." I grunted from a particularly vicious thrust. "Sold only in drugstores. Not like the lousy stuff they sell in filling stations. A guy

might as well use Saran Wrap. I've heard of some who do."
He turned me around. "You don't have cancer of the ass. Or
if you do, I can't find it." Then he said, in what I thought was one
of the saddest voices I'd ever heard: "You know, in forty years
of rectal examinations, I've yet to find a single cancer. Not one."
But I wasn't listening. I was determined to make him admit the
hypocrisy of it all. "Go on down to the drugstore," I said bitterly,
watching him strip the glove from his hand and drop it into a
basket. "But a vasectomy? Not hardly."
He raised his pale eyes from behind his rimless glasses. "Vasectomy? Vasectomy?"
This was ten years ago, and I was afraid even *he* hadn't heard
of the goddamn word. It wasn't something that was exactly on
everybody's lips. Spermicide was the big word in those days,
foams of one kind or another, the rhythm method, and other
things that didn't work. But vasectomy was a different story. I'd
wanted one the first time I ever heard of it. Cut the passageway
and tie it off with catgut. Let the little bastards try to get out then.
But it wasn't as easy as I'd thought. The doctors would take one
look at me and say I was too young.
"What if you change your mind later on?" they'd say.
"Then I'll just have to live with it," I'd say.
"Not good enough," they'd say.
Then they would patiently explain that it was what was called
a mutilating operation and that if I ever changed my mind, I
could come back on them and sue.
"Don't you have insurance?"
"I do," they'd say, "and I plan to keep it. The answer is no."
I was cleaning up with the dainty piece of paper the doctor had
given me with averted eyes after the finger probe. Finally, after
he was sure I had finished, he said: "My partner'll give you one
if you like."
I was, as they say, overwhelmed. "You mean a vasectomy?"
"Right."
"Why the hell didn't you tell me this six months ago?"
"You didn't ask." He turned back to what he was doing. "Make
an appointment with his secretary when you leave."
The young thing sat behind the glass partition, dressed in

starched white uniform, long hair hived on her head, appointment book open in front of her. Her tiny teeth were straight and
blinding as she smiled her question.

"I'd like an appointment with Dr. Brown."

"Of course," she said. "And what is the nature of your problem?"

"I want a vasectomy."

Her face fell. Even her hived head seemed to shrink. "Vasectomy?" she said.

"Anytime on Tuesday'll be fine," I said.

She talked while she wrote in her little book.

"Are you married?"

"Yes."

"You know your wife'll have to come down and sign for it."

"My *wife*'ll have to sign for *me?* Hell, I'm practically five years
older than she is."

"Doctor requires it," she said.

"I've already told her I was trying to get one. And she doesn't
care."

"Do you have children?"

She was through writing in her book now, and I was feeling just
terrible about the whole thing, but feeling worse about being
slapped around by this girl, who was herself a child, who couldn't
have been out of high school more than a year, if that long.

"Is all this just general conversation, or is there some point to
it?"

"Doctor will want to know."

"I've got two boys."

She shook her head sadly. "*Just* two."

"What the hell's wrong with two?"

"Please try to control yourself," she said. "You can see the
doctor next Tuesday at two-thirty. In the meantime, your wife'll
have to come in and sign a few forms."

"My wife'll have to come in and sign a few forms? What kind
of forms?"

"Tell her to bring some identification, too."

I was beaten by then, and I knew what they were up to and that
there was no way for me to win. "What kind of identification?"

Her young motherless mouth got grimmer. "A marriage license would be nice. And two other pieces. Something like a driver's license, maybe."

If I could have got behind the glass with her, I'd have choked her. But I couldn't, so I just said, "Right," and left.

My wife, Sally, went down and had to suffer even greater humiliation than I because although she was only twenty-six, she looked eighteen—still does, for that matter—and they gave her all manner of hassle, including the fact that I might be fairly useless as a husband if I let the doctor fool around with me "down there."

Sally never lost her smile. "If it's what he wants, it's all right with me."

"But you're the other half," said the grim-faced child in charge of forms.

"You've read her her rights," I said. "For Christ's sweet sake, give her the forms."

"I *do* wish you'd keep a civil tongue," the girl said, but she handed over the forms.

I thought I was going to get cut the following Tuesday, but as it turned out, that was just talk time. I sat across the desk from the doctor, and he explained to me what I already knew: all about the vas deferens being the duct that carries sperm from the epididymis to the ejaculatory duct; about how once the thing was cut, chances were it couldn't be fixed again.

He put his fingertips together and looked at me across his desk. "Mr. Crews, do you hate children?"

"I love children," I said. "I just happen to think that two's enough."

"What if something happens to them—they die—what then?"

"I will've had two. I think that's my share. Besides, I could adopt some."

"Suppose something happened to your wife and the woman you wanted to marry wanted children of her own and you couldn't give them to her?"

"Then obviously she'd be the wrong woman for me to marry, wouldn't she?"

"Your answers come very quickly," he said.

"I've thought about it a long time."

He looked down at his chart. "You have two boys?"

"Yes."

"And you're thirty years old?"

"Right."

"How would next Thursday be?"

"Next Thursday'll be sensational."

"Three o'clock then. We'll do it right here in the office under local anesthetic. Won't take but fifteen or twenty minutes." I was already up to go when he asked: "Do you have Blue Cross/Blue Shield?"

"Yes."

"They'll pay for half of it. The operation itself costs seventy-five dollars. Sit back down. There's one other thing. Some men become impotent, or nearly so, after a vasectomy. There's absolutely no anatomical reason they should, but they do."

"I'll take my chances," I said.

"See the nurse on the way out," he said, bending to his charts again.

I saw the nurse on the way out and suffered her fierce looks while she made an appointment for me. "I come from a very large family," she said as she wrote. "A very large family.

"Be here a half hour before: at two-thirty." Her dark face darkened. "And have your wife come sign before. No wife to sign, no operation."

"She'll be here."

Another nurse approached from behind the one in the booth and handed me a little paper cup about the size of a thimble. "We'll need a specimen before you go."

I looked at the cup in my hand. "A specimen of what?"

"Don't be wise."

I really didn't know. Then I did. "Where?" I said.

"The rest room is down the hall on your left." So I took the little cup and went down to the rest room and jerked off into the little cup. In a long life of feeling like a fool, that may have been the high point. Thirty years old, husband and father, jerking off into a cup the size of the end of your thumb, in some anonymous room with a sign on the wall that said: "WASH HANDS BEFORE

LEAVING." I was scared to death I'd miss the thing, but I didn't, and when I brought it out, she slabbed a bit onto a piece of glass and put it under the microscope.

"My God," she said, "they're beautiful. Really strong tails." She looked up from the microscope. "You want to see?"

"No."

"But they're *yours.*"

"Not for long, they're not," I said, and walked out.

Sally came down and ate her ration of shit, showing everything from her birth certificate to her fingerprints, signing an affidavit that we did in fact have two boys at home and it was all right to cut her husband's string loose.

The doctor prepped me himself. I was lying naked in a chair that reminded me of the kind the old-time barbers used. He was very businesslike and efficient. He shaved the few hairs there where he was going to cut at the top of my scrotum. He'd already given me a couple of needles, and everything he meant to cut was dead to the world. He looked up at me.

"This is it," he said. "You sure you want to go ahead with it?"

"Cut," I said.

And he did. Two tiny incisions. Snipped a couple of lines, tied them off, and sewed up the incisions. The whole thing was done in twenty minutes.

"You are going to have to come back several times and let us have specimens. There'll be live sperm for a while, but finally there should not be any at all."

I beamed upon the doctor. "Sir, you're a prince among men."

He beamed back at me. "Not really," he said.

For the next several times I went in, the nurses glowered at me, their young bellies yearning for that packed-full-of-life feeling and knowing that that there was at least one man less in the world capable of helping them realize their dream. The sixth time I loped my pony in the tiled, sterile bathroom and brought the little cup of come to the nurse, she turned up from her microscope with the most hopeless look I ever expect to see in my life.

"Well, you're done," she said. "It's nothing here."

I went out of the office smiling. I've been smiling ever since.

Going Down in Valdeez

I was standing there in front of the Pipeline Club in a fine, misting rain with my hand still on the door of the taxi that had brought me in from the airport to Valdez, Alaska (pronounced *Valdeez*, so that the last syllable rhymes with *disease*, by the folks who lived thereabouts, folks who do not take the pronunciation of their town lightly and who are subject to become very pissed very quick if you do not come down hard on the *eez*, drawing it out in a long sibilant *z*); I was standing there looking at a legless man where he sat on the sidewalk on his little wheeled dolly, a beatific look of ecstasy on his thin, pale face as he looked not back at me but up into the cold, slanting mist, and the lady cabdriver was saying for the fourth time since I got into her cab: "These goddamn *new* people think they own this goddamn town, but I'll tell you one goddamn thing: They don't own it yet."

I was stunned with exhaustion. The flight from Atlanta to Chicago to Seattle to Ketchikan to Juneau to Yakutat to Cordova had left me confused and disoriented. Then my ordinary morning terrors had been compounded by the flight from Cordova in a Piper Aztec, bouncing and dropping and tilting through winds that anywhere else in the world would have been called a hurricane.

The ecstasy on the legless man's face had changed to a gentle, bemused satisfaction. I turned to see if the taxi driver was looking at the legless man. I thought she might tell me about him, tell me maybe that he was a religious mystic famous in Valdez for seeing through to the secret heart of things. But she was still staring curiously up at me, and through her clenched teeth, she said: "You just goddamn remember that."

"Look, lady," I said, but she was already squealing in a U turn, roaring off toward the airport.

When I started across the sidewalk, the legless man put his padded fists down and gave himself a shove, shooting his little dolly past me. I stopped, blinked. There on the cement where the legless man had been sitting were two symmetrical, perfectly formed human turds. I turned just in time to see the man and the dolly being lifted by two young boys into a camper on the back of a Ford pickup. I knew I'd been given a sign. Because I believe most devoutly in such things, I knew I had been given a sign to reckon with.

Inside the Pipeline Club I asked the bartender for double vodka and tonic with no ice and then found myself a corner where I could lean my head back against a wall and collect myself.

When I got off the Alaska Airlines plane in Cordova, the flight up to that point had only been exhausting. An hour later, when I got into the Piper Aztec, it went from exhausting to terrifying. We were in heavy rain and wind under a lowering sky. It couldn't have been much more than noon, but it seemed like dusk dark. I was the only passenger, and I rode up front by the pilot. He looked to be in his early twenties, wearing Levi's and a work shirt. His damp hair was hanging in a wet curling bang over his eyes. He was impossibly young to be taking me up in an airplane.

"What airline is this?" I shouted over the noise of the engine. The Aztec was unmarked except for numbers on the fuselage, and I thought wildly as we approached the runway that I was on the wrong plane and, such being the case, I could get off.

"Chitina," he shouted back. "We do ferrying work for Alaskan over to Valdeez."

He moved the throttle to full rich, and the plane shook and groaned, its little wings flapping like a crippled bird's. "Listen," he screamed, "the ride'll be a little choppy today. But I think it'll be all right."

He thought it would be all right. Yes, indeed. Once aloft, I opened my eyes and watched him expertly light a Lucky Strike while the horizon tilted everywhere about us. I asked him where he'd learned to fly, thinking perhaps the Army or the Air Force.

"Aw, it's just something I picked up back in Texas. Always been interested in it and I just picked it up."

His name was Jerry Austin. From Austin, Texas. There was a story that the town had been named for some of his people somewhere back there. He didn't know if it was true. Thought it might be a lie. But you never can tell.

"Only been up here in Alasker three months. Hope to git a job with a jet out of Anchorage. Don't know if I can, though. Ruther not fly this rig up here in the winter."

We had been in the air for about twenty minutes when we turned away from the coast, following a wide body of water up between two mountains that rose 4000 or 5000 feet above us on either side.

"Valdeez Bay," he shouted. We had come out of the rain now, and the day had brightened under patches of blue sky showing through the clouds. "Right up yonder beyond that rise is Valdeez. This is where the tankers'll come in to pick up the oil off the pipeline." He looked down at the shimmering surface of the bay. "Seems a shame to ruin that water. Won't be fit to wash your feet in when they git through with it." He pointed off to the left as he banked the plane. "There she is."

From the air Valdez looked like a mobile-home court. It was a city on wheels. House trailers were jammed into every available space.

"What's that over there?" I asked.

"That's four hundred miles of steel pipe. Thirty-foot sections. Four-feet diameter." He looked at me and smiled. "Made in Japan. It's stacked over there right where Valdeez used to be."

"Used to be?"

"A few years back Valdeez was wiped out by a earthquake and tidal wave. When they built it up again, they moved it up here."

We were coming in fast now toward the airport. All manner of heavy machinery—packers and stackers and dirt buggies and backhoes and scrapers—raced about over the barren landscape. For no apparent reason, two helicopters hovered a half mile away on the side of a mountain. Raw lumber was everywhere, stacks of it, and the naked sides of buildings in various stages of construction shone in the sun but only briefly because as we made our approach, the sky closed again as if by magic and a misting rain began to fall.

"Jesus," I said, "is that a dirt runway?"

"Yeah," Jerry said, putting his cigarette out with one hand and bringing us in with the other. "But when they finish over there" —he pointed to the madly racing machinery—"when they git through over there, you'll be able to bring a 727 in here."

The lady cabdriver laughed when I told her to take me to a motel. "No rooms in this town. None. I can check if you want me to, but there won't be any." She got on her radio, and sure enough, there were no rooms.

"Take me to a bar then," I said.

After I'd had enough vodka to steady me down, I asked the bartender to sell me a bottle.

"Not but one place you can buy a bottle of vodka in Valdeez. Just a block over there. Pinzon Liquor Store. Truck Egan's place."

"Egan?" I said, the name trying to remind me of something. Then I knew where I'd heard it. "Say, he's not. . . ."

"That's right," he said. "Governor of Alaska's brother. Truck's the smart one in the family. Shit, Bill Egan's on the phone two, three times a day, asking Truck what to do."

I walked through the rain across Egan Drive to the Pinzon Liquor Store on Tatitlek Avenue. Truck Egan was a very small man with wet eyes, a sad, gentle face, and a badly twisted hunchback. His long, slender white fingers trembled as he put the vodka in a bag.

There were no other customers in the store, but he didn't want to talk. Or rather, his sister, Alice, an imposing lady with bluing hair, didn't want to talk, and that seemed to discourage Truck. It was apparent Alice was displeased over the prospect of anybody writing anything about Valdez.

I got back into the rain and walked toward a neon sign I'd seen from the taxi coming in from the airport advertising the Club Valdez. Egan Drive is the main street going through town. It is wide and paved with sidewalks and curbstones. But once you turn off that and head up toward the place where the house trailers are stacked in cheek to jowl, up toward the little marina where the fishing boats swing at anchor, the streets dissolve into mud and potholes and rock. Packs of dogs scavenge in overflowing dumpsters and garbage cans, snarling and fighting among themselves. Scraps of lumber and twisted sheets of corrugated tin litter the edges of swampy streets. Construction is going on everywhere in and among the house trailers. Even the Alaska National Bank of the North is in a house trailer, but they're building right next door, going at it with hammer and Skilsaw, and even as I write this, they might be out of their house trailer and into something new and fine.

The Club Valdez was one enormous room, a bar across the front, two pool tables in the back, and, in the space between, maybe ten or twelve round wooden tables. The smoke was heavy. The jukebox was playing Charlie Pride. A lone couple two-stepped across the bare wooden floor as a line of men at the bar watched them.

I got a vodka and went to the head. The sweet smell of grass clung to the damp calcimined walls, and clouds of smoke hung in the air, mixing nicely with the odor of vomit and piss. "My, my, my," I said to myself while I watered off, "it's everywhere, even here in Valdeez."

As if on cue, a boy popped out of the stall. "You wanta buy some?"

I looked at him and thought, *Now, ain't you a dumbass?* but I said, "What you selling?"

He had on a beaded headband and a fringed leather jacket over greasy Levi's stuffed into mud-spattered cowboy boots.

"What you lookin to buy?" The words turned to grits in his mouth, and it occurred to me that most of the talk I'd heard since I'd been in town, including the taxi driver's, had been Grit talk.

"What you selling a lid for?" I asked.

"A weighed ounce," he said, "is worth ninety dollars."

"Not to me it isn't," I said.

"All right then," he said, "sixty dollars."

"You're hurt," I said. "Something's burned in your fuse box."

He shrugged. "People expect to be robbed up here. Anythin is worth anythin you can git for it. But sixty's all right. Sixty wouldn't cheat me."

"I bet it wouldn't," I said. As I was going out the door, he went back into the stall.

I went to the bar and watched the couple two-step. The girl was very skinny and she had a baby with her. She had thoughtfully tied it to a chair with a leather belt. She and the man went back to the table between numbers to chug some beer and pet the baby. She gave it a sip from time to time, and the baby sat strapped to the chair, gurgling and mewling contentedly, now and then nodding off. Which reminded me I was looking for a place to put my head down.

"Writin a letter home, are you?"

I looked up from the notes I was scribbling. The man was on the stool next to me. He seemed to be about as drunk as I was. I would have guessed his age at thirty, but he had a marvelously weathered and ruined face. On his hard hat was a faded McGovern sticker.

"Yeah," I said. "I'm just writing the old lady it ain't nowhere to stay in this town."

"You just git in?"

"Yeah."

"You ain't got on yet?"

"Not yet, but I'm supposed to git on."

"You got some cash money in you pocket?"

"I wouldn't come off up here without some cash money."

"Go out yonder to the airport then and tell Dave Kennedy I sent you. My name's Bugger Wells. Kennedy's building a camp out there the other side of the airport. It'll cost you, but you can stay. Ask anybody out there for Dave Kennedy. You won't have no trouble."

The cabdriver took me to a tiny two-story building that had an outside stairway leading to the top. The second floor was a single room with a half partition. The whole thing couldn't have been more than twenty feet square. Maps and overlays and blueprints and papers of every sort were stuffed into shelves along the walls. Two Teletype machines rattled next to the semipartition. A polar-bear skin covered the top of a dun-colored couch. The bear's mouth was open, and its stunned marble eyes stared past me through the window where the helicopters still hovered in the distance and the yellow, growling machinery still raced about over the airport. Dave Kennedy stood at his desk, the top of which was a foot deep in papers, most of which seemed incredibly dusty. He was on the phone, cradling it between his shoulder and right ear. His left ear was pinned against his head and grown shut.

A lady in corduroy trousers sat in the corner at a typewriter. She stopped typing and looked at me. I told her what the guy at the Club Valdez had told me.

"Valdeez," she said. "You say *Valdeeez!*"

"He was right," said Dave Kennedy, who had just put the phone down. "You can stay at the camp. Thirty-three dollars a day. You looking for work?"

I decided to tell him what I was doing in Valdez.

"No way," he said. "Take you a year to write this and you still wouldn't have it right. You'd have it wrong. The only way to measure what's happening here? You know? You want me to tell you? I'll tell you. A six-inch ruler made out of rubber that stretches to seventeen feet. That's how. Nothing like this ever been done. And you can't worry because a ruler's got twelve inches to the foot. In Valdeez, there may be twelve feet to the inch. OK?"

The explanation seemed to satisfy him immensely. It tended to confuse me, but I thought better of asking him to explain it. I'd noticed a National Car Rental sign downstairs and asked if I could get a car. Rent you a plane if you want one, he said. I said, no, a car would do nicely. While the girl was writing out the ticket for the car, Dave Kennedy took me over to the window and pointed. "See where they're building down there?" It looked to me as if they were building *everywhere* down there, and I told him so.

"No, no," he said impatiently, "there by the trailer. Right there with the silver top. Go in there and ask for Hap. Hap, the cook. He'll fix it. Give him the money."

I found Hap in a house trailer that had been converted into a kitchen and dining room with enough seats to feed 54 people. Directly next to it, a whole covey of carpenters was building a permanent dining hall that would eventually feed 600.

Hap was feeding some of the early night crew when I got there and he asked me to wait. I sat at a table, looking at a cup of coffee he had given me and thinking how nice it was going to be to put my head down, when a foreman came in. Like most of the men there, the foreman's skin was ruined from the wind and the sun and the snow. He had what looked like might be skin cancer across the bridge of his nose. He was pissed when he came in. He kicked a couple of chairs, hustled his balls, and sat down. He started talking loudly, a little out of breath, to nobody in particular.

"I'll tell you one damn thing: if you pick up something in this town, don't set it back down. Because if you do set it back down even for a minute, it'll be another price when you pick it up." He got off his chair, hustled his balls again, sat back down, crossed his legs, uncrossed them, and sat kicking one heavy boot against the other. "Went into town there to buy a damn alarm clock. Wanted to make sure the crew was up and ready. Went in the store there. Didn't have but one kind of clock. Looked like a piece of shit, but I thought it'd get us up. Young kid behind the counter. Asked him how much it was. Said he didn't know, but the boss was next door and he'd run ask. While he was gone, I picked up one of the goddamn things. Had a sticker on it said six dollars and fifty cent. Kid come back and said the boss said nine dollars and fifty cent. I told the kid the one in my hand said six-fifty. He said he just knowed what the boss said. Fuck it, I didn't want to stand around there all day talking to a shirttail kid, so I bought it. Brought it down here to camp and the goddamn thing quit in the middle of the night. Crew was half a fucking hour late. Took the goddamn thing down there a while ago. Man runs the place said he was sorry, but it was as is. *Sold as is.* No refund, no nothing. But the sonofabitch *did* say he was sorry. I told him to stick it up his ass, and I hope the alarm went off. I'd already checked all over town and there weren't no more clocks. Not another goddamn one in town. I guess he knowed it too because when I told him I'd have to buy another of the goddamn sorry things, he looked me dead in the eye and said just as slick as you'd want: 'That'll be twelve dollars and fifty cent.' "

Hap came out of the kitchen and took my money, $165 for five nights, and gave me over to a bull cook named Paul, a dark boy of about twenty-two with very white teeth and short, curly hair. On the way over to where I would be bunking he explained to me that a bull cook was the all-round good guy in camp who made the beds, carried the trash, swept the floors, and did whatever else was necessary to keep the bunkhouse crew happy.

The bunkhouse in this case turned out to be a house trailer. The entire camp was made out of house trailers joined together by a walkway and covered over with a little roof. Each trailer had a deep sink, a bathroom, and slept five men. The floors were covered with gold-speck carpeting, and the walls were all paneled with imitation wood. It was exactly the sort of thing that would have passed for elegance in Waycross, Georgia. Paul told me there was a washing machine and dryer in the back that I could use for nothing. If I needed anything, I should let him know. When he left, I walked outside and sat on an empty gas can. It was gray and still raining, but the sun was brilliant and brittle as glass high on the sides of the Chugach Mountains where they rose 5000 feet and better on all sides of the town. I was finally at the end of the line, Valdez, Alaska.

Alaska is an awesome place where exaggeration and outrage are the norm. It is a place where Eskimos live and work in cold so extreme it often reaches 80 degrees *below* zero. Three percent of the state is made up of active glaciers and ice fields—20,000 square miles—more than is found in the rest of the inhabited world combined. It is a land of unimaginable wealth that we ripped off from the Russians on October 18, 1867, for about two cents an acre. The shortest distance separating North America from Asia is between Little Diomede and Big Diomede islands. On Little Diomede a picture of Abraham Lincoln hangs on the schoolhouse wall. In the schoolhouse on Big Diomede is a picture of Karl Marx. Everything about Alaska stuns the imagination—including the proposed trans-Alaska pipeline. To understand what is happening to the town of Valdez, to the people there, it is necessary to have some notion of the dimensions, the magnitude of the pipeline itself.

In the northernmost part of the state, between the formidable mountains of the Brooks Range and the Arctic Ocean, lies the North Slope. And it is there at Prudhoe Bay that the trans-Alaska pipeline will rise. It passes the Sagavanirktok River, the Atigun

Valley and crosses the mountains of the wild Brooks Range itself through the 4500-foot Dietrich Pass; and from there it goes south to the Yukon River and on south, passing only 15 miles to the east of Fairbanks. Once past Fairbanks, it goes into the Alaska Mountain Range, where it will reach an elevation of 3500 feet as it crosses the Isabel Pass before descending into the Copper River Basin. The line then climbs the Chugach Mountains and descends through Keystone Canyon into Valdez, the nearest year-round ice-free port capable of accommodating tankers of the size that will be needed to haul the oil to West Coast refineries. The distance covered is exactly 798 miles.

The line itself will be buried when the terrain it crosses is solid rock or well-drained gravel. When it is not buried, it will be raised on special pipe supports. It will go over rivers and under rivers —more often than not under them—and when it does go under rivers, it will be encased in concrete four inches thick.

The pipe out of which the line will be constructed comes in sections about 40 or 60 feet long, 4 feet in diameter, with thicknesses ranging from .462 inches to .562 inches. In Berkeley, California, where the pipe was tested, a section of it was subjected to a maximum force of 2.52 million pounds and a lateral deflection force of 459,000 pounds before it wrinkled. There is, as I write this, a total of 418.54 miles of this pipe stacked and waiting in Valdez. It was made in Japan and the first shipment arrived in Valdez September 13, 1969, the last shipment October 21, 1971. The other pipe-storage yards are at Fairbanks and at Prudhoe Bay.

By the best estimates, there are an incredible 9.6 billion barrels of oil on the North Slope, and that is said to be as much as the combined reserves of Louisiana, Oklahoma, Kansas, and half of Texas. When the pipeline is completed, the oil will go into it hot (at times as hot as 140 degrees Fahrenheit) and remain warm throughout the line because of the heat of the twelve pumping stations along the route and the heat generated by the friction between the oil and the pipe itself. Initially, the line will move 1.2 million barrels a day—that's 50.4 million gallons—but ultimately it is designed to move 2 million barrels a day. Under normal pumping conditions, there will be, at any given moment, approximately 11,000 barrels, or 462,000 gallons, in any single mile of line. When the line first begins pumping, the oil will move about 2 miles per hour inside the line; but when it reaches capacity, the oil will travel at something just over 7 miles per hour.

The entire line will be under computer control, with a monitoring station in Valdez. At the first sign of a loss of pressure, which would mean there had been a rupture or a leak somewhere along the way, the entire line could be shut down within twenty minutes. Shutting down a system that includes almost 800 miles of line and that much moving oil would create tremendous backup pressures, so designers have contrived to build into the lines a series of valves and overflow tanks to accommodate that pressure. All tank facilities will have dikes built around them for protection against earthquakes. The Valdez terminal, which will be across the bay from the actual city of Valdez, will be constructed on solid bedrock far above the highest recorded seismic sea wave.

All of this planning and designing and construction is being carried out by the Alyeska Pipeline Service Company. Alyeska was formed in August of 1970, by Amerada Hess Corporation, ARCO Pipe Line Company, SOHIO Pipe Line Company, Exxon Pipeline Company, Mobil Alaska Pipeline Company, Phillips Petroleum Company, BP Pipeline Company, Inc., and Union Alaska Pipeline Company and is owned outright by these eight companies today. Certainly, it would appear that the designers have done everything they could do to prevent despoiling a beautiful irreplaceable wilderness by visiting ruination upon a balanced, though delicately so, animal and plant life.

But there is some question as to whether what they have done is enough. There is the matter of those caribou, for instance. Everybody has heard about the pipeline and the caribou—that magnificent herd of animals balanced off nicely on the scales of progress against this magnificent herd of people, you and I. There are better than 205 million of us; there are only 450,000 of them. Each of us—every man, woman, and child—uses an average of three gallons of oil a day. Numbers count for something, by God. So what does Alyeska intend to do about the fact that 450,000 caribou are up on the North Slope every summer to calve and then migrate through the Brooks Range, where they are sure to encounter the pipeline? Where sections of pipe are aboveground and would interrupt the natural migratory patterns of the caribou, Alyeska will build underpasses for the animals to walk through. That's right, *underpasses.* Will the caribou walk through the underpasses? They'd damned well better if they want to get to where they've been going for hundreds of years.

What of the spawning of fish when they are laying all that pipe under all those rivers? Simple. They are going to time the operation so they won't be putting the pipe down when the fish are spawning. But will the fish spawn after their natural beds have been upset by inevitable noise, vibration, and the ubiquitous debris of construction? Many of us hope so, but many of us doubt it.

Alyeska also plans to time its construction to minimize the disturbance to Dall sheep, a rare species, grazing and lambing in the Atigun Canyon. But they will be disturbed, however minimally, and nobody can predict with certainty what the outcome will be. The peregrine falcon is an endangered species, and yet there will be many places along the pipeline where the peregrine falcon nests. It is stupid and absurd to say the pipeline work will not disturb and upset the peregrine. *Anything* disturbs and upsets the peregrine, so delicate is its nervous system and so finely attuned is it to the natural rhythms and cycles of the earth.

Many people who love the idea of the pipeline will point out to you that Alyeska doesn't want or need much land to carry out its project—a ridiculously small percentage of the state as a matter of fact. The right-of-way will extend only 25 feet on each side of the 4-foot pipeline, and if you add all the additional working space required for the job, it will only come to about 7680 acres, or 12 square miles. The state of Alaska contains 586,412 square miles. That figures out to be .002 percent of the total area of the state. But it is not, of course, *what* they want, it's *where* they want it. The quarrel comes from the fact that the 12 square miles form a thin knife-edge line and therefore a barrier of some sort, if nothing but an access road, across the entire interior of Alaska from the Arctic Ocean at Prudhoe Bay to the Bay of Valdez.

The final nut buster is that there are men who have every

reason to know about such things who think we did not need to go onto the North Slope to start with. One of these men is Barry Commoner, director of the Center for the Biology of Natural Systems at Washington University in St. Louis. In a *Playboy* "Interview" of July 1974, he said: "It's been estimated that the oil on Alaska's North Slope may provide the U.S. with a two-or-three-year supply. So we've extended the country's oil resources from, say, 20 years to 23 years. For that, we may permanently wreck the ecosystem in Alaska. Is it worth it? I don't think so."

But all this has been hashed over. And for every expert you can find who thinks the pipeline is a horror, the oil companies can find five who think it is an unmitigated blessing. In the meantime, the actual welding of the line has not started; but those miles and miles of pipe are lying there in Valdez, waiting. Barges are on the way from Washington State, loaded with supplies. Men and equipment arrive every day. The town is gearing up as best it can for the onslaught. Dave Kennedy is completing a camp to house 600 men. Another camp is going up to house 1700 men. And across the bay at the site of the proposed terminal, Fluor Alaska, Inc., is about to start construction of a camp where 3500 men will stay. Valdez will change from a village of about 1000 people to a boomtown of 17,000 in the next few years. There is a tension, even a violence, in the air of Valdez, poised on the brink of becoming something it has never been before. What that something is, nobody knows. But you can hear it in the growling machinery, the whine of ripsaws, the constant beat of hammers. You can smell it in the smoky bars. You can see it in the faces of the people.

I was standing out on the dock in the rain, freezing, while they headed and gutted fish. That morning Dave Kennedy had asked me down at the camp if I knew why the men had to drink so much in Valdez. No, I told him. He said you had to stay as wet on the inside as you were on the outside, so you wouldn't warp. I had done the best with it I could, but I was beginning to warp bad. The boy standing beside me, whose name was Chris Matthews, stood not as I did with my back to the rain but rather with his face into it, looking out toward the flat gray water of Valdez Bay. He didn't seem to notice the rain or the wind even though my teeth were chattering so I could hardly talk. The rain was fine as mist and driven by a thin, cold wind. Chris was sixteen years old with corn-colored hair cropped close and a mouth full of broken teeth. He had just brought the fish in off the boat where it was anchored out in the flats off Cordova. A seaplane had taken him and the fish off the boat. He was a quiet, almost shy boy, but when he spoke, his voice carried the flat authority of a man who had been around the block.

"It's a seaplane that'll take you off the boat and bring you in for fifteen dollars. Cain't bring my boat in. Got a Indian fishing out there with me. Good man. But a drunk. I bring him in, I cain't git'm back out again."

He was popping the heads off the salmon, expertly ripping their bellies, lifting out long pink roe, and dropping it into a zinc bucket at the end of the bench. Directly he quit with the fish and wiped his hands on the end of his shirt. He walked over to the edge of the dock and spat in the water. Straight across the bay from where we were standing was the site of the terminal where tankers would take the oil off the pipeline. Even from there we could see the yellow scrapers and dirt buggies and Cats, small as ants, digging away at the mountain, preparing for Fluor Alaska to build a camp for 3500 men.

"We'll all end up working for Fluor," he said and spat again. "The money's too good."

We went back over to the bench where Chris' daddy, Bob Matthews, and Bob's partner, Johnny Craine, were finishing up with the fish. Johnny's wife, Lynn, was packing them into long fish boxes.

"We'll freeze'm and sell'm locally in the winter," Chris said. "Ain't no fish here then much. Sell'm wholesale for forty, forty-five cent. These reds will bring that; the king'll go for a little more maybe."

"Let's go across the street for a drink," somebody said.

Wet, smelling slightly of fish, we went up the ramp with the fish boxes to the pickup truck. We walked across the muddy, unpaved street to the Club Valdez. It was late afternoon, and the bar was beginning to fill up. Four couples were two-stepping to Merle

Haggard. The boy ordered a Coke and I got a vodka. The others asked for Olys, by which they meant Olympia beer. I never heard anybody order any other kind of beer but Oly while I was in Valdez. I know there were other kinds of beer there because I had been into several Budweisers myself. But everybody else drank Olympia because goddamn it was Alaskan beer. They didn't care what people Outside drank; they drank Olympia. (*Outside* is the word they use for anyplace that is not in Alaska. Sometimes they'll refer to the Lower Forty-eight, but mostly it's Outside.) Native Alaskans, as well as people who are not native Alaskans but who have been through one or more Alaskan winters, have a tremendous contempt for people Outside. And like people everywhere, they do not gladly suffer fools to instruct them on the error of their ways. It is common to see bumper stickers saying: "SIERRA CLUB GO HOME" and "WE DON'T GIVE A DAMN HOW YOU DO IT OUTSIDE."

Earlier, out on the end of the dock, Chris had been standing there kicking one rubber boot against the other when he looked up and said: "Family of pukers."

I looked where he was pointing and saw a man and a woman and a child coming down to the dock from a fifty-foot yacht with raised fishing chairs and curtains on the windows of an enclosed cabin. The man was double-knitted and color-coordinated and wearing a braided cap at a jaunty angle. The woman was pants-suited in something phosphorescent pink.

"Pukers?" I said.

"This is one of the best fishing waters in the world—commercial, sport, anything. People like them there come from Outside with they damn boats and git one of us to guide'm. Only thing is, they spend all day puking. Pukers ought not to have boats."

I eventually learned that *puker* had become one of the kinder generic words for anybody from Outside.

Johnny got up to dance with his blond and handsome lady, Lynn. They sailed smoothly about the wooden floor, Johnny's cheek pressed against hers, she humming the words to the song softly, the two of them two-stepping as only people can who have been together thirty years and better. Lynn had followed Johnny to Valdez, but Bob's wife was Outside. She didn't like it in Alaska.

Johnny and Bob had been partners for twenty-one years, worked dirt jobs all over Alaska, had been up on the North Slope together back in the early days. They were Cat drivers and together owned some heavy equipment they leased out. They were just about to bid on the sewage contract the town of Valdez was going to put out in a few days.

A friend of theirs came in and Bob waved him over. He was lean, not big but set up thick in the shoulder and narrow in the hip. His hands were wedge-shaped and laced with heavy veins. His eyes were dark; his hair thick and straight and black. He was a little drunk. The lady with him was slender, with flat cheeks and deep eyes and a beautifully formed mouth. Bob introduced us. His name was Jay and hers was Chris. They were both native Alaskans. He was Irish and Indian. She was Eskimo.

She hugged my neck like a good buddy and said: "You met your first full-blood Eskimo in the Club Valdeez." Then to her husband: "Show'm what you got for Father's Day, honey."

Jay wasn't feeling good. He looked at me, "Gone come up here and write it all down in a week or two, are you?" I told him I didn't think I'd get it *all*, no. I was feeling about like a snake by then myself. "You know where I just come from?" he said.

"Show'm what you got for Father's Day, honey," his wife said.

"I'll tell you where I just come from, a meeting with the pipeline people; Impact Meeting, they call it. Had a goddamn Texan there, ten-gallon hat, cowboy boots, sunglasses, and he was telling us what to expect from these Alaskan winters." His voice was thin and bitter. "Telling us how to dress and what to do—you know, the dos and don'ts of Alaska. I sat there wondering how in the hell I got through forty-some-odd years up here without a goddamn Texan to tell me what to do."

His wife didn't like the way things were going. "Somebody ask him what he got for Father's Day. A gold watch is what I gave him."

Jay shook his head and drained his Oly. "Goddamn Texans took over this state and never fired a shot."

His wife said: "You know what Father's Day meant? It meant I could go back for seconds." She laughed nervously. She had tremendous teeth.

"You know the difference between cowboy boots and farmer's boots?" asked Jay. "Farmer's boots got the bullshit on the *outside.*"

His wife came over and took his arm. "I want to dance," she said. He didn't seem to want to, but he got up, anyway, and they two-stepped away to Hank Williams, Jr.

A lady, rather heavy and smelling of talcum, had joined us at the table and had begun a long story in a sour, quarrelsome voice about what was happening to food prices.

"We're not all on the pipeline money, you know," she said. "A eight-ounce can of vegetable juice, the kind I like and all, jumped from seventy-nine cent to a dollar and three cent in one week."

I'd walked around town that day myself, seeing what the stores were like. There was not a single bar of hand soap in any store in all of Valdez. Neither was there any milk. None. A Coke, a small one, cost fifty cents. Generally anything that is brought in by truck is very expensive, if you can get it at all. Anything that is flown in is, given the scheme of things, fairly reasonable. Meat, for instance, comes by plane, and round steak in the grocery store was $2.25 a pound.

Jay and his lady came back to the table, and he was in a better mood. He showed us the gold watch she had given him for Father's Day. He said he was going to be a grandfather any day now. Except for his beat-up face, he looked thirty. He was forty-two.

His wife started telling me how her mother used to make ice cream. When she got to the place where her mother was adding seal oil, she suddenly stopped and said, "Do you boogie?" I told her I'd boogie her back off. "Goddamn, let's do it," she said. And we did, but it was science-fiction boogie, because we had to do it to "Tie a Yellow Ribbon Round the Old Oak Tree."

We came back to the table, and Jay put his hand on my arm. "You serious about writing about this?" I told him I was. "Then I want to tell you," he said. "I'm native Alaskan. I never went Outside until I was grown. Still haven't been Outside but two or three times in my whole life." He waved his arm to include the room. "There's not but seventy thousand of us. Think about that. This country and there's not but seventy thousand natives. We're

Eskimos, Aleuts, Indians, and people like me, a cross, but born here and raised here. And this pipeline's gone kill us, kill the country." He was speaking with great intensity, his face flushed, his hand where it held my arm gripped hard enough to hurt. "Ruin it all forever."

I thought he meant the pipeline itself, running across the interior of the country. I thought he was talking about ecology.

"Shit, no," he said. "I was Outside a couple of years ago in a bar and a couple guys started in on me about how the line was gone ruin Alaska and they had a river right there in their own state that'd kill a horse if he was to drink out of it. They're so full of shit in the Lower Forty-eight. Let'm look to their own backyard before they start telling us what's ruining our country. What's gone kill us is the scumbags that'll follow the line, follow the men and the money. The Alaskan people are delicate—the seventy thousand—so . . . so . . . innocent. You know innocent?" I told him I knew innocent. "It's not the workers. Hell, the men are all right. Look at'm up there." We turned to look at the long line of men at the bar, solemnly staring at three couples two-stepping over the smooth wooden floor. "Scumbags always follow construction, but there'll be scumbags here like they've never been scumbags before. This job is so big, the money's so. . . . Look, a laborer on this line'll make seven, eight hundred dollars a week. A guy driving a dirt buggy can make twelve hundred a week. The companies put these men in camps, feed'm, give'm a place to sleep. All that money's free and clear. Only a few of'm got their wives up here. So what'll the men do? They'll give their money to scumbags. And I don't give a shit about that. You think I give a shit? But this job's going to draw every high roller, promoter, hype artist, con man, pimp, and dopester. . . . It's gone suck'm up here from Outside. And once they're here, it'll be all over. They'll go through this country, every city, every town, every village, like maggots through meat."

He stopped and chugged an Oly. The whole table had grown silent, listening. It was a little embarrassing, because he was so obviously sincere, so impassioned about something he could do nothing about.

The boy, who had sat all this time drinking a Coke, said in his flat, laconic voice: "That's why I'm staying on the boat. Me and that drunk Indian. They'll have to come take me off that boat."

Everybody laughed, and the boy's daddy, Bob, slapped the table with the palm of his hand and said: "Hey, let's go have a fish fry!"

I said I'd go by Truck's and pick up some beer and meet them at their trailer. After they had gone, I had another vodka and thought about the mess that was Valdez, Alaska, and how pleased I was that it was their mess and not mine, or, if in some larger sense it was mine, that I wouldn't have to deal with it. I'm a coward that way.

I'd gone by a couple days before to see the mayor, but he was out delivering the mail, had a mail route. The mayoralty turned out to be one of those dollar-a-year jobs. So I dropped by to see the city manager, Mr. Lehfeldt, a neatly dressed man with slicked-down black hair and nervous eyes. He in effect told me he was scared to death. "There's not enough sewers and there's not enough water and I had a meeting with Alyeska last week. . . ." He stopped and drew a deep breath before his tight, petulant voice ran on. "And they're talking about coming in here to start building housing for a thousand supervisory personnel. That's more than all the permanent housing in the rest of Valdeez put together!" When I got through talking to Mr. Lehfeldt, the mayor was still out delivering mail.

So I stopped by to see Police Chief Dave Ohler, a big man with enormous hands, whose gentle, whispery voice almost put me to sleep even though I only spoke with him for a minute or two. He seemed to see no cause for alarm in the fact that there were only three men on the police force. "Course, we've got a state-trooper office here with two men permanently assigned to it, so that gives us five officers, and we've only got at this moment about two thousand people in town." What about when it jumped to 5000 or 6000 or 10,000? Well, he wasn't sure. But so far things seemed to be going along OK. "I guess we can expect some trouble, but so far everything in town seems to be pretty clean." Drugs? Whores? Not that he knew of.

I went over to the Pinzon Liquor Store for some beer and vodka. Alice wasn't there, but Truck was still as reticent as ever.

We exchanged pleasantries about the weather, and I went back out into the rain. Just as I was getting into the car, a guy called to me from across the street. There were two of them, both young, both bearded, sitting in a Volkswagen bus.

"Step over here a second," the one on the near side called. I walked over to the bus. The one behind the wheel leaned toward the window. "You want a tattoo?" he said.

First I thought I'd heard him wrong; then I thought he was crazy. "No," I said. "No, I don't want a tattoo."

"Listen," he said. "I'm from L.A. I worked for Lyle Tuttle. You know Lyle Tuttle?"

"No," I said.

"Tattooist to the stars," he said. "He's the one tattooed Janis Joplin.

"How you know you don't want one? You ain't seen my work. Pete, show him my work." The boy nearest me got out of the Volkswagen. I took about three steps back when he stepped down to the street. I was pretty freaked by then. "This here's Pete. He's a walking advertisement for my work." Pete shucked out of his shirt, held his arms out, flexed, and slowly turned. He was intricately and beautifully illustrated. From neck to navel he was a complicated network of interlocking eagles and jaguars and anchors and hearts and legends written in a kind of Germanic script. I couldn't take my eyes off him. Among other things, he must have been an iron freak. Muscles, as he turned, rippled and slid, ridged and quivered, making the smooth, multicolored skin come alive, pulsing in an undulant motion.

"Jesus Lord," I finally said.

"See," the guy in the truck said. "You don't know what you want. I got lots of designs you can choose from, or I'll work from something you design. We're camped right out. . . ."

"I've got to go see some people," I said. "They're waiting."

The illustrated iron freak was still turning, and I could not bring myself to say I didn't want one of his tattoos. They were too beautifully and skillfully done to tell him that.

"OK, that's OK. Come by our place anytime."

He told me where they were camped, out beyond the Pipeline Storage Yard on the road to Anchorage. You turned left on the first dirt road beyond the yard.

I was just turning to go when he said: "One last thing. You wanta buy a watch?" He whipped open the door to the bus and there in a shallow suitcase must have been 150 watches of all kinds—wrist, pocket, and pendant.

"When I got more time to look at them," I said. "When I come for my tattoo, maybe."

"Good enough," he said and closed the case.

Bob Matthews was already cooking the fish when I got there. He was doing it outside even though it was raining. They walk through the rain in Valdez the way the rest of the world walks through sunshine. They don't seem to notice it. I went inside and drank with Johnny Craine while Lynn made coleslaw and cooked cornbread. A guy came in and said hello and asked if he could take a shower. Lynn told him sure and said there were towels by the sink.

"That's something you get used to up here quick," she said. "Somebody says hi; then they ask you if they can have a shower. Nobody's got any water up here much, you know."

Bob came in with the fish, and we ate and drank and told sea stories. No alcohol is allowed in the pipeline camps up on the North Slope by the oil companies because the men are working in such cold weather that a drunk could easily wander out into the snow and freeze to death. So Lynn baked a cake for Johnny one Christmas, hollowed it out, put a quart of whiskey inside, and sent it to him. (I think I understand that story, but I'm not sure.) Up on the North Slope no engine is ever turned off during the winter months. Tractors, Cats, trucks run day and night for the good reason that if anything ever shuts down, you can't start it again. Rubber tires shatter like glass. Bob told a story about getting outstanding on some bootleg stuff and decking an Eskimo only to wake up later that night to find the Eskimo outside on a Caterpillar bulldozing down the camp.

And so it went late into the night, through outrageous quantities of fish, cornbread, slaw, and beer and vodka, until we were all full, talked out, laughed out, and sensationally drunk. At which time I thought I was going back to the camp, and I'll never know how it happened (maybe I just wanted to see the illustrated man again) but I ended up out on the road to Anchorage, left on the first dirt road past the Pipeline Storage

Yard. None of it's too clear, but I do remember sitting in a trailer with these two guys explaining that my right leg was game, a really bad knee, broken, torn, bad cartilage, unrepairable, and saying that I thought I needed hinges on that knee, four tattooed hinges, one on the front and back and one on each side. I think I was joking. It's all very hazy. Anyway, that's the last thing I remember.

I woke up the next morning in the rented National car with a pounding head and a dry mouth. I thought at first an ant or maybe even a bee had stung my right arm, was stinging it. I looked down to knock it off and damned if I didn't have a tattoo. A hinge on my right elbow. I was still parked in front of the trailer where the tattoo artist and his walking advertisement lived, and I went bellowing out of the car, my head hurting ninety miles an hour, into the trailer. The two guys were asleep on a ratty bed.

"You sonofabitches," I was shouting, "you tattooed me!"

Their eyes were open now. One of them yawned and said, "That's right."

I started yelling and screaming that you just didn't tattoo somebody when he was out on his ass, that I never would have agreed to being tattooed, that only assholes got tattooed and I was not an asshole. And then I really started foaming at the mouth when he told me it had cost me $65. Out with the old wallet. A quick look. Sure enough, I was lighter by $65.

"You bastards, what if I get hepatitis?"

The iron freak got off the bed, his eagles and jaguars flashing, walked right up and leaned into my face and said softly: "If you get hepatitis, you'll turn yellow as shit."

As I was driving back to town, I said to myself: You have been rolled and permanently discolored in Valdeez, Alaska.

The whore was twenty-two and her name was Micki (spelled with two *i*'s that way). Her husband's name was Buddy. They were from Los Angeles.

"So, you know, I'm reading the paper one morning and the wire service has picked up a story about a girl who got permission to go up on the North Slope and sell subscriptions to *Argosy* magazine. Two months later some security people stopped her.

She had five subscriptions to *Argosy* magazine and nineteen thousand dollars in her pocket.

"So, you know, we were swinging down in Los Angeles, right? I mean, you know, Micki was turning four or five guys a party anyway. So I said why not go up there and make some money? Micki said sure, why not? In three years we'll retire to France forever."

"The Riviera," said Micki.

We were in a mobile home, a double wide. Micki had come out of her little room and was sitting in a housecoat. Buddy was tricked out in the best tradition of pimpdom. He was all ruffles and lace and stacked heels and wraparound goggle-style amber sunglasses and a gold earring and on and on. He'd been going through this long number about how cool he was (I think he'd read Iceberg Slim's autobiography) when Micki leaned forward in her chair and said, looking at my discolored, swollen, scabby hinged elbow: "How long've you had that?"

"About three days," I said.

"Is the guy here in Valdeez?"

"Who?"

"The man who gives tattoos."

"Yes."

"Buddy," she said, "I want a tattoo."

"Bullshit," he said.

They were immediately in an awful argument. He'd flown her out to Seattle not long ago for a little R&R, and she'd seen the movie *Papillon*. She wanted a tattoo of a butterfly on her ass. He shouted that she wouldn't be able to fuck for a week with a tattoo on her ass. Just look at that goddamn hinge on his goddamn elbow! She screamed she wouldn't turn another trick if he didn't get her a tattoo. It was very embarrassing. I hate to witness family disputes. But he relented finally and stomped out of the room. He wasn't gone but a minute before he was back, zipping himself into a pair of muddy Levi's and buttoning a mackinaw that was torn and raveling at both sleeves.

He shrugged. "I have to get out of my good stuff and put on this shit when I go out of the trailer."

He wanted me to go with him, but I told him the tattoo artist and I had had words. He didn't like me and I didn't like him; further, I thought they were doing a bad thing getting the butterfly, at least from the man out by the Pipeline Storage Yard. But Micki was adamant, and Buddy left with the directions I gave him. While he was gone, we talked about her situation there in Valdez.

"They mostly want head. Hell, I don't mind giving head. I'm in the business. It comes with the package."

"Well," I said, because she had paused and I didn't know quite how to react to that, "it's so cold and wet here in Valdeez."

She didn't understand what I meant by that any better than I did. She regarded me blankly for a moment. "I think they think I might have the clap or something. Shit, we got a doctor who looks after me. See, most of'm have their old ladies Outside in Seattle or up in Anchorage and they fly out to see'm every couple of weeks and I don't think they want to risk carrying home the clap."

She'd broken out a little cellophane bag and dumped a small hill of white powder onto the table in front of her. While she talked, she chopped it fine and then laid it out in little rows with the edge of a razor blade.

"Like I say, it don't matter to me, but you'd be surprised how many insist I swallow. In a long day that can work out to a lot of come."

With considerably more show than I thought was necessary she took out a $100 bill—going to some pains to make sure I knew it was a hundred—rolled it up, put one end in her right nostril, her thumb against her left, and leaned forward over the table and snorted a row of coke. Then she gave her left nostril the same shot.

She smiled a laid-back smile. "I figured out one day I took nine yards of cock. Later on I won't have to work so hard. Once all the men are here and the camps are full, Buddy plans to expand to take some of the load off me. Maybe then, too, Buddy can wear his clothes on the street. It kills him to have to get out of his fine things to go out, but Valdeez is still so small and our cover's not good enough to let him flaunt himself. He wants to flaunt himself."

The telephone rang, and she answered it. "Yeah, if you come right over."

The guy must have been calling from the corner because he was there in about four minutes. He was a fisherman. He reeked of salmon. She took him into her little room. In less than five minutes they were out again. She sat down and snorted another row of coke.

"This has got to be one of the greatest places in the world to work. These guys are so horny I can bump into them and they come. Of course, everything has its drawbacks and disadvantages. That poor creep probably hasn't had a bath in a month." She gave me her dreamy little smile again. "I washed about six inches of him. It'll be the last bath he has until he sees me again."

The telephone rang. She picked it up, listened, then put her hand over the mouthpiece. "How soon do you think Buddy ought to be back?"

"He ought to be back now," I said.

"No," she said into the phone. "No, not even later. Call tomorrow."

I commented that business seemed to be good, trying to make it as objective and professional as I could, just the sort of thing you might say to a used-car dealer who had lately opened a lot and was trying to establish himself.

"Oh, this is slow," she said. "The middle of the week is never any good much. But weekends? You ought to see weekends. It's a madhouse around here. They all seem to be hornier on weekends."

I asked if it was a Friday, a Saturday, or a Sunday when she took the nine yards, because I'd done some quick, easy arithmetic in my head and—using a modest six inches as a standard—found six guys to the yard, times nine, and got the, at least to my mind, phenomenal number of fifty-four.

"It was a Sunday," she said. "Sundays are always good here."

Buddy came in with the illustrated iron freak and the tattoo artist. They were both carrying stuff: alcohol, gauze, swabs, a little metal case that held the electric needle.

They were very friendly to me, as though nothing had happened out there at their place three days ago.

"How's your 'too?" said the iron freak. "You ready for another one?"

"No," I said.

"They're addicting," said the artist. "Everybody comes back for another one, and then another, and pretty soon you'll look like Lyle Tuttle."

"I've never seen Lyle Tuttle," I said.

"Tattooist to the stars," he said.

"You told me," I said.

"Well, he's got more pictures than Pete here. Right, Pete? Lyle Tuttle's got no space left."

"Great," I said. "That's just great."

Buddy went immediately and changed into his street-corner flash. Micki was looking over some designs the artist had brought over. He had plugged in what looked like a baby-bottle warmer to get some steam to sterilize his equipment. While he made all these motions of cleanliness—hospital conditions, he called them —I couldn't help noticing that his fingernails were extravagantly dirty. Micki finally found the butterfly she wanted. It was a big thing, nearly as big as my hand, with blue, green, and yellow in its wings.

Buddy came out and looked at the design she had chosen. "Good Christ," he said. "You'll be out of commission for a week."

She said: "You know as well as I do I do most of my work on my knees." He started to protest again, but she stopped him by saying, "Shut up, Buddy, or I'll send you back to Los Angeles."

While she was lying face down on the couch, pulling her robe up around her shoulders and sharing the last few rows of coke with Pete and the artist, Buddy leaned in close to me and said behind his hand: "Regular pimps get treated with respect. Hell, they're gods to their girls. Right? Am I right?"

I told him I'd heard that what he said was true.

"Don't ever hustle for your wife," he said. "You get no respect."

I told him I'd remember that. We turned to watch the artist at work. He was swabbing down Micki's cheek. She had a fine ass. The little machine with the tattooing needle in the end of it made a sound like a small eggbeater. The artist held it lightly in his hand and, I was pleased to notice, made quick, sure strokes with it. After each stroke, he swabbed the stroke with an alcohol-soaked piece of cotton. Micki lay with her face turned to the side and her eyes closed. She never once flinched.

Buddy, the first time the artist missed with the cotton swab and the blood coursed down off her snow-white ass, grabbed his mouth with his hands and said: "Oh, oh, blood, my God, the blood!" and ran to the rear of the double wide.

Finally, the tattoo was done. And a handsome tattoo it was after the colors were traced and blended into the wings and all the blood was wiped away. There was a slight redness around the edges of the butterfly, but other than the redness it might have been painted on with bright watercolors instead of embedded in her flesh with an electric needle. In a few days, of course, it would swell. It would scab. It would turn ugly, and if Micki couldn't keep her fingers off it, there would be infection—not much, but still infection—a little pus, a little blurring of the line with scar tissue. But as everybody knows, if you want a tattoo (and why in God's world would anybody want one?), you have to run the risk of infection, of pus and scar tissue.

It was no doubt gratuitous, even sentimental, but looking at the butterfly on the young whore's ass, I thought of the long snaking pipeline falling from Prudhoe Bay across the interior of Alaska to the Bay of Valdez. I thought: If Alaska is not our young whore, what is she? She is rich, but who can live with her? She is full of all that will pleasure us, but she is hard and cold to the bone. And if we scar her, leave her with pestilence and corrupted with infection, irrefutably marked with our own private design, who can blame us? Didn't we buy her for a trifling sum to start with?

Watching the freshly wiped butterfly that had so lately been bloody, knowing that before it would be beautiful again it must first be scabby and unlovely, I came to a kind of bilious outrage and depression. It was a green and sour thickness I could taste on my tongue. It was a taste and feeling that would stay with me for weeks after I left Valdez.

I stood up, made my apologies for leaving early, and, without waiting for Micki to answer, went through the door into the fine, misting rain. I walked back toward the car in the dark thinking about the town out there, the people I'd met: Dave Kennedy building, Hap cooking, Chris on the flat with the drunken Indian fishing, Johnny Craine's wife cooking and giving showers to those who had none. I thought about it all and watching the bloody butterfly going on Micki's snowy cheek; finally, all I could think of or remember with any pleasure was that over in the Club Valdez they were still two-stepping. Charlie Pride was singing and Hank Williams, Jr., was next and at the bar, a long line of quiet, almost solemn men watched the dancers two-stepping, gliding over the smooth wooden floor, their faces touching, the lips of the women parted, softly humming the words of the song.

Tip on a Live Jockey

One of the great passions of my life is horse tracks and everything connected with them. I've been known to spend an entire day at a track in a fever of pleasure without betting a dime. A while ago I drove the entire length of Florida to watch a boy named Gene St. Leon work. I went for one reason: St. Leon is a good, young jockey. He has that single-mindedness of purpose that will take him where he needs to go, make him into what he needs to be.

But for the moment it's all hustle and scratch. St. Leon does not have scores of people lavishing praises upon him, protecting him from the press and other people, and nursing along his great talent in the delicate way that teenage jockey Steve Cauthen has. But it is, at least to me, of no great consequence. All you have to do is see St. Leon on a horse in the stretch to know that he is one of the really good ones.

On the December day I saw St. Leon, it was 72 degrees under a brilliant sky at Calder Race Course in Miami. The vague, not unpleasant fragrance of horseshit hung everywhere about the $30 million complex, floating over the two lakes in the infield, mixing nicely with the manicured shrubbery, the flowering plants, and the scent of combustion from the Gray Line tour buses lined up at the curb. Thousands of bettors, men and women, rushed across the macadam parking lots, their strident voices as tense and semihysterical as if they had been going to a public hanging. But this was more serious than death. This was as serious as money.

In the jockey room, the little men waiting to go up in the irons were getting ready. The people who bet have place and show, but the jocks have only the nose. The winner's share of a $10,000 purse is around $6000. The rider gets 10 percent of that, $600, good pay for about a minute and thirteen seconds' work. But for riding a second-place horse, maybe one-tenth of a second off the pace, the jockey makes $55. No jockey enjoys riding for lunch money.

So the jocks were putting themselves together. Some were unbinding knees done up the night before with Ace bandages and liniment, some were sitting in the whirlpool, and some, the unfortunate ones, had been in the steambox pulling (losing) weight. It is not unknown for a rider to go into the box at nine in the morning and come out at eleven-thirty, pulling as much as nine pounds in 150 minutes of steam. That's no easy thing to suffer. He comes out stunned and dazed, just in time to go out and ride.

There must have been twenty or twenty-five riders in the room, mostly naked or wrapped in towels, and each rider took a turn stepping on and off the huge scale.

If you care at all about doing a difficult job well, if you care about discipline and condition, a jockey stripped down will make you stare in an unseemly way. They are beautiful because they are perfect of their kind. They have been reduced to essence. Ligament and muscle—each separate and distinct—meld onto bones insistent under diaphanous skin and utterly without subcutaneous fat. They carry their little asses, which resemble two hardboiled eggs wrapped in a towel, like running backs on a football team carry theirs.

It takes tremendous guts to get on a 1000-pound thoroughbred and get boxed in at forty-five miles an hour with maybe a dozen shod hooves pounding up your back and the hooves of your own horse clicking as they strike the horse in front of you. The guts it takes is manifest in everything jockeys do, from the way they walk, to the way they look at you, to the way they talk or—as is so often the case—don't talk.

Gene St. Leon was sitting in a chair just inside the door of the jockey room. He was naked except for a towel wrapped around his hips, and he did not appear happy. The day before, he'd had five mounts and had not been in the money on any of them. He was not accustomed to such performances from himself. He holds the Calder record for the most wins in a season, 149, which he set in 1973 at the age of nineteen. Currently, he was in a head-to-head battle with Charles Baltazar for the winningest jockey of the Winter Running at Calder. Yesterday Baltazar had brought Ming Princess home for a winner for the first race. The score today stood 29 to 27, with Baltazar leading. St. Leon looked up and saw me. He had known for a week that I was coming to watch him. I was worried about getting in his way and told him so.

"You won't get in my way," he said. "I won't *let* you get in my way. One other thing, I don't like to talk just before I ride." He turned on what I think of as his racetrack face; when he gets near a horse, his eyes go flat as nailheads and have about as much depth.

St. Leon started dressing. I went out into the sunshine, where grooms were leading the horses to the walking ring. Eight men, all dressed in blue caps and white shirts, came single file from the jockey room, each of them carrying a saddle. These were the jockeys' valets, men who assist the riders by helping them dress, who carry the saddle to the paddock, who take the saddle after the postrace weigh-in, and who sponge down the jockeys between races.

Presently the jockeys came out. They did not go to the paddock but stood around in the walking ring. They had their game faces on now; the time for talking was over, and they were ready to work. This race was for three-year-olds at seven furlongs (seven-eighths of a mile).

The horses, saddled now, were being led around the walking ring. A voice called: "Riders up." The jockeys were given a leg up, and they took one turn around the walking ring before they went onto the track. Gene St. Leon, sitting lightly as a leaf in the weighted saddle, which is not much more than a leather pad, was up on a horse named State Three.

The crowd was really funky now, a lot of pushing about by bettors consulting tip sheets and each other. On the sixth floor of the main building, the caller, binoculars strung from his neck, announced over the public-address system: "One minute to post time."

When he spoke, a piece of the crowd came out of the stands like a wave breaking and washed down to the rail, all babbling in a voice that only risking money can induce.

"The horses are in the gate."

Across the infield a great rhythmic surge of color broke from the gate, and the sound that every horseplayer lives for, a sound that is a kind of poetry, rose into the bright air. Far away the solid feet of hooves, here on the rail the single baying cry of the bettors, and over it all the calm lilting voice of the caller, and then, as the horses turned into the stretch, the shouts and the whistles of the straining jockeys, the incredibly sharp snaps of the whips. And finally, as they came out to the wire, the horses' breathing like snorts of pain.

St. Leon rode third or fourth all the way to the top of the stretch, where he moved between horses and brought State Three home a winner by a quarter of a length.

The jockeys were breathing almost as hard as the horses, their faces drawn, their eyes a little mad. St. Leon stepped on the scales, had his weight recorded, and handed his saddle to his valet. St. Leon had four more mounts this day, but the next one was not until the fourth race, so I went to the track restaurant.

I was sitting with a jockey in a restaurant overlooking the track. He asked me not to use his name if I wrote what he was going to tell me about his business.

"I have to go out and ride with those bastards," he said. "I could get hurt."

The lady he was with was having a chef's salad and a martini. She was having many martinis. The jockey ignored her except when she became too aggressive. She ignored her salad, but not her martini, and amused herself by touching the jockey, putting her finger in his ear, petting him like a dog, and fumbling at something under the table. Patiently and without looking at her, the jockey took her hand and put it up on the table.

"But, baby," she said. He ignored her and ordered another

club soda. He had ordered nothing to eat. I thought he might be keeping his weight down to ride at this meet.

"I ain't riding," he said. "Everybody and his brother's down here. Summer, maybe there'll be seventy riders here. In the winter, I bet there's three hundred seventy here. That ain't why I'm not riding though. I just wanted some time to goof."

I asked him about honesty at racetracks.

"The horse got the spitbox," he said, "but a rider can't get caught unless someone stumbles on him. And even then he's got to have really bad luck to get nailed." He sighed, moved his lady's hand off him again, and said: "Drink your drink, Dolores." Again to me: "The one, two horse in every race got to go to the spitbox instead of back to the regular stable and get their piss checked for dope. But the jocks ain't got a spitbox. They don't get checked. A lot of bad shit goes down at the track, man. There's always a trainer somewhere that'll daylight a horse, train him in the middle of the night. That way the times—the right ones anyway—won't get set down."

"You ever bet a horse?"

"You got to be shittin me," he said. "You almost never find a jockey who does."

"Still, some guys do win," I said. "I mean, consistently win."

"You ever know one?"

"No."

"I don't either."

"St. Leon's up in this race," I said.

"I hope he does good for you."

I went down to the rail and watched the jockeys go to the gate. This was the fourth race of seven furlongs for fillies and mares, three years old and upward. St. Leon was up on a mare named Star Dewan carrying 117 pounds; Charles Baltazar's mount was the Number 8 horse, Worthy Notice, carrying 116 pounds. Baltazar won the race. Gene St. Leon brought the mare in dead last.

That night at dinner St. Leon told me about females in general and mares in particular. "A mare's like every other broad in the world—you don't hit her at all and she won't run; you hit her too much and she sulks."

We were on the ninth floor of the Holiday Inn overlooking Calder. In the moonlight it all could easily have been part of some half-demented French king's garden: carefully shaped infield lakes, transplanted palms, symmetrical in their placement, and finally the oval track exactly one mile long surrounding everything.

"You know they sew'm up, don't you?" St. Leon seemed to say it with some satisfaction.

"Sew up who?"

"Mares."

"Sew'm up how?"

"You know, their . . . sew'm up."

There was a curious shyness and delicacy in the way he talked. I never so much as heard him say "damn" in the time I was with him.

"It saves a lot of temperament," he said. "When they quit and become brood mares, they just snip'm open."

For dinner St. Leon was having a small steak, a tiny salad, and one glass of champagne, which he took in cautious, extremely precise sips. It would last through the meal.

Maybe because sewing and snipping were still on my mind, it came to me to ask him about female riders.

"I've got a girl cousin who is an apprentice jockey right now," he said. "Can you imagine hiring a hundred-and-ten-pound woman rider when you could hire a hundred-and-ten-pound man for the same money, same job? Women are not as strong as men and not as coordinated." He smiled. "A girl can't even get a whip in her left hand without putting it in her mouth first."

"Still, they do get hired."

"Yeah, they get hired. Mystery, ain't it? Is there any sport where a woman is equal to a man? Does Chris Evert have a chance against Jimmy Connors? Where is the woman golfer that's got a chance against Jack Nicklaus? There's not one. And no woman can outride me. She may be on better stock and I may get outrun. But no woman can outride me. If I'm head to head in the last furlong, it takes a lot of rider to get by me. I don't think *anybody* can outride me. Nobody."

"You have much trouble with weight?"

He shook his head. "I would if I weren't so weight-conscious. At any time of the day or night I know what I weigh within a few ounces. I stay at a hundred and ten."

"But don't you like to eat?"

"Like it? I love it. But you can grow right out of your job in this business. A lot of guys end up selling real estate or something. Myself, I'd rather buy it than sell it." He paused to watch the bubbles in his champagne. "I want to be like the Shoe [Willie Shoemaker]. Now you take the Shoe. You call him up and he might not answer his phone." He leans across the table toward me. "The Shoe don't *have* to answer his phone *no* time. That's what I want, to get free. And riding's my ticket home."

"What would you do if you couldn't ride?"

"It'd kill me if I couldn't ride. Don't know what I'd do. I was down on the track at six-thirty this morning breezing horses. I didn't have to be; I wanted to be. If I wasn't with you now, I'd be at home reading the racing form. I want to know everything about horses."

"You have many days like today when you ride four horses out of the money?"

"This is a funny business," he said. "You gotta roll with what happens. Balance is the thing. One year you could make a hundred twenty-five thousand dollars and the next only twenty-three thousand dollars. And your agent gets thirty percent of that. But it all comes in cycles. I never look back. You got to live for the next one. You get tired, down on yourself sometimes, but you can't take that to the track with you. I'm going out there tomorrow and *win.*"

Gene St. Leon won the first race the next day and was within two wins of Baltazar. Neither of them rode in the fifth. Baltazar was up on Strawberry Pop in the sixth, but the race was won by jockey Earlie Fires on Tanya Lady. Both of them rode in the seventh. Baltazar did nothing, and the best thing St. Leon could do was ride the show horse.

"If I'm not first," he told me in the jockey room, "I'm so disappointed and mad at myself, most times I don't know where I've finished."

In the eighth race Baltazar did not ride. St. Leon, on The Big

Machine, ran fourth. He had good position all the way, but the horse just didn't have the steam. "I can go to the whip if I need to," St. Leon explained, "but there's no use beating a horse to death that just ain't got it in him to win."

Jockeys know that the horse is at least 80 percent of the race. The jockey can only hold the horse at the right time. Move him at the right time . . . look for the opening in the pack . . . ride to the horse's strength. All jockeys know these things, beyond which they can do nothing. And yet in their secret hearts I believe the great riders think they can *make* a horse win. If a jockey believes in his own greatness, and if he does not win, then the jockey thinks in some strange, perhaps unknowable way that he let the horse down. No jockey ever told me this, but after listening as carefully as I can to what they say, to their attitudes toward racing, that's what I've come to believe.

By the ninth race St. Leon had ridden one win and one show in four starts. Not good enough. Outrage is the best word to describe the look of him as he came out to ride a horse named Can You Beat That. No tantrums, no kicking things, nothing verbal. But the outrage was there in his physical attitude.

Baltazar was on Clem's Candy Man, carrying the same weight as St. Leon's horse, 116 pounds. In the walking ring the jockeys didn't look at each other.

When the horses broke from the gate, it was apparent that St. Leon was riding well on a horse that was running well. You knew he could feel the horse coming through the bit into the reins in his hands. You knew that between his knees the plunging animal seemed an extension of himself.

"Sometimes you get on a horse," St. Leon told me, "and right away you and the horse are together. The horse knows what he expects out of you and what you expect out of him. I don't know how, it just happens."

This was the fifth time he'd been on a horse today, each time hunkering over the horse's neck with his entire weight carried on the muscles just above his knees. But coming down the stretch in this race, if St. Leon was tired he did not show it. He got the horse's head out front, and he was going to the whip good. "A horse wants to lose," he had said. "You got to *make* him win. He gets the lead sometimes, and he thinks it's all over. He just stops running. That's when you go to the stick."

They were driving to the finish now. St. Leon's knees were right, his arms and shoulders pumping and pumping, rowing the rhythm of the horse the way a man rows a boat, and the horse was stretched low to the ground, driving. St. Leon brought Can You Beat That across the wire, a winner going away.

When he took his saddle to the scale, his face showed nothing of triumph. He might have been looking at a knife. He stalked off to the jock's room.

There was one race left, the tenth, and Baltazar was not riding. St. Leon, who had 29 wins to Baltazar's 30, rode a perfect race on Callalittlelater. This time when he crossed the finish line, he stood straight up in the irons, his right fist over his head.

As Gene St. Leon himself said, "It all comes in cycles." In the same week he tied Baltazar for leading jockey, St. Leon overslept one morning and failed to be in the jockey room in time to report his weight for the first race. He stood in the jocks' lounge and watched on closed-circuit television as another jockey rode St. Leon's scheduled mount to an easy victory. St. Leon was very still for a moment, and then, since he had to report his weight for later races, he went over and stood on the enormous scale. He watched the needle in the wide glass face swing and stop. His weight was fine. Then his right fist whipped out in a vicious hook that shattered the glass. Miraculously he was not hurt. He paid the cost of repairing the scale—$150.

Somewhere right now Gene St. Leon is going up—or dreaming of going up—to do his high-speed balancing act . . . and it's like the first horse, the last horse, the only horse he'll ever ride.

Tuesday Night with Cody, Jimbo, and a Fish of Some Proportion

Cody came into the bar sometime before midnight with a big brown paper sack in one hand and an open can of Pearl in the other, shouting that he'd just caught a bass, a big one.

"Damn thing must go twelve, fourteen pounds," he called down the bar, waving the sack and signaling the bartender for another Pearl. Then: "Hell, give everybody another drink. I feel good . . . gooooood!" He threw back his head and howled the last word like a dog cutting a hot trail.

While Mac was putting up another round, Jimbo, a tall, big-jawed boy about Cody's age, said: "Git it outen the sack then and let's all have a look."

Cody set his new Pearl down on the bar and reached into the sack.

"Fore you even bring it out, though," said Jimbo, "I got two one-dollar bills says whatever you got in there don't weigh ten pound." He looked around at the other five or six guys sitting with him and winked broadly, showing his blunt, widely spaced teeth. "Probably ain't even a bass."

Cody stopped with his hand in the sack. "Don't try to ruin my fun, Jimbo."

"I ain't tryin to ruin nothing. You want my two dollars or not? Ain't nobody else gone take it. Know you probably got a speck in there, or maybe a catfish."

Cody still hadn't taken his hand out of the sack. "You tryin to ruin my fun?"

"One thing I noticed," said Jimbo. "Ever time you git drunk, your fish git heavier. I just thought to make myself two dollars."

Cody wasn't drunk, but he was drinking pretty good for a Tuesday night. If I'd been inclined to do it, though, I would've offered the bet myself, because that paper sack didn't look like it had twelve pounds of fish in it. But I hadn't known these boys long, and it wouldn't do to act pushy. Besides, as short a time as I'd been around them, I knew it was a very private thing that was going on between Cody and Jimbo. They were good friends, had been for years, and out of a great respect and mutual admiration they often locked up toe to toe and beat each other severely about the head and shoulders.

The first night I'd started drinking in the bar, Jimbo had shown Cody his knife in an argument that started over whether they were going to watch Loretta Lynn on the television or listen to Johnny Rodriguez on the jukebox. Nobody'd been cut, but Cody did manage to loosen Jimbo's earlobe with a shot in the side of the head with a half-empty beer pitcher. It did not surprise me at all to see them two nights later drinking together. They were laughing and playing a Grit version of the dozens with each other. The only sign of their TV-jukebox thrash was a nasty clot of blood on Jimbo's ear.

"There's mine, sumbitch, if you even *got* two dollars," said Cody.

When Jimbo got his money on the bar, Cody whipped his bigmouth bass out of the sack. There was a discreet silence along the row of stools. Cody glanced from the silent faces to his fish and back again.

Jimbo said: "That fish has lost weight."

As if on signal, the stools scraped back and everybody headed for the little room in back where Mac kept a scale he used for weighing barbecue and roast beef. Cody threw the fish on the scale, and the needle swung and held at nine and a half pounds.

"It's something wrong with that scale," said Cody.

"Mac, is it something wrong with that scale?" asked Jimbo.

Mac, a great bartender: "I don't *think* it's anything wrong with that scale, but I ain't ready to say one way or the other if it's right or if it's wrong."

"You owe me two dollars, boy," said Jimbo.

"Wait a minute," said Cody, chewing for all he was worth. "How many is it here thinks this scale is right?"

Before it was all out of his mouth—because we could see what was coming—everybody had headed back to the bar, including Mac. We sat down and sipped the round Cody had bought and listened to them shouting over the scale in the little room behind us.

I sat there drinking a vodka and feeling good, feeling the way a man does when he knows he's home. A month earlier I'd moved off Lake Swan, where I'd lived for five years. The move meant I had to give up Lonnie's Tavern in Putnam Hall and find a new place to sit and drink while thinking over my little ball of wax. So I searched out Mac's place the way other men might search out the right wife or the right church. No blasphemy intended, but I learned a long time ago that for many of us *where* we drink is more important than *what* we drink, more important even than *if* we drink, because a bar that's right is a place you can go and sit for hours in the friendly supportive dark, sipping warm Coke and eating endless bags of fried hogskins, greasing and regreasing your stomach after some mild outrage in the same bar the night before.

Such a bar should never be crowded. If a bar's crowded, you know immediately it's no good because there are never enough people who know a good bar from a bad bar to cause a crowd. A crowded bar always pours a lot of things like Tequila Sunrises and Black Russians, drinks that have nothing to do with the pleasures of whiskey.

Not too long ago, I was drinking whiskey with Madison Jones in Alabama and a boy at the table ordered a Bloody Mary. When it came, Madison watched the thing for a moment and said: "What's in one of them, anyhow?"

The boy said: "Well, it's a little tomato juice and a little Worcestershire sauce and some salt and just a touch or two of Tabasco and. . . ."

"You put a little hamburger in that you'd have a whole meal, wouldn't you?" Madison said.

Just so. Whiskey with food is fine, but putting whiskey and food in more or less equal amounts in the same glass is uncivilized.

And just as uncivilized is a bar that has things in it that are too new. Formica or chrome won't do unless it has been dinged so many times and encrusted so deeply with the leavings of countless nights that it is unrecognizable. Say it's sentimental or romantic or silly, but I'm convinced nothing new will work with whiskey because whiskey is never new. It's old and it likes old things.

Once when I was a boy, my uncle and I drove to the county line to have a drink. I'd never been to the place where he took us, a plain place with uncovered wooden floors and heavy wooden tables with benches instead of chairs. We bought a bottle and sat down with it. Being young and inexperienced in such matters, I proceeded to tell my uncle that he ought to try going to a bar I'd been to several times on the other side of the county because it was closer to home. What I hadn't stopped to consider was that while it was closer, it was also filled full of glass and plastic and other shiny things.

My uncle set it all straight by snorting through his nose and saying: "I was over there about two years ago the first time. Last time, too. I'd soon drink my whiskey in a drugstore."

Cody had finally paid Jimbo the $2, which Jimbo spent on several of Mac's pickled eggs, half of which Cody ate himself while Jimbo shouted to the rest of the bar to watch *by dammit* what Cody was doing. Watching them was a whole lot better than watching TV, because even though they were playing, it was play with blood in it. They were deadly earnest and by now fairly deadly drunk.

Shortly after midnight they began to discuss the merits of their pickup trucks. Jimbo pretty much wanted to limit the conversation to the last two pulls they'd had, because he had won them both. But Cody kept pointing to the record of total pulls printed on tablet paper hanging from a nail behind the bar. The tablet paper clearly showed that out of twenty-two pulls, Cody had won fifteen of them.

"You ain't got the reflexes of my granny," Cody said. "An that poor ole lady's been dead four years."

That apparently was enough to do it. They bet $10 and headed for the parking lot. The rest of us, including Mac, followed them outside, where they backed their pickups tailgate to tailgate. The parking lot was an empty field about three acres big with an oak tree in the center of it. We stood under the oak tree smoking and drinking while Cody and Jimbo fastened the two trucks together with logging chains. Some of the men laid off small bets on one or the other of the trucks.

One of the men went over to drop a white handkerchief for the start. Cody and Jimbo were both in the cabs of their trucks, engines whining, peaked out. They watched the white handkerchief in their rearview mirrors, and when the handkerchief dropped, they popped their clutches and the trucks fishtailed and disappeared in rooster tails of dust that rose two stories high.

Unlike horse pulling, there are no rules in pickup pulling. Somebody has to ask, often *beg*, for it to stop. He has to scream out of the window that he's been *beat!* And also scream whatever else the other guy might want him to.

Cody still had his mind on the fish. He was dragging Jimbo around and around the field at what looked to be about twenty miles an hour, scattering us from under the oak tree like a covey of quail, as he leaned out of the window with the bloated fish by the tail and screamed: "How big's the goddamn fish, Jimbo?"

Jimbo was spinning for all he was worth, but he could find no traction, none at all. He finally—when it looked like he was about to be thrown over—stuck his white face out of the cab window. "Beat!" he croaked. "Beat! I been beat! *Beeeaatt.*"

Every time Jimbo shouted he was beaten Cody seemed to haul him around the field a little faster, and from Cody's raging face came the maniacal demand: "How big? How big's my goddamn fish?"

Jimbo was totally out of it now. He fought the wheel, trying to keep it right as Cody seemed to find a little more speed.

Finally: "Ten! Ten!" shouted Jimbo, almost losing his truck in a tight turn.

"How big?"

"Twelve."

"How big?"

Now Jimbo made it a question, a hysterical question: "Fourteen? Is it fourteen, Cody? Fourteen?"

Cody lightened up, and they came to a stop in the swirling dust. He got out of his truck swinging his fish like a bell. He'd stopped chewing his teeth, and his eyes had gone suddenly sane. He walked back to Jimbo's truck and said: "Yep, I think fourteen'll do her."

Jimbo came bellowing out of the truck, and they would've probably locked up right there if we hadn't got between them. Jimbo was yelling that Cody had weighted his truck, put weight on it, and by God he'd find it.

Cody, his face flushed and his mouth beginning to chew again, said: "It's virgin. My truck's virgin, Jimbo. Don't say nothing about my truck."

"Weighted!"

"Virgin!"

It was a standoff, and God knows what would've happened if Cody, like a lot of other men before him, hadn't let victory overload his tongue. He suddenly blurted: "My pickup can pull your logger. Bring that logging truck down here and this little old GMC'll cut the nuts off it." He reached over and patted the rear fender of his truck the way men in an earlier time patted the withers of their best horse.

Jimbo calmed right down. His voice was sweet as a baby's after a warm bottle. "Pull my logger?"

Cody did a little shuffle in the dust. "This little old GMC *wants* that logger."

"My logger's settin dead on ready."

"Git it."

Jimbo turned on his heel, got in his truck, and spun out of the lot. We stood watching him leave. The truck he was going for had once been used to haul logs to the pulpwood mill. Jimbo had converted it to take watermelons to Cordele, Georgia. Both Cody and Jimbo worked with their daddies on two of the biggest watermelon farms in North Florida, the watermelon capital of the world. Years of tossing thirty-pound melons up to a man on a high-sided truck from first light to first dusk had given them bodies so keyed up, coiled, and ready to strike that if they weren't actually heaving melons, they literally did not know what to do, how to act. The problem resolved itself in random violence full of joy and love masquerading as anger. Nobody ever said it, but everybody knew it. It was this knowledge that gave the senseless, meaningless, childish moments late at night a certain and very real dignity.

We had time to go back into the bar and have a drink and eat bloody roast beef sandwiches on rye with a little mustard. Mustard is allowed in a good bar, but there is never any mayonnaise. Mayonnaise won't do. And it cannot be explained. Either you know right off that mayonnaise doesn't belong in a bar or you can never know. The absence of mayonnaise in a good bar is a part of the natural order of things, like a rock falling *down* when you turn it loose instead of falling sideways.

We heard the logging truck and got outside while Jimbo was still backing up to Cody's pickup, smiling and whistling something that was not a song.

"Wanta go for twenty?" said Jimbo. "That way I'll get my ten back and you'll only be down ten yourself."

"Make it light on youself," said Cody.

They got in their trucks, and the handkerchief was dropped. Cody popped the clutch on his pickup, and when he hit the end of the chain, he came to a dead and sudden stop as though he'd been chained to the oak tree in the center of the lot. Jimbo looked at him through the rear window and then moved off slowly with little more trouble than he might have had if he'd been pulling away from the curb. Cody's truck was spinning and whining, but Jimbo, now and then showing his quietly vicious smile in the rear window, wound out across the field without even breaking traction. When he took second, he didn't even grind the gears, and by the time he went through the first tight turn—slinging the pickup through an arc of about seventy-five feet—he must have been doing twenty-five or thirty. In the middle of the arc, Cody stuck his head out and screamed: "Whoa! Wwwwhhhoooaaa!"

But Jimbo didn't slow down, and he didn't look back anymore. He dragged Cody all over the lot, and when he tired of that, he dragged him across the highway, hitting the median as he went, blowing one of Cody's front tires. Cody gave up trying to control his pickup and leaned out of the window instead, confessing everything he could think of to confess: that he was beaten, that his fish was a runt, that *he* was a runt, and that his pickup was, too. Jimbo finally got enough of whatever he was after and brought Cody back across the highway and stopped under the oak tree. When they got out of their trucks, they were both soaked with sweat and very sober. Cody still carried his fish by the tail as he came to lean on the fender of the logging truck with Jimbo.

"That was a ride," said Cody.

"It's not just the sort of thing a man'd want to do ever night."

Cody seemed to see the fish in his hand for the first time. He half turned and laid it on the hood of the logging truck. And that's where he left it as the two of them—without ever taking the chains off their trucks parked there under the oak tree—went back into the bar.

The Car

The other day there arrived in the mail a clipping sent by a friend of mine. It had been cut from a Long Beach, California, newspaper and dealt with a young man who had eluded police for fifty-five minutes while he raced over freeways and through city streets at speeds up to 130 miles per hour. During the entire time he ripped his clothes off and threw them out of the window bit by bit. It finally took twenty-five patrol cars and a helicopter to catch him. When they did, he said that God had given him the car and that he had "found God."

I don't want to hit too hard on a young man who obviously has his own troubles, maybe even a little sick with it all, but when I read that he had found God in the car, my response was: *So say we all.* We have found God in cars, or if not the true God, one so satisfying, so powerful and awe-inspiring that the distinction is too fine to matter. Except perhaps ultimately, but pray we must not think too much on that.

The operative word in all this is *we*. It will not do for me to maintain that I have been above it all, that somehow I've managed to remain aloof from the national love affair with cars. It is true that I got a late start. I did not learn to drive until I was twenty-one; my brother was twenty-five before he learned. The reason is simple enough: in Bacon County, Georgia, where I grew up, many families had nothing with a motor in it. Ours was one such family. But starting as late as I did, I still had my share, and I've remembered them all, the cars I've owned. I remember them in just the concrete specific way you remember anything that changed your life. Especially I remember the early ones.

The first car I ever owned was a 1938 Ford coupe. It had no low gear and the door on the passenger side wouldn't open. I eventually put a low gear in it, but I never did get the door to work. One hot summer night on a clay road a young lady whom I'll never forget had herself braced and ready with one foot on the rearview mirror and her other foot on the wing vent. In the first few lovely frantic moments, she pushed out the wing vent, broke off the rearview mirror, and left her little footprints all over the ceiling. The memory of it was so affecting that I could never bring myself to repair the vent or replace the head liner she had walked all over upside down.

Eight months later I lost the car on a rain-slick road between Folkston, Georgia, and Waycross. I'd just stopped to buy a stalk of bananas (to a boy raised in the hookworm and rickets belt of the South, bananas will always remain an incredibly exotic fruit, causing him to buy whole stalks at a time), and back on the road again I was only going about fifty in a misting rain when I looked over to say something to my buddy, whose nickname was Bonehead and who was half-drunk in the seat beside me. For some reason I'll never understand, I felt the back end of the car get loose and start to come up on us in the other lane. Not having driven very long, I overcorrected and stepped on the brake. We turned over four times. Bonehead flew out of the car and shot down a muddy ditch about forty yards before he stopped, sober and unhurt. I ended up under the front seat, thinking I was covered with gouts of blood. As it turned out, I didn't have much wrong with me and what I was covered with was gouts of mashed banana.

The second car I had was a 1940 Buick, square, impossibly heavy, built like a Sherman tank, but it had a '52 engine in it. Even though it took about 10 miles to get her open full bore, she'd do over 100 miles an hour on flat ground. It was so big inside that in an emergency it could sleep six. I tended to live in that Buick for almost a year, and no telling how long I would have kept it if a boy who was not a friend of mine and who owned an International Harvester pickup truck hadn't said in mixed company that he could make the run from New Lacy in Coffee County, Georgia, to Jacksonville, Florida, quicker than I could. He lost the bet, but I wrung the speedometer off the Buick, and also—since the run was made on a blistering day in July—melted four inner tubes, causing them to fuse with the tires, which were already slick when the run started. Four new tires and tubes cost more money than I had or expected to have anytime soon, so I sadly put that old honey up on blocks until I could sell it to a boy who lived up toward Macon.

After the Buick, I owned a 1953 Mercury with three-inch lowering blocks, fender skirts, twin aerials, and custom upholstering made of rolled Naugahyde. Staring into the bathroom mirror for long periods of time, I practiced expressions to drive it with. It was that kind of car. It looked mean, and it was mean. Consequently, it had to be handled with a certain style. One-handing it through a ninety-degree turn on city streets in a power slide where you were in danger of losing your ass as well as the car, you were obligated to have your left arm hanging half out the window and a very *bored* expression on your face. That kind of thing.

Those were the sweetest cars I was ever to know because they were my first. I remember them like people—like long-ago lovers—their idiosyncrasies, what they liked and what they didn't. With my hands deep in crankcases, I was initiated into their warm, greasy mysteries. Nothing in the world was more satisfying than winching the front end up under the shade of a chinaberry tree and sliding under the chassis on a burlap sack with a few tools to see if the car would not yield to me and my expert ways.

The only thing that approached working on a car was talking about one. We'd stand about for hours, hustling our balls and spitting, telling stories about how it had been somewhere, sometime, with the car we were driving. It gave our lives a little focus and our talk a little credibility, if only because we could point to the evidence.

"But, hell, don't it rain in with that wing vent broke out like that?"

"Don't mean nothing to me. Soon's Shirley kicked it out, I known I was in love. I ain't about to put it back."

Usually we met to talk at night behind the A & W Root Beer

stand, the air heavy with the smell of grease and just a hint of burned French fries and burned hamburgers and burned hot-dogs. It remains one of the most sensuous, erotic smells in my memory because through it, their tight little asses ticking like clocks, walked the sweetest, softest short-skirted carhops in the world. I knew what it was to stand for hours with my buddies, leaning nonchalant as hell on a fender, pretending not to look at the carhops, and saying things like: "This little baby don't look like much, but she'll git rubber in three gears." And when I said it, it was somehow my own body I was talking about. It was *my* speed and *my* strength that got rubber in three gears. In the mystery of that love affair, the car and I merged.

But like many another love affair, it has soured considerably. Maybe it would have been different if I had known cars sooner. I was already out of the Marine Corps and twenty-two years old before I could stand behind the A & W Root Beer and lean on the fender of a 1938 coupe. That seems pretty old to me to be talking about getting rubber in three gears, and I'm certain it is *very* old to feel your own muscle tingle and flush with blood when you say it. As is obvious, I was what used to be charitably called a late bloomer. But at some point I did become just perceptive enough to recognize bullshit when I was neck deep in it.

The 1953 Mercury was responsible for my ultimate disen-chantment with cars. I had already bored and stroked the en-gine and contrived to place a six-speaker sound system in it when I finally started to paint it. I spent the better half of a year painting that car. A friend of mine owned a body shop, and he let me use the shop on weekends. I sanded the Mer-cury down to raw metal, primed it, and painted it. Then I painted it again. And again. And then again. I went a little nuts, as I am prone to do, because I'm the kind of guy who if he can't have too much of a thing doesn't want any at all. So one day I came out of the house (I was in college then) and saw it, the '53 Mercury, the car upon which I had heaped more attention and time and love than I had ever given a human being. It sat at the curb, its black surface a shimmer-ing of the air, like hundreds of mirrors turned to catch the sun. It had twenty-seven coats of paint, each coat laboriously hand-rubbed. It seemed to glow, not with reflected light, but with some internal light of its own.

I stood staring, and it turned into one of those great scary rare moments when you are privileged to see into your own predicament. Clearly, there were two ways I could go. I could sell the car, or I could keep on painting it for the rest of my life. If 27 coats of paint, why not 127? The moment was brief and I understand it better now than I did then, but I did realize, if imperfectly, that something was dreadfully wrong, that the car owned me much more than I would ever own the car, no matter how long I kept it. The next day I drove to Jacksonville and left the Mercury on a used-car lot. It was an easy thing to do.

Since that day, I've never confused myself with a car, a confusion common everywhere about us—or so it seems to me. I have a car now, but I use it like a beast, the way I've used all cars since the Mercury, like a beast unlovely and unlikable but necessary. True as all that is, though, God knows I'm in the car's debt for that blistering winning July run to Jacksonville, and for the pushed-out wing vent, and, finally, for that greasy air heavy with the odor of burned meat and potatoes there behind the A & W Root Beer. I'll never smell anything that good again.

The Knuckles of Saint Bronson

Charles Bronson walked away from the crew and cast, off down the railroad track, across the high trestle, and stood with his back turned to the place where the next shot was being set up for a movie called *Breakheart Pass.* When he is shooting in the studio, he will—if he is not in his dressing room—take a chair in the farthest corner and sit there alone, looking apparently at nothing. But here at the tag end of the Bitterroot Mountains, high above a little town called Reubens in northern Idaho, he habitually simply walked away from the train and waited to be called to do the shot when it was ready. Everybody saw a lot of Charles Bronson's back. His characteristic gesture was to show his back to the largest number of people possible. I never heard anybody say he thought Bronson did this to be offensive or hostile or even unfriendly. It was just part of who Charles Bronson is. A very large part. So while dozens of property men and makeup men and wranglers and grips and cameramen shouted and wrestled with lights and reflectors and generators, Bronson quietly walked back down the Union Pacific track, across the trestle, and stood looking into the valley below, several hundred feet almost straight down, where a little stream breaking over white rocks caught the brilliant sun.

He stood utterly still, and I tried to remember what that way of standing reminded me of. And then I knew. Charles Bronson stands like a pit bulldog. He somehow manages that kind of balance with only two feet. It is the kind of balance only the very finest athletes, the world-beaters, have. As a matter of fact, some world-beaters *were* on that train with us—one of the world's great fighters, Archie Moore; Joe Kapp, who was always known as a man who would stick his head in the fire and because of it took the Minnesota Vikings to the Super Bowl; Ben Johnson, who set a calf-roping record of 12.5 seconds at the Pendleton Round-Up in 1949; and Yakima Canutt, World Champion Cowboy in 1917, 1919, 1920, and 1923—but the greatest *natural* athlete on that train was Charles Bronson. Or so I became convinced in the time I spent with him.

So symmetrical is he that it is impossible for him to make an ungraceful move, and it is from that symmetry that his bulldog balance comes. It begins, though, in his bones, the balance does. His bone structure is straight and true and absolutely without flaw. Don't let anybody ever tell you he is bandy-legged or bowlegged, because he is not, even though some writers have described him so. His legs are the most heavily muscled part of his body and the fully developed quadriceps might make him appear slightly bowlegged to someone who did not know what he was looking at. But I did know, and he is not.

"May we have the actors, please?"

It is Ron Schwary, assistant director, the man responsible for setting up the shot, getting things ready for the director, Tom Gries. He thinks he has it now and is calling for the players: Bronson, Ben Johnson, and Charles Durning. They've done this scene before. Better than half the day has gone into shooting an action that will take less than a minute on the screen. A couple of lines have been blown. A couple of marks have gone missed. The cameras were wrong for whatever reason at least once. But then Bronson noticed that the scene itself was being played wrong. Or so he thought.

Bronson: "The audience can see there's no use for this rope. It makes more sense for me to go down the embankment at the end of the trestle."

"If that's the way you think it ought to be played," said Gries. "Yeah, OK. Just make it look good."

"But," said Johnson, "it's a line here Durning s'posed to say about he might slip off the rope and escape. Hell, we ain't got a rope now."

Gries smoothed down his scalp with the palm of his hand (his head is shaved as slick as a baby's ass). "All right. Here. Durning can say something like: 'He might try to get away' "—Gries looks up now toward Johnson, smiling—"and you just give him a cowboy answer."

The crew repositioned the cameras and the lights for the shot. Now Schwary was calling for the scene to be shot. Far down the track, I saw Bronson's shoulders lift. He often breathed deeply before starting a scene. Then he turned and came directly toward us down the track. He had maybe twenty-five yards to walk. The trestle was very uneven, with crossties and broken rock. But Bronson, coming across it, could have been walking over a ballroom floor. He came as smoothly as a model with a book on her head. And he never looked down. He never does. No matter how rough the ground. And yet his feet go unerringly to the place where they need to be. No bounce. No wobble. No hitch in his gait. But he does not glide. Or float. He seems to be suctioned to the earth, growing from it, joined to it even when he's moving over it. And as he comes straight toward you, you see that his center of gravity is very low in his body. Truly, his center of gravity must be in his cock or directly behind it. He does not smile. He rarely does, and when he does, it looks like it hurts him. Since his features are so distinct—heavy, even—you'd think they would also be mobile. Not so. No expression is his habitual expression.

He stopped on his marked spot. Shook his shoulders. Breathed. Relaxed inside that incredible cock-of-the-walk posture. The director went over and stood head to head with him for a brief moment. Then he looked up at Johnson.

"Are we all ready?" he asked.

"I think I got the line," said Johnson.

"The line?" Gries said.

"The one I give to Durning when he says he might try to escape."

Gries held his hands up, palms out. "Don't tell me," he said. "Just let me hear it when we shoot it."

The assistant director raised his megaphone. "Kill all radios. Kill the AC generator. Could we have quiet on the set, gentlemen? *Roll'm!*"

The director leaned slightly behind the camera and called: "Action!"

Bronson went down the slope like running water.

Durning: "He might try to get away."

Johnson: "He might *shit,* too."

"Cut!" said Gries. "Good. We'll play it just like that."

"You're gone keep it like that?" said Johnson.

"I thought the line was great," said Gries.

"Well," said Johnson, "there's another movie I cain't take my old mother to see."

"All right, once more, please!"

Charles Bronson came back and lined up to shoot the scene again. While they made some last-minute adjustment with the cameras, he held his spot, looking to neither the left nor the right. He spoke to nobody. Nobody spoke to him. All around him, men were laughing and joking and talking. Only he was still, his eyes so hooded he could have been asleep. The grab-ass went on. Johnson had found a turd that had dropped from one of the train's toilets onto the track. He said: "I believe they got yore spot marked right here, Durning." Bronson does not turn to look. He almost never does.

Gries calls over their heads: "We seem to be having too much fun, gentlemen. A little more seriousness, *please.* " But his tone says he is joking, too. Everybody laughs. Except Bronson. They all look like they're having a hell of a lot of fun. Except Bronson. Not only does he look like he is not having any fun, he looks as though he has never had any.

Everybody has something to say about Charles Bronson. Everybody. Sometimes it's very short: "Can't act." Or: "I don't like violence; I don't like Bronson." Or: "Sumbitches say he cain't act. But he can." They come, opinions do, from all directions.

When my twelve-year-old boy, Byron, found out I was going to see Bronson, he raced to his room and came back with a *Mad* comic. "Give that turkey this and see what he says." After admonishing him about calling distinguished people turkeys, I looked at it. The cover was Bronson. Death Wish Bronson bringing death to muggers, turning on the steps in Central Park, firing his evil gun at evil hearts everywhere, all the while squinting like the end of the world.

A couple of hours later a college professor I know, who is just so goddamned intellectual he won't eat onions, sighed, looked out of his office window, and said sadly: "There must be something wrong with me, I *love* Charles Bronson. If Robert Redford was over there under a tree jerking off, I wouldn't walk across the street to see it. But Bronson? Well. . . ."

The next morning, going through the Atlanta airport, I stopped by Benny's for a drink. Benny is a great fat fag friend who always gives me a drink when it's too early for the bars to be open at the airport. We sat in the back of his little shop, I drinking vodka, he drinking some abomination before the Lord called a Tequila Sunrise.

Benny, a little breathless, said: "The French call him *le sacré monstre.*"

"Run that by again, Benny?"

"The sacred monster. *Le sacré monstre.* That's what they call him. Only the French could have hit it straight on like that. The Italians call him *il brutto;* that means the brutal one or the ugly one or something like that. Whatever it is, it's not as good as a sacred fucking monster."

"How come you know so much about him?"

"I see all his movies. I read every single word written about him." He swallowed his Tequila Sunrise and made another. "Doesn't everyone?"

"Why?" I said. "Why do you read that stuff and see all the movies?"

He held up his hand. "One: I think he's a great actor. And two: I admire him for the money he makes."

"How much does he make?"

"I don't know for sure, but I read somewhere a million dollars a picture. See if you can find out for me, will you?"

"I'll try," I said.

(Note: I don't know for sure, either, Benny, but here is the best information I could get: on *Breakheart Pass,* he got $1 million for showing up. All expenses are covered: the house he and his wife, Jill Ireland, rent in Lewiston, Idaho, cars, food, two governesses for their four-year-old daughter, Zuleika, and so on. Plus $2500 a week walking-around money. Plus ten points of the picture. Now, Benny, even allowing for your 20 to 40 percent Hollywood hype, that's still a lot of cheese, any way you cut it.)

When I was about to go, Benny said: "Somebody at *Playboy* doesn't like you."

"Everybody loves me everywhere," I said.

"So maybe they'll send you to interview Mount Rushmore next," he said. "From everything I've read, the second head from the left on Mount Rushmore talks more than Charles Bronson."

"I wouldn't have taken it if it had been an interview," I said. "I'm just supposed to hang out and see what happens."

We had a couple of more drinks and I left. Ten days later, when I got back home, I was met at the airport by a guy named Jingo, whom I've known for maybe four years. He's a kind of reject from someplace like Oakland, California. He wanted big-time degeneracy but couldn't handle the freight and so ended up in a small North Florida town wearing a lot of tattoos, riding a greasy Harley 74, a chain around his waist, a mouthful of blunted and yellow teeth, and a compulsion to get into fights he can't win. He's always beat up bad: swollen eyes and cut lips, and nostrils clogged with black blood.

There's only one flight a day into the little town where I live. He had been meeting the plane from Atlanta for the past three days.

"I got the whole thing figured," he said.

"What whole thing?" I said.

"Jesus," he said, "didn't you go see Bronson?"

"How'd you know that?" I said.

"Then you did?"

"Yeah."

"We're gonna sell him," Jingo said.

"Sell who?"

"Bronson, for Christ's sake."

He'd caught me at the place where you get your luggage. I had my bag now. "Tell me tomorrow, Jingo. Or, better, wait until next week. I'm tired."

He grabbed my arm. "You know what we can get for Bronson's sock?"

"His what?"

"Sock. Sock, dammit. *One* sock."

I could only stare at him.

"Fifty, maybe sixty bucks."

"Jingo, I don't *have* Bronson's sock."

"Who's gonna know? Tell me that. Who? We can say you ripped off his dirty-clothes bag. Right? We can also take a bite out of a piece of bread. Say you got it off his plate when he wasn't looking, after he was through, you know? A fucking piece of stale bread, we get sixty, maybe a hundred dollars. His *mouth* touched it, you see?"

"Jingo, go home," I said.

He gave his little I'm-only-shitting smile, which was not funny at all but had much of the malice of the world in it, and said: "You can put out a contract on a man's hand in New York for six hundred dollars. You realize what we could sell his knucklebones for?"

It was quite a long time before I could convince Jingo we were not going to peddle the knuckles of Saint Bronson or any other bogus mementos.

He kept saying everybody else was selling Bronson and there was enough for everybody to have a piece of the action. Everybody was selling him. Yeah. I was reminded of the publicity man who sat in the screening room at Burbank with me three days earlier while I watched a movie called *Breakout*. When it was over and the lights came up, the guy said: "Stripped to the waist, Bronson's money in the bank." It wasn't so much what he said as how he said it. He positively leered. I felt like rearranging his teeth for him. But I let it pass, because I didn't think it would have pissed Bronson off if he'd been standing there. After all, he refers to himself as a product that has to be packaged and sold a certain way, just like—as he is fond of saying—a bar of soap.

I met Bronson the first time standing beside the flatbed railroad car that housed the kitchen on the picture train. He was yelling up to the cook that he wanted a bacon-and-egg sandwich. The kitchen had a sign on it that said: "YOU CAN WHIP OUR TATERS, BUT YOU CAN'T BEAT OUR MEAT." And another that said: "KEEP THE WEST ALIVE: BALL A COWBOY TODAY."

It's just a chuckle a minute, folks, when you are around your heavyweight movie people.

Bronson's publicist, a delightful and generous man by the name of Ernie Anderson, introduced me to Bronson. We shook hands, and Bronson went back to the business of getting his sandwich.

Ernie took me by the sleeve and pulled me aside. "Now, don't crowd him. For God's sake, don't crowd him. Because if you do, see. . . ."

Ernie told me that only about 900 times. We left the Lewis and Clark Hotel that morning at daylight, loaded into minibuses with the rest of the crew and drove southeast about twenty miles, out past Culdesac, through the Nez Percé Indian reservation, finally stopping at Reubens, where the train was waiting. On the drive out, Ernie kept telling me how hard Bronson was to talk to, that he might not talk at all.

"Listen," he said, "when Charlie is in a bad mood, I'm furniture. That's all I am, I'm just like a piece of furniture."

Frankly, I didn't give a shit if he talked or not, because I was at death's door after coming down with a severe case of drunk the night before. I'd managed to cleverly secrete a flask of medicine on my person, however, and was only looking for the right moment to get well. Bronson doesn't drink, though—except for about one bottle of Campari every two pictures—and I didn't want to blow the whole goddamn assignment on the first day just because I needed a drink. I probably should not have had the vodka out there to start with. I'd already had to sign a release saying that if I got hurt accidentally or otherwise, I couldn't sue the production company. But it was a cold mother up there in the snow and wind and ice of Idaho, and I couldn't bring myself to go off to the mountains dry and unprotected from the chill. I was determined to keep it to myself, though, since Ernie had gone to some trouble to impress upon me Bronson's aversion to alcohol.

"Listen," he said, "when we were shooting *Breakout,* the character Charlie plays always had a beer in his hand. All the time. One beer after another. Well, for Charlie, we had to put mineral water in the cans. You know how much it costs to put mineral water in beer cans?"

I told him I did not. What I didn't tell him was that I found the idea a depressing perversion of the natural order of things. Mineral water, for God's sake? Isn't that what little old ladies drink so their bowels'll move?

"OK," said Ernie. "It's all right. We can get in his car."

Apparently, Bronson had given him some sign that he wasn't in such a bad mood that we'd have to be pieces of furniture. We walked along the track, following Bronson, who was now chewing away on his sandwich.

He stopped by a gun-metal-gray boxcar that was spotted with blisters of peeling paint. He reached up and took hold of the sliding side door—the same kind of sliding door you see on all boxcars—and pulled it back. *Voilà!* The star is home! I could see before I got inside that it was heavy gravy, at least a couple of hundred thousand dollars' worth of boxcar. Red carpeting, color-coordinated kitchen with yellow cabinets, stove and refrigerator, color television, electric lights, walls paneled in heavy black wood, acoustical ceiling. The middle of the car was a kind of living room. At each end was a rather large dressing room complete with bed, lighted mirrors, and bath.

I eased myself down at a table and tried not show how shaky I was. Bronson went immediately to the stove and started making coffee. He turned and squinted at me through the smoke of a cigarette dangling from his lips.

"Coffee?"

"Yeah," I said, "I'll have a cup."

I could see the cups at the end of the counter, and I started to get up to get one.

"No," he said, "sit still. I'll get it."

"Someplace I can take a piss?" I said.

Standing at the sink, he motioned with his head. "Back there."

It was a large bathroom done in an off green, containing your basic chemical shitter. I doctored myself and came back out feeling better about the day and the world at large. Bronson had left the sliding door open, and I stood in the doorway looking out. The steam engine gave two blasts of the whistle, and we started to move forward.

Behind me, Bronson said: "This used to be a hunting car used by railroad executives." *Hunting* comes out in two distinct syllables—hunt-ing—betraying his years of work at the Pasadena Playhouse and elsewhere, trying to get rid of his Russian-Lithuanian accent. He got rid of the accent, only to replace it with a way of talking that suggests he learned English as a foreign language. But the choppy way he separates words into distinct syllables gives a strange and considered force to what he says. "They left the outside of the car the way it was so they could leave it on sidings and nobody would be tempted to break into it."

He brought a cup of coffee to the table. Then he took a chair over to the open door and sat staring out at the snow and broken rock slipping past as the train climbed into the mountains. Unlike most people, Bronson has no trouble letting a conversation fall to silence. There is no such thing as an awkward silence around him, because you come to understand early on that silence is his natural state, or so it was with me, and I was content to sit and listen to the rhythmic clack of the train wheels and watch him burn up cigarettes, which he does with a certain single-mindedness. He does not chain-smoke, but almost, and has since he was nine years old.

But he says as soon as *Breakheart Pass* is in the can, he'll quit permanently. For a man whose discipline makes him climb ropes at the age of fifty-three, work with a speed bag and a heavy bag, do flying karate kicks, abstain from alcohol, eat vitamins like candies, his addiction to cigarettes and coffee does seem strange. But such discipline also means he will probably succeed in quitting now that he has decided to do it.

I had been talking to Ernie, who was sitting quietly at the table across from me, when Bronson turned from his place at the door and said: "Where do you come from with that accent?"

"South Georgia," I said. "Down around the Okefenokee Swamp. A farm." And then, in the garrulous way I have that would make me the world's worst interviewer if I ever tried to interview anybody, I went from talking about farming to talking about mules, about how I didn't learn to drive a car until I was twenty-one, because we never owned a car. "I still don't know anything much about cars, but I know a hell of a lot about mules."

"So do I," Bronson said. "They still had mules in the mines when I was a boy in Scooptown, Pennsylvania."

When I mentioned the mules, his face changed. He smiled, but not with his mouth. It was all done with his eyes. When you are close enough to see the green specks that float in his eyes, you suddenly realize what amazing eyes they are. He can smile with them, snarl with them, make an absolutely indifferent wall with them, or use them to make himself accessible—or at least to the extent that he is ever accessible, which is not often and not very.

"But it's all changed there now," he was saying. "The mules are gone; the slag heaps, for the most part, are gone. Hell, they've even got grass planted in the yards, green growing things everywhere. All different than it was."

The mules are gone from Bacon County, too. I told him that there had not been any mules there since I left to go into the Marine Corps when I was seventeen years old. Then, for whatever reason, I got into telling a story about a drill instructor brutally and literally beating the shit out of a boy on Parris Island.

"Yeah," he said. "There are a lot of bastards like that. I met my share of sonofabitches in the service. I remember back during World War Two, when I was in gunnery school at Kingman, Arizona, the squadron had a party. This sergeant's wife wanted to dance with me. Great big fat woman. Hell, I didn't want to dance with her. *Nobody'd* want to dance with her. I told her no. Little later, the sergeant comes over to me and wants to know why I've been propositioning his wife. Apparently, she'd gone over and told him I'd been after her. I told him I hadn't propositioned her and I wasn't interested in her that way or any other way. So he wants to fight. Fight a sergeant, when I'm a private? I didn't need that, and I knew it. I back off. He follows. I back. He comes on. I back all the way down the dance floor, until I'm against the wall and I can't back any farther. So I picked the bastard up and threw him. For some screwy reason, I thought if I didn't hit him, I wouldn't get in trouble. So I threw him. When he landed, he broke his arm. I got six months' hard labor, carrying sides of beef into the mess hall and cans of garbage out of it." He stops talking, and an introspective, almost bemused look comes into his eyes. He turns to stare into the deep valley below the trestle we're crossing high in the mountains.

In the time I was with Bronson, I came to believe that while he would not back off from trouble, he would go to considerable trouble to avoid bullshit. To fight over a fat lady you don't know and have no interest in is bullshit and Bronson knew it, so he let the guy back him down the floor. There is so little bullshit in the man that he will do almost anything to keep from having to deal with the bullshit in somebody else. But after he's backed as far as he can go, if pressed, he will break your arms for you. He is, in fact, the straight-on, tear-your-balls-off kind of guy that he so often portrays with such power on the screen.

"You cannot lie to the camera," Gries told me. "It ultimately sees through to who you are, touches the basic quality of your character. That's why Nixon came off so badly in the debates with Kennedy. And that's why Bronson can so successfully play the kind of roles he plays. He brings tremendous authenticity to them. He makes you believe."

When he was telling the story of the fight, I realized that when he has something he wants to talk about, he is articulate and talks with great animation. He just doesn't seem to want to talk much with very many people. And particularly, he doesn't want to talk to every Tom, Dick, and jag-off sent by some newspaper or magazine to interview him. When a reporter is sent out by, say, *The New York Times* or some other equally prestigious publication, the reporter thinks Bronson ought to fall down in a faint, slobbering to please him. When he doesn't, the reporter writes that Bronson is inarticulate and hostile. The truth is no more spectacular than this: he doesn't talk when he doesn't want to, and he is hostile only when he has something to be hostile about—which seems to me a damn fine way to be.

Bronson was smoking and drinking coffee and staring at the snow-crusted countryside. I was talking with Ernie about critics —in this case, literary critics. "I think a hell of a lot of writers quit writing or don't write any more than they do because they can't stand what critics write about them. A guy named James Boat-wright reviewed a novel of mine in *The New York Times* and he wasn't just unhappy that I had written the novel, he seemed unhappy that I was alive." I looked over at Bronson, the weight of whose gaze I had felt fall upon us, and said: "I think some actors have probably been run off the screen for the same reason."

"You have to ask yourself who you wrote the book for," Bronson said. His voice was more violent than it had been, because it had gone utterly flat and laconic. "Did you write it for the critic in Los Angeles? For the one in Rome? In New York? In Hong Kong?"

I allowed as how I had known what he was driving at for a long time.

"You won't satisfy them all," he said, "so to hell with them."

Did he read what critics had to say about him?

"Sometimes reviews are sent to me by my agent or somebody and I'll glance at them. But I don't make any effort to see reviews. No, I actually don't read them much."

"I stopped reading reviews of my novels," I said, "except for one or two lousy fuckers I compulsively read because they are such bad critics and bad people. They obviously don't like books at all. That's probably why they became literary critics, so they could say shitty things about books."

"Some men make their reputations like that," he said. One massive shoulder tightened under his jacket. "And they all have their little pet bitches. There's a lot of pear-shaped guys, like that Jay Cocks, who think if an actor is in shape, he can't be any good." He turned to look through the door again, his glowering stare more hooded than ever.

Time magazine's Jay Cocks tends to turn up in conversations with Bronson, who is already on record as saying: "One way or another, I'll get that man. Not physically, but I'll get him."

The train came to a banging, couple-rattling stop on the edge of a high trestle between Craigmont and Craig Junction, about 4000 feet above where we had started two hours earlier. Bronson caught the edge of the door and dropped lightly to the ground. He was already halfway back to where the scene would be shot before Ernie, who went out ahead of me, could get out of the car.

They were shooting at the very back of the train, which meant I could sit in the caboose and watch the action and stay warm. The caboose was paneled in heavy, carved, hand-fitted wood. Comfortable couches lined the walls. When I got there, Kapp and Moore were talking. Shortly, Richard Crenna, who plays the governor of Nevada in the picture, and Ed Lauter, who plays an Army colonel, came in. It was warm and I took off my jacket. Kapp saw the hinge tattooed on the inside of my elbow and fell out.

"You got it wrong," I said. And I tried to explain that some guy had mistakenly put that on me in Alaska while I was hurt bad from alcohol, that I had no other tattoo and that I had not consented to the hinge.

Joe Kapp said: "That's what you *think* you did. That's the way you *remember* it. But as soon as I saw you, I knew you were the kind of guy who would get a tattoo on the head of his dick."

Which only goes to show that a man can be a great quarterback, a natural leader of men, and still badly misjudge character.

Ben Johnson came through in an enormous sheepskin-lined coat, a cud of tobacco in his cheek, his U.S. marshal's gun strapped tight to his leg, and demanded: "Where you boys got that goddamn shitter hid? I cain't find it." Somebody directed him deeper into the car, where the dressing rooms were, and he bulled on through, chewing and wheezing.

Gries, who had just come in and sat down, waiting for the cameras and lights to be positioned outside, laughed and said: "When I called Ben and told him I needed him for this picture, he said: 'Do I git to ride a horse?' I said yes. He said: 'Do I have to talk much?' I said no. He said, 'I'll take it.'"

Outside, the wind had picked up. I could hear it and knew that out there in that weak sunlight, with the thin mountain wind whistling down the valley, it was one cold mother. The actors who could ducked into the caboose from time to time, if only to stay for a minute, trying to warm the ends of their fingers and their freezing noses.

Except Bronson. He stayed outside, with all apparent patience, waiting to be called to give his lines. He had walked back down the track and stood by himself, throwing rocks, some of them as big as a five-pound bag of sugar, at a target only he could see. He threw them as though it were a workout, regularly and without stopping.

Crenna was in his first picture, *Red Skies of Montana,* back in 1952, with Bronson. He had one line. He was allowed to say: "I could eat a hamburger." Bronson didn't have any lines at all.

I told Crenna what Bronson had said about critics. "Oh, yeah. Sure," he said. "You know right off that some critics will pan this film simply because it's a Western. Other critics will pan it because it has Bronson in it. *Only* because it has Bronson in it. A knee-jerk reaction. Some critics will start out by having fun with the title. *Breakheart Pass.* 'Don't break your heart with boredom by seeing *Breakheart Pass,*' something like that." He stopped talking and watched Bronson for a moment through the window. "I don't think reviews get to Charlie much, though, unless they're especially personal. In the twenty-five years or so I've known him, he's not changed much. He's his own man. Stays pretty much to himself. If he cares what other people think of him, he doesn't show it."

Kenny Bell, a still photographer, came in and sat down. He had been on four pictures with Bronson. I asked him about Bronson's reputation for being temperamental on the set, for blowing up.

"Almost never," he said. "Charlie's a professional. I've been on eighty-four features and I've never seen an actor who was more professional than Charlie. He always comes on the picture knowing his job. He's always got his lines. And he expects everybody else to be the same way. But there is one thing, and you can put this in caps: when somebody fucks up and keeps on fucking up, Charlie doesn't hesitate to let him know about it. But if the picture's right, Charlie's right. That's the way he is."

I went outside and walked down the track. Bronson gave me a quick, uninterested glance. He threw another rock and then turned toward me. He watched me, and it is difficult to convey the feeling Bronson gives when he looks directly at you. He has a way of *focusing* himself on you, and it is literally a pressure you can feel on the surface of your skin. As I walked toward him, I didn't have the slightest notion of what I would say to him. Certainly, I did not know I was going to ask him a question; there is ample evidence on the record to show that he does not much like pointed and direct questions. And it was too early to risk putting him off. But there was something that I *did* badly want to ask him, and it popped out before I knew I'd say it.

"I've read where you said, 'I don't have any friends and I don't want any friends. My children are my friends.' Did you say that?"

He looked at me for a long four-beat, which is a thing he often does, as though he were considering very carefully what he wanted to say. "Yeah," he said finally, "I said that."

"Doesn't that strike you as a strange thing to say?"

"No."

"Jesus, come on," I said. "It is strange, too. *Everybody* has friends. What reason is there not to have friends?"

"There's no reason not to have friends. Just the opposite is true. There's every reason to have friends. But I don't think you ought to have friends unless you're willing to give them time. I give time to nobody."

It was cold and dark, though still early, and I was tired, too tired to sleep, so I walked around Lewiston, thinking of what were purported to be the facts of Bronson's life, at least what I had been able to find out from him and from others.

He was born Charles Buchinsky, a name that he used in the first eleven of his pictures. He changed it to Bronson during the McCarthy years, because Buchinsky sounded Eastern European and therefore suspect. The Pennsylvania coal-mining town where he spent his early years was ugly and dirty and poverty-stricken. There was never enough money and never enough food for him and his fourteen brothers and sisters. If he talks about anything at all, he will sooner or later get back to those early, terrible years. You don't have to listen very closely to what he says to know that as a child he felt nobody loved him, that nobody cared whether he lived or died. He worked in the mines until he was old enough to escape by joining the Army during World War II, in which he served as a tail gunner in a B-29. (There have been writers who have maintained he did not serve as a tail gunner in World War II, that it is all a fabricated publicity story. I believe he did. I even *know* he did, even though I have no hard evidence to prove it. My

evidence is the sound of his voice and the look in his eyes when
we were telling sea stories, I about the Marine Corps, he about
flying. At some point, he raised his hands and began to talk about
the placement of his thumbs on the cool, curved firing mecha-
nism of the gun. It was enough for me. He has had such a weapon
in his hands. And he has heard shots fired in anger.)

After the service, he fell in love not with acting but with the
money actors made. He didn't have to be very smart to know that
it beat the hell out of shoveling coal. He became attached first to
the Philadelphia Play and Players Troupe, where he designed
scenery. From there he went to study and work in the Pasadena
Playhouse. Starting with something called *You're in the Navy Now,*
he became the guy who held the horses. He held the horses in
fifty-two pictures before anything much happened. He was the
presence, the muscle, the body that rarely spoke, always the
menace in the background. The heavy, but not the superheavy.
He didn't become superheavy, and consequently, his star didn't
really begin to shine until 1968, when he starred in a French
production called *Adieu, l'Ami.* It was a huge success in Europe,
and it was in Europe that Bronson came into his own. Today he
is bigger in Europe, the Orient, and the Middle East than any
other actor, and in the United States he is as big as anybody. I
am, of course, talking about box office, selling tickets. How good
an actor he is is another thing. Some of his pictures have just torn
my ass with boredom—*Mr. Majestyk* and *The Stone Killer,* to name
two. In others, I loved him. He made the hair get up on my neck,
made me want to eat tacks, in pictures like *Rider on the Rain,* which
still has to be the best thing he's ever done, and *Hard Times,* which
I saw before it was released while on this assignment. *Hard Times*
is a simple, stark, gutsy, down-but-not-out, back-against-the-wall
melodrama. I thought the story had enormous holes in it, that the
relationships between the characters were not clear—particularly
the relationship between Bronson and the character played by Jill
Ireland—but Bronson didn't write the story, he only acted in it.
Somebody else has to take the responsibility for the story. His
responsibility is to make a character named Chaney believable.
He does. Or at least he did for me.

Chaney is a bareknuckles fighter. He will fight anybody, anywhere, and the only money he makes is money he makes betting on himself. The fights are not legal, are not staged in arenas. They take place anywhere—in warehouses, train yards—and anything goes, including biting, kicking, gouging, as long as the fighters are on their feet. James Coburn, a fine journeyman actor, turns in a creditable performance, and Strother Martin gives what I think is his best performance ever, even superior to his role as the prison warden in *Cool Hand Luke.* It is a testament to Bronson's work in this picture that when the three of them are on screen at the same time, Bronson simply blows them away. Even as hard and as well as Coburn and Martin work, they remain little more than props to Bronson's performance. But while Bronson's acting is superior, the story is vapid, and while it will undoubtedly do tremendously well at the box office, Bronson himself will catch a huge ration of shit because of the way the picture is put together. But that is the nature of critics. Even when they know something is wrong, they rarely know where to place the blame.

I was thinking all of that while walking through the damp, wintry streets of Lewiston, more than a little mystified by the phenomenal, inexplicable success of this not-so-good ole boy from Scooptown, Pennsylvania, when it occurred to me that Lewiston *made* Bronson. If his success lives anywhere, it lives in Lewiston. Isn't Lewiston middle America? Doesn't middle America force-feed the rest of the world its values and aspirations? Doesn't the rest of world lust after what Lewiston has already acquired? The rest of the world says it is not true. But wouldn't Frenchmen and Germans and Japanese sell their souls to slip into suburbia down by the Clearwater River on the outskirts of Lewiston? Of course they would.

So I thought: The town must be pretty well stirred up because Bronson is here. Why don't I go listen? Hollywood is a huge, extremely complex, multimillion-dollar machine whose sole purpose is to put the skin on baloney. Surely, Lewiston has as many baloney eaters per capita as anyplace else in the world. I determined to spend an evening among the wild baloney eaters, and immediately I felt better.

In Lewiston, on a Saturday night, you can go to Bullwinkles Tavern out on Main Street, where you can drink a little beer or wine or win a little money on one of its six pool tables. Or you can truck on out of town on the N and S Highway to a great bar called The Stables, where the John Horse band is working out, putting down some tight, inside sounds. It's a place where you can get a little vodka to clean you up and, at the same time, be hassled by the guy who owns the place if you happen to have a tape recorder with you and no papers saying you're on assignment from *Playboy.* After you give the guy at The Stables about as much shit as you figure you can without being arrested, you can move back into town to Effie's, a great little place that serves nothing hard but where you can lie back in a booth with a Coors and what has to be the biggest hamburger in the world. (One of the guys from the picture went down and photographed the thing. Incredible. Big as a plate and thick as your wrist. Lady told me Ben Johnson had been in there twice to scoff on one.) Or you can go to Curley's in North Lewiston, or The Huddle, or the Long Branch Saloon, or Smitty's (The Barrel) across the Snake River in Washington. There is no shortage of bars, and if you make a few and listen closely on a Saturday night, you'll hear the voice of the world talking on about how it is to be in love with Bronson.

"Come here. Hell, you can see it from here. I'll show it to you." The lady is wearing what looks like a nurse's uniform and is an absolute lake of fat. I've watched her drink seven cans of Coors. She takes a can down in two hits. Her body is never at rest. Her shoulders slosh and gurgle. Fat runs down and laps like waves when it hits the shoreline of what must be a girdle at her waist. She gets off the barstool and leads us to the back door. She has three friends with her, two ladies and a man. The two ladies are tiny, hurt things with spots of mustard and catsup on the front of their dresses. I figure they must be waitresses. The man is the husband of one of them, but I never find out which one. The fat lady goes through the door sideways and out into a dark little alley full of hungry cats and rusting water heaters.

She points. "Him and Jill lives right up there."

"Where?"

"Up there on the hill, looking down. You can see it."

"Where the light is?"

"Right there."

"Jesus, he's up there right now."

"What you think he's doing up there?"

"God, I don't know, he—"

"Doing what everybody else does, I imagine." The man's thin, reedy voice comes out of the dark unconvincingly. You know he does not believe it. Neither does one of the ladies.

"Charles Bronson don't have to do what everybody else does."

"No, I guess he don't, at that," says the man.

"When you got what he's got, you do just what you damned well please."

"He can take him a bath or eat him a steak or him and Jill can go up in a airplane and look down. He ain't like you and me."

"Let's git us another Coors. At least we can do that."

It's getting on toward midnight now. The bar is heavy with smoke. The drinkers are tired and a little stunned. You can see them beginning to fade toward Sunday. But suddenly everything is stirred up, everybody's awake, calling to one another across the dance floor. Somebody has come in with Bronson's autograph.

"I was in the Pay-Less, the wife and me, when I seen him over in radios. He was in there with his wife and his little girl, just a tiny little thing—"

"Zuleika. Her name's Zuleika."

"I walked over there to him and—"

"What'd he do?"

"I almost give'm my pipe to sign this paper with, but I didn't. Damn, was I nervous. The closer I got to him, the more my chest closed up. I got next to him, I could hardly breathe."

They are all crowded around the bar now, where the paper with his signature is spread out.

"Writes messy, don't he?"

"I think it's beautiful," says a young barmaid, her fine blond hair caught at her neck with a clip. "Just beautiful." Her hand goes out and her fingers touch the name. Her nails are red as blood, and the paint is chipping on her thumbnail. Her fingers tremble slightly as they touch the paper, and her chapped mouth goes soft and slack and lovely.

"Don't git that French-fry grease on it."

"I wouldn't ruin that name for nothing in the world."

"I'd like to come up against him just one time."

"I don't know if you would or not, Ted."

"He ain't tough. Hell, you can look at him and tell he ain't tough."

"You go to all his pictures, Ted, you know you do. Every last one of them."

"I didn't say I didn't go to see his movies. I said I'd like to come up against him one time. I'd like to break his goddamn face for him, that's what I'd like to do."

"We ain't drunk. Not real drunk, anyway."

"Why's she got her head on the table?"

"She's tired. She worked hard today. I ain't seen you in here before."

"I ain't been in here before. I'm here to write a thing about Charlie Bronson. I came up from Florida."

"Write a thing?"

"A piece for a magazine."

"You lying sonofabitch."

"No, it's true. Really."

"Have you seen him?"

"Talked with him today the first time."

"I got a picture of him. Got it out of a magazine when I found out he was coming. Got it in my room. I got a room over by the tissue factory."

"What do you think of him?"

"And you talked to'm today, huh, just today?"

"Right."

"You know, you got eyes just like his. You're both all wrinkled and ruined around the eyes."

"Neither one of us can see. So we squint. He wouldn't be Charles Bronson in Coke-bottle glasses, would he?"

"He cain't see?"

"I don't think very well. He's got glasses, but I've never seen'm wear them. But he's got'm."

"You cute and you got eyes just like his. You got the same cute eyes. Where you staying?"

"Over at the Lewis and Clark Hotel."

"Did you see that sign they got in the bar over there? Says: 'PLEASE DON'T HIT THE ACTORS IN THE FACE.' "

"They're clever as hell, those movie people."

"I went over there, hoping I'd see *him,* but *he* never showed up. I did meet a fella from the picture, though. He was a [deleted]. His name was [deleted]. He didn't wanta do nothing but butt-fuck me, though. Said if I'd butt-fuck him, he'd take me out there on the train and innerduce me to him. I'da done it if I thought it was the truth. But it was a lie and I known it for a lie."

"You cain't believe everything you're told, all right."

"But you really are writing about him? Been right up close to him and all?"

"Close as I am to you right now. That's what this is for. It's a tape recorder."

"A tape recorder? I thought it was a radio. You got me on there?"

"Yep."

"You got him on there?"

"His tapes is back in the room."

"I wouldn't mind going back to your room and hearing them tapes. And to boot, I wouldn't mind fucking them cute eyes of yours right out of your head."

"I'm working. I never mess around when I'm on a job."

"You always drink this much when you working?"

I went back to the bar in the hotel and had one drink. When I got up to the room, I needed to put down some notes before I went to sleep, so I took off my clothes, broke out a bottle of vodka, and climbed up in the bed. But before I did, I turned on the television. I lay there writing and sipping. But then a voice, a disturbingly familiar voice, impinged on what I was doing. In a way that I am not able to explain, it was scary, like a nightmare, like something unnatural and unreal, as though you had got a letter and opened it up and found it was from God.

I reluctantly raised my eyes, and there full screen on the television was Crenna's face looking straight at me. I had spent a long time talking to Crenna that day. He is originally from Los Angeles, but he might have been from the Okefenokee Swamp in Georgia, so well did I get on with him. My kind of people. *But now he was in the box!* His face was coming through the wire. His voice was all fantasy and hard-edged diamonds. I had spoken to him as a man only that day, but now, in a celluloid and plastic alchemy, he had become part of my dreams. He was staring at me. I snatched the cover off, got up, stumbled over, and hit the OFF button. I stood at the window, looking out over the darkened city of Lewiston. It *is* fantasy. It *is* magic. And none of our dreams are safe from it. We are all—all of us—part of the wild tribe of baloney eaters.

Each time they reshoot the scene Bronson has to climb the steps of the tender, jump down to where the fuel is, walk over that to the locomotive, and appear in the doorway, where he squats. It doesn't sound like much, but after you've done it ten or twelve times, it becomes a little much. A few times the trouble has been the camera. Scott Newman, Paul Newman's son, who is playing a young soldier, has run out of frame twice and missed his mark once. Earlier he leaned too far out the window and went right off camera. And yet each time, Bronson does it again, nothing showing in his face.

"I give time to nobody." That line has been running through my head ever since he said it and particularly today, watching him work. It was said by one of the world's most famous husbands and fathers. He insists that Jill and their six children (all but Zuleika are from earlier marriages) travel with him. The time and energy he devotes to travel arrangements, tutors, governesses, sometimes as many as 100 pieces of luggage and negotiating whole floors of hotels to accommodate such a family, are phenomenal. Jill told me that Bronson insists upon the entire family having dinner together every evening. A full, slow dinner. She said it is one of his happiest, most contented moments.

"I give time to nobody." He has been working at a frantic,

almost hysterical pace. Remember, for twenty years nothing happened. Then things began to break, but it all didn't really get off the ground until *Death Wish,* which in terms of a long career was only yesterday. Now he's working like there's no tomorrow. As I write this, *Breakout* has just been released in Europe. It was supposed to begin showing in theaters in this country in July. I had to rush out to Burbank to see his next film, *Hard Times,* because they were sending the only print they had to Europe to be shown to theater owners there. And he was already shooting *Breakheart.*

Standing in Colgems Square outside Producers Building Number Three, where we had just seen *Hard Times,* Bronson's agent, Paul Kohner, was talking to Larry Gordon, who was the producer of the film. They had a fine cut on the picture, but it was not color-coordinated, the music for the sound track was not ready, and there were jumps and bleeps in some of the dialogue. But I had flown there on a few hours' notice, because they were shipping it off to market.

Kohner was not entirely happy about it. "You're releasing this picture too early," he said, "after *Breakout* has had only five weeks. A Bronson picture needs more than five weeks. It deserves more than five weeks."

"As long as there's a nickel left in *Breakout,*" said Gordon, "the theater owners are not going to run *Hard Times.* But we've got to get it to them. They're hot for it, and we've got to get it to them."

Kohner demurred for another moment, but with a marked lack of conviction, and then changed the subject. "All right. The picture's fine. All you have to do now is find another one for Charlie."

"We've already got it," Gordon said.

"Good. I hope so," said Kohner, "because we have nothing for the fall."

Meanwhile, Bronson is in Idaho, shooting *Breakheart Pass.*

Meanwhile, he's got to have made $5 million in the past eighteen months.

Meanwhile, they have nothing for the fall.

What, one asks oneself, is the goddamn hurry? Is Bronson a bubble the men around him believe will finally burst? Did the man wait twenty years to be a flash in the fucking pan? Must they send his pictures out like baloney on a production line, feeding the public as many as it can possibly swallow before throwing up? It is, as any fool can see, a self-fulfilling prophecy. Bronson deserves better. Even if he doesn't want better, he deserves better. When he is genuinely interested in the script, as he was in *Rider on the Rain,* and when the story plays to his strong suit, he is an excellent actor. Strother Martin, a fine actor himself, is on record as saying: "Many years ago, I saw Charlie play an immigrant who was learning to read and write for his citizenship. Most eloquent. I've always admired him very much."

They had taken a break. Thirty or forty people headed for the coffeepots. I happened to be in front of Bronson. I drew a cup and offered it to him.

"No," he said, "you waited in line. I'll get my own."

After he had his coffee, I followed him out to the edge of the gorge, where he was staring at the ground, making patterns in the snow with his boot. I was still thinking about "I give time to nobody." And I was wondering how it felt to have waited this long for what had come to him. Because I knew from my own experience that when you wanted to do a thing, whether you were very good at it or whether you were only a journeyman craftsman, if you could not do it, it was a kind of death.

The day before, Jill Ireland had told me, "You get caught in this acting thing and you almost can't do without it. You want a job. But you can't get one. You know you can do it, but, damm it, you can't do it unless someone asks you to. It's enough to drive you to suicide when you can't work."

And I was standing beside a man who had waited as long as anybody had ever waited for stardom in the history of the movies. I decided to try the sort of direct thing he doesn't like.

"You mind talking?" I said.

"No," he said, "I don't mind."

"Are you bitter about holding all those horses, man? About having to wait so long to make it?"

"No, I'm not bitter. That's all gone. I don't think about it."

"I read somewhere . . . I seem to be always telling you I read something and—"

"It's all right," he said. "I don't care."

"I read about your saying your ma sold you. You wouldn't tell me about that, would you?"

"Not a lot to tell. I don't even know it for sure. But as far as I'm concerned, I *know* it. She was always threatening to sell us. Then one summer she said she knew where I could get a job. She took me to upstate New York. I saw the money change hands. It was two Polish onion farmers she sold me to. When she left, I knew, I mean I *knew* it right away. I wasn't just working for these men, they *owned* me. It showed in everything they did with me."

He said it all in a flat, even voice, without emotion. Which I found profoundly moving. So I watched him make patterns in the snow with the toe of his boot, until I remembered that Yak Canutt had said that Bronson was one of the greatest natural stunt men he had ever seen. It was a way to change the subject, so I did.

"Do you ever consciously study films in an effort to learn ways of doing certain physical things on the screen—falling, rolling, things like that?"

He actually smiled, the only time I saw him do so in the time I was with him. "I watch films to see what *not* to do."

It fit what I thought of him at that moment. Bronson's been around enough blocks to find out whatever he needs to know. He does not suffer advice gladly. Ernie Anderson said that when they were filming *Hard Times,* they brought a consultant on location to show Bronson how to jump out of a moving boxcar. He told them to get the guy the hell out of his way, saying: "I know more about jumping out of boxcars than he does."

The director called for the actors. Bronson turned and walked away. Anybody else would have said something like "See you later" or "Take care" or *something,* but Bronson simply walked off. But it did not bother me at all. He says only what is necessary to say, and I like that, I like it a lot.

One of the last things Jill Ireland said to me was: "I hope he has a long life and time to do all the things . . . and enjoy the money he's made."

So do I.

The Hawk Is Flying

I was jogging between Lake Swan and Lake Rosa on a ridge full of blackjack oak when I saw the hawk, tail feathers fanned and wings half spread, beside a clump of palmetto about twenty yards off the dim path. From the attitude of her wings and tail I first thought she was sitting on a kill, maybe a rabbit or a rat, but then she turned her wild dandelion eyes toward me and I knew that she was there in the sand not because of something she had killed but because she herself had almost been killed. Blood was dark and clotted on the trailing edge of her right wing. Some sorry bastard had brought her down with a gun and then not had the decency to find where she fell.

I stood there in the path for a long time, deciding whether or not to kill her. I knew the chances of keeping her alive were slim after she'd been hurt. But leaving her wing-shot in the dirt like that would take more meanness than I thought I could manage. At the same time, though, I knew the right thing to do would be to step quickly across the sand and kick her to death. I watched her where she sat quietly, feathers ruffled now and unafraid, and I knew I was not going to find it in myself either to leave her or kill her. There was nothing to do but take her up and try to save her.

Because the direct stare of a man is terrifying to a hawk, I kept my eyes averted and slowly circled to the edge of the palmetto, where I knelt in the sand. Her sharp, hooked beak was open from heat and exhaustion, and her peach-colored tongue beat like a pulse with her rapid breathing. From her size and plumage she was obviously a red-tailed hawk, less than two years old and in her prime, but even so, she would have a nervous system as fine and as delicate as a Swiss watch and be subject to death by heart attack or apoplexy if she was not handled carefully. I would need not only whatever skill I might have but also enormous luck, since she would rather die than submit to me. Moving very slowly so as not to disturb her any more than was absolutely necessary, I took off one of my Adidas shoes and rolled down a long one-size-fits-all sweat sock I was wearing. Then, moving the hand that held the sock out in front of her so that she would follow it with her eyes, I eased my other hand over her back and pinned her wings down so she could not beat them against the ground. Her shallow, rapid heart trembled under the fine bright feathers of her breast. I tore the toe out of the sock and put it around her neck like a collar and rolled it down until she was encased in a tight tube of elastic cotton. All that was visible was her head at one end of the sock and talons at the other.

On the long slow walk back home, the only sound she made was a soft clucking very much like that of a chicken. I held her as loosely as I could because I was worried about the heat of my hands and the way she was wrapped. I really expected her to die, but apparently she was not hurt as badly as I thought. By the time I put her on my bed her breathing had slowed and she had grown calm under the tight sock.

I sat down and opened my desk, and there, nearly filling the bottom drawer, was leather from all the years I had kept and trained and flown hawks. On top was a pair of leather welder's gloves, the right one bloodstained between the thumb and forefinger. And under the gloves were several pairs of eighteen-inch jesses and two four-foot leashes and fifteen hoods, each one with the size and date it was made cut into the top of it, and finally four tiny brass falcon bells and as many shark swivels, used to join the jesses to the leashes.

I took the hoods out of the drawer and arbitrarily selected Number 7 to fit to the hawk's head to see if it was lighttight. It was too big, so I tried the next one down, Number 6, which was nearly right. When I went to Number 5, the fit was perfect, so I drew the leather hood strings, and the hawk, in total darkness now, lay utterly still. With a pair of scissors I carefully cut away the sock. I put on the leather gloves and with my right hand under her breast lifted her to stand on the floor. In the darkness and confusion of the lighttight hood, she stood without moving while I looped the leather jesses around her legs and attached one of the bells to a tail feather. I then attached the ends of the two jesses to the shark swivel and hooked the other end of the swivel to a leash. Her blood-clotted wing hung half spread from her body. I ran my fingers gently along the leading edge to see whether or not the bone was broken. It was not. The flesh was torn, but not badly, and I was able to remove four tiny bird shot from the wound with a pair of tweezers without cutting away any of her feathers. With the leather glove covering my wrist, I touched her legs from behind, and as all hawks will do, she immediately stepped up and back, her talons gripping my arm tightly enough to hurt through the quarter-inch leather.

It has always seemed an awesome mystery to me that any hooded hawk anywhere in the world will step in precisely the same way if the backs of its legs are touched. It was true when Attila the Hun carried hawks on his wrist, and it is still true. Presumably it is something that will be true forever. It is part of the reason men have been fascinated with the art of falconry through all the centuries of recorded history.

The hood was the only way I could possibly keep her while her wing healed because without the hood she would beat herself to death at the end of the jesses. A hood makes a hawk's movements and reactions predictable, but there is something about it that is disgusting, too. To make a hawk as docile as a kitten, to reduce even the biggest and most magnificent raptor in the world to something any child can carry, has always caused a sour ball of shame to settle solid as bone inside me.

I made a perch for her out of a broomstick attached to the top of a ladder-back chair and put her on it. She gripped the perch and sat as still as if she had been killed and stuffed. Eventually she would move, but only a little. She would lower her head and rake at the hood with her talons, but not for long, and the period of quietness would give her some chance of staying alive until she healed. I drew the blinds on the windows and stood watching her in the darkened room, thinking again of the perverse pleasure and unreasonable joy, dating all the way back to my childhood, that I have found in meat-eating birds.

One of my most vivid memories is of riding bareback on a mule in the pinewoods of South Georgia and seeing a buzzard walk out of the stomach of a dead and bloated cow, a piece of putrid flesh caught in its stinking beak. And right behind that memory is a hawk swinging into our farmyard and driving its talons into the back of a screaming chicken and flying toward the darkened tree line on the horizon. And necessarily linked to that memory is my grandmother immediately cooping up all the chickens except one puny biddy left unprotected in the yard with arsenic on its head for the same hawk to come back later and take away toward the same dark tree line, never to be seen again. A bird that drinks blood and eats flesh seemed to me then, and seems to me now, an aberration of nature, and I have always thought it must be for this very reason that I have been driven to capture, train, and fly hawks, to participate in the thing that I find so abhorrently and consistently beautiful.

I left the room and let the hawk sit in silence for the rest of the day and that night. I knew there was some danger she might die of shock or thirst. But unless she was kept still so the damaged wing could start to heal, she would surely die from exertion.

Toward the end of the next day I went down to a feedstore and bought a biddy and carried it dead into the room where the hawk sat on her perch, more alert now, shaking the bell with her tail feathers and holding the damaged wing closer to her body and turning her hooded head toward me as I came to the perch. The blinds were still drawn, and I knew after the long blind night of the hood she would not be afraid of me if I did not look directly at her and made no sudden movements. I held the biddy between the thumb and forefinger of my right hand while I slipped the strings at the back of the hood and drew it away from her head.

I held the biddy about six inches away from the perch and stood very still while the hawk raised the feathers on her head and looked from the glove to my averted face and back again. She had to be hungry, perhaps dangerously so, but I was not going to feed her unless she stepped to my hand. I was not surprised when she had not taken that step after I had held the food in front of her for nearly an hour.

Finally, I backed quietly to the door and left her sitting unhooded in the darkened room. I didn't know how long it would take before she stepped to my glove to eat. But she had to do it or I could never release her and let her fly free again. The problem was simple enough and even easy to solve if she would just cooperate. If she did not lose her fear of me and step to my glove to eat, I would not be able to work her to a lure. And if I could not work her to a lure, I'd never be able to strengthen her wing enough so she could hunt for herself again, because it would take from three weeks to a month of inactivity for her wing to heal, and after she sat on a perch for a month, she wouldn't even be able to fly to the top of a tree, much less catch a darting rabbit. The choice was brutally necessary: either she lost her fear of me and ate off my glove or I would starve her to death.

Fortunately, most birds of prey—except owls, which are too dumb to do much with—react favorably to patience and calm persistence. After two days on the perch without food, half the time wearing the hood I put on her to accustom her to it, the hawk stepped to my glove and ate the biddy right down to the feet. The next day I gave her strips of beef heart and began taking her outside and fastening her leash to a block of wood where she could weather in the sun and bathe from time to time in a shallow pan of water. There are few things in the world more beautiful to me than a hawk rising from the water and slowly turning in the sun, wings stretched and fanning on the air.

There was no infection, and even though the red-tailed hawk did finally lose two of her flight feathers, she was soon flying the length of her leash to my glove. But her eyes and feathers were dull, and she was extremely weak. With no work, her appetite had gotten smaller and smaller until she was eating barely enough to stay alive.

Twenty days after I brought her home, I decided to start flying her to a lure. I didn't think she was ready for it, but I was afraid she was going to die if she didn't start taking more food, and the only way she was going to do that was if I worked her.

The lure is a pillow-shaped piece of leather with a freshly killed chicken's head tied to it along with a nice bit of bloody meat. I introduced her to the lure in the room where I kept her, letting her fly to it and eat with it caught between the thumb and forefinger of my glove. When she had become thoroughly accustomed to it, I let her go entirely without food for thirty hours and then took her to a wide, empty field and set her on a portable perch. I fastened her jesses to a twenty-foot length of light but very strong nylon cord. From a distance of about seven feet, I showed her the lure, swung it round and round before finally offering it to her on the glove. Her bobbing head followed the bloody meat, and then, giving a short, startled cry, she flew to it, her talons stretched and ready.

By the end of two weeks I had lengthened the nylon cord to sixty yards. At first there were a few lapses when she swerved away from the lure and headed straight up. But she didn't have to be jerked out of the air many times by the cord before she was convinced she was somehow irrevocably joined to me and the lure.

Five weeks after I took her crippled and bleeding out of the sand, she was flying free, diving at the lure as I swung it in long arcs over my head, finally catching it high in the air and powering to the ground with it. As she sat on the lure eating, I would quietly walk to her and touch the backs of her legs with the glove and she would step up and back, finishing her meal on my arm.

I kept her longer than I needed to because I had come to love her, probably because she did not love me, and never would. She was as wild the day I flew her free as she was the day I found her. Hawks are not your friend and do not want to be. They are incapable of love, and I have for a long time thought that was precisely why I so much loved them.

One Sunday morning, trying to do it mechanically and without thought, I drove sixty miles to the Okefenokee Swamp with the hawk hooded so she would stay quiet. When I had taken the canoe five hours deep into the black-water cypress, I unclipped the falconer's bell, slipped her jesses, removed the hood, and threw her from my wrist toward the bright blue sky. I had taken her as deep into the swamp as I could because she had lost her fear of man and at least here she would have some chance of survival. But given the number of fools with guns, I did not think that chance very good, even though she had been freed in the middle of a national preserve.

For a long time I heard her high trailing cry above me. But I never looked up. I felt bad enough as it was.

Television's Junkyard Dog

I came out of the Sheraton-Universal Hotel at nine in the morning into a blinding sun under a brilliant sky and walked into a landscape covered with tourists. There was a row of them lined up cheek to jowl directly across the macadam drive where limousines and cabs and private cars pulled through. The tourists all had their little cameras pressed to their faces or strung from their necks. I'm sure I couldn't have looked as bad as I felt because I felt pretty bad. My Levi's and T-shirt were specked with blood from the night before when two guys took what little cash I was carrying off me in an alley in Pasadena. The tiny cut in the top of my scalp made my head feel as if one of those mean Irish teams had been playing soccer with it.

One of the tourists rushed out of the line and threw down on me with his camera, all set to pull the trigger.

"Are you anybody?" he demanded.

"No," I said, "I ain't nobody."

He let his camera down on its strap, his face fell into a kind of angered sorrow, and he walked back to take his place in the line without saying anything else.

In the telephone books at the hotel, Universal Studios advertises itself as the biggest studio in the world, trying to get tourists —and God knows they get them—to take the tram rides through the place and see how they make bridges collapse, how they part the Red Sea and make a train run away. Besides all this, the tourists are promised action-packed live stunt shows and a tour of the famous 420-acre back lot. Three trams leave every half

134

hour. The tourists are exhorted to Catch Hollywood in the Act and Learn Some of Hollywood's Best-Kept Secrets.

As the taxi was nosing its way through streets jammed with trams on its way to Stage 37, where Robert Blake was filming an episode of *Baretta,* I couldn't help thinking the secrets advertised by Universal must be among the worst-kept in the world.

When I got on the set, Blake was sitting in a chair, immaculately dressed in a white suit with a vest over a pale blue shirt. They were doing, and continued to do all day and into the night, a courtroom scene. Everybody knows, even people who have never seen one, that a sound stage where a picture is being shot resembles a very crowded room where somebody has just yelled: "FIRE!"

Men and women rush about everywhere, calling to one another, in some instances screaming to one another, and it is at first glance unimaginable that anything coherent ever emerges from the chaos. But it isn't long before you realize it is a very *controlled* chaos. Everybody knows what he's doing, and he's doing it with all possible haste and precision. They are making an hour show, in six or seven working days, week in and week out.

One of the men talking to Blake, John Ward, an actor, dialogue coach, and occasionally a director, introduced me to Blake. Ward has known Blake twenty years and has been with him on and off during all that time. He is Blake's right hand.

Just as I was about to speak, a thin man rushed up to Blake with a note on yellow paper. He had a look on his face I'd once seen on a fox that had unsuccessfully tried to chew its leg out of a trap during a long night. He kept the note while he breathlessly explained that it was a list of shots the producer said they had to shoot again. Then he handed the note to Blake, who wadded it into a tight little ball and threw it behind him. He hadn't even glanced at it.

"Tell'm we ain't shooting a fucking thing over!"

The man's face got quietly desperate. "But he said. . . ."

Blake's face darkened a little, and he shouted: "Tell the asshole *I* said we ain't shooting *nothing,* not one goddamn thing over!"

With the guy still standing there, his mouth formed as though he would say something else, Blake turned to me, and we shook hands, his face already easy and smiling again. He tapped me on the shoulder and said: "I'm in the middle of a little shit, man, I'll be with you in a while."

"It's cool," I said. "I'll just hang about and watch."

What I watched in the next couple of hours was Blake dictating scenes that had not yet been written, improvising on ones that had, winging it, talking to the director—no, *telling* the director what should be done and how it should be done—listening to and arguing with the cinematographer who has shot every one of the *Baretta* episodes, a tiny man with a great white mustache named Harry Wolf, a man who won the Emmy in 1976 for his work on the show, another of the few men Blake obviously loves and has explicit trust in. He also managed to get in an incredible amount of cursing and shouting about wardrobe, dissolves, cuts, about whether a scene needed to be shortened or lengthened or even included at all. Nothing, not the smallest detail, escapes his attention and utter concern. And despite the most brilliantly dirty mouth in the industry and a manner that is decisive to the point of brutality, all the people on the set seemed to love him.

Energy comes off Blake like heat off a stove, and everybody else lives off it. He came on the set at nine that morning, and he would be there long after dark, that energy still cooking.

He came over to where I was and said: "I don't know how you want to do this, but anytime I'm in that chair and you want to talk, do it. It won't bother me."

"We'll get to it, no problem," I said.

He left me standing by the wall, my motorcycle knees killing me from the night in the Pasadena alley, my damaged head ducking lighting screens being lowered on ropes from the catwalks high above the set, dodging as best I could men pushing wheeled cameras, and trying at the same time not to get my gimpy legs caught in the tangle of cables strung everywhere over the set.

Blake carries his weight from the waist up, most of it in his arms and shoulders and chest. Even through the coat he was wearing, you could see the rolling muscle down each side of his spine flex and pump as he walked. He's not a tall man, maybe less than five nine, and he's not heavy, but when you stand next to him, he seems much bigger than that.

While another set was being lighted, he came by and said: "Let's go out to the trailer and talk."

The trailer was one of those long coach affairs, air-conditioned, with a kitchen and beds and couches. A thick shag covered not only the floor but parts of the walls. He went directly to a little shelf and dipped a generous spoon of snuff behind his lower lip. He looked over his shoulder and gave me that quizzical little-boy smile that he can do sometimes, a smile that half the women in America have dreamed of taking to their hearts, not to mention their breasts.

"These mothers have got me hooked on snuff again," he said, and sat down on a couch across from me.

"Used to dip myself," I said. And then: "That work out there must get you pretty rank at times. Saying the same two lines for ten takes, those boiling lights. All those people."

"You're probably here on the worst day in the entire history of *Baretta.* There's nothing duller than this Perry Mason shit."

I asked him about working in television as opposed to working in movies.

He gave that look he can sometimes do, the look half the men in America wish they could screw their faces into when they need to get out of a hairy situation on a Saturday night. "In the first place in television, here at Universal, nobody listens and nobody cares. As far as most people are concerned, they just as soon turn out Perry Mason or Donald Duck, it don't make no difference. Cause once you sell the hour, as long as it's on the air, it don't matter. You're on the air, or you ain't on the air. It ain't like a movie, where the better you make it, the prouder you are, the more people go see it. Or it's like writing a book—movies, I mean —the more of your heart you put into it, the more satisfying it is, the longer life it has. In television, their theory is put the money in the pot: once it's on the air, forget about it, screw it.

"And they don't spend any money on it cause you're gonna get the same price from the network whether you spend three hundred thousand dollars or four hundred thousand dollars. The less you make it for, the more money you get out front. Nobody gives a damn. The only people who care are my troops. The gorillas. The people down here on the set."

He stopped and spat, apparently swallowing a little snuff juice at the same time. It seemed to satisfy. "Who's the director out there, his name?" I asked, not really caring one way or another. I only wanted to get this wild man talking, talking about anything, because the moment I saw him, before we ever spoke, I felt a strange blood bond, an almost painful shock of recognition. It was all the more painful because as contradictory as it may sound, I did not know what I had recognized.

He shifted his snuff a little and said: "It don't matter. This episode is being directed by a guy named Robert Douglas. Directors on television are transients. They come and go. Every episode. The guild says you gotta have a director, so you stick a director in the chair. And it's like sticking a broomstick in the chair. The show directs itself anyway. There are maybe two or three good directors in television. The rest are atmosphere."

I was sitting in an office big enough to stable a team of draft horses, waiting for a man who I had been told was the best editor in New York. He had just bought my sixth novel—the contracts signed, the money paid—and now I had come 1000 miles to get the editorial advice I'd been assured would make a good book better. Since this was the first book of mine his house had published, I'd never met the man. He came breezing in, nodding his head and calling me Harry—folksy as hell—and sat in the middle of the floor, even though there were couches all over the place and a perfectly good chair behind a desk that a grown man could have slept on.

He immediately went into a long, detailed monologue about the trouble he'd been having with his nose. At first I wondered if I'd come to the wrong place, and then I wondered what reason he might have for thinking I gave a good goddamn about his nose. He did, however, finally lean forward right in the middle of a history of his left nostril and say: "Now, Harry, about your book. . . ." I leaned forward. He leaned forward. This was what I'd come to get: the word, the brilliance of genuine literary direction. "Here, Harry, is what you've got to do." I waited as he concentrated to get it just right. "Harry, you've got to open the end of your novel up and let it breathe." I sat, stunned, waiting to hear what he would be able to follow that line with. But he seemed to have finished. "Let it breathe?" I said. He touched his sick nose gingerly with his forefinger. "Right," he said. "That would be my advice: open up the end and let it breathe." I stayed in his office for two hours trying to discover what that could mean and then left without ever knowing. I never saw the man again, but I often wondered what a man like that might be called. After all these years, Robert Blake had just told me. He was not, for instance, a goddamn stupid sonofabitch. He was *atmosphere*.

They were about to shoot part of a scene that Blake had just finished writing, a scene with a beautiful lady judge doing a number on Detective Baretta. Baretta is on the stand, and as usual, he is in trouble for breaking the law he is sworn to enforce. He has illegally obtained evidence against a loan shark by going into the shark's car without a search warrant.

Everything is ready on the set. The good gray bailiff is in place, along with lawyers and extras sitting on the courtroom benches. Electricians and cameramen and a crowd of other men and women are waiting for the magic moment, forty-two people in all, as I counted them, all sweating under enormous lights flooding out of the ceiling. Quiet is called for, the scene is marked, a horn goes off.

The judge is supposed to say: "An automobile is private property, Detective Baretta, just like an apartment or home. To break in without a warrant is illegal. You must know that."

Baretta's answer is supposed to be: "Yeah, I know dat. And I also know dat thirty percent interest is illegal. A fifteen-year-old girl borrowing fifty dollars and still paying on it two years later is also illegal. *I know dat!*"

When the director calls "ACTION," the beautiful judge delivers her lines in a fine and official voice. Detective Baretta begins: "Yeah, I know dat." Then he pauses. He turns toward her. He leans in on her desk. This wasn't in the rehearsal, but she responds naturally, relaxed, playing to him, knowing as she does that Blake often improvises. Their faces are close, little more than a foot apart. Detective Baretta says: "Yeah . . . I know and I also know dat . . . dat. . . ." He's looking dead into her beautiful eyes, and he finishes by saying: "Licking and sticking and dicking are illegal, but it's right out there on the street." He breaks up in laughter. Then he screams out: "What was dat line? Gimme dat sonofabitch again."

As they get ready to try it again, he goes over to the cinematographer, whispers something to him while embracing the little man with a massive arm.

Much later, after many, many takes of the same scene, we were back in the trailer talking about the few people who show a little class, which took Blake straight to the little man he's hugged, Harry Wolf.

"He's been here from the day this show started. He's been in the trenches, he's fought and bled to make the show what it is. Last night he came up to me, and you know what he said?"

"Tell me."

" 'You can fire me anytime you want.' Classy guy. I love him. Just won the Emmy for *Baretta* and they had the nerve to call up and tell him some shot was outta focus. Or some other bullshit. He says you can have my resignation anytime you want. He don't work for them anyway. He works for me. No, he works *with* me. He's one of my brothers, one of the people who make the show work.

"An all the other assholes up there who wear suits and everything don't amount to a row of ratshit in a windstorm, none of'm. They don't listen and they don't care."

Blake got up and ditched the snuff and lit a cigarette, or rather he didn't light it right away. He puffed on it dry for a long time, which is one of the things he does, before eventually putting a match to it. While he did it, I was thinking of the things I'd heard him say on TV talk shows about being Little Beaver in the Red Ryder series of movies, about how his mother had put him on that goddamn horse when he didn't understand what was going on anyway, and besides, he was scared of horses to start with. I told him I'd heard him talk on television about his mother and the Red Ryder thing but that I'd never heard him say anything much about his father. Was Little Beaver the first thing he did in Hollywood?

"I came out here and won a contract at MGM in the heyday of

MGM, in the time of Judy Garland, Spencer Tracy, and the rest of'm. I started in a thing called *Our Gang*. I was Mickey."

"Christ, I never knew that."

"Yeah. Well. An about my father? He was pretty sick in the head. As a matter of fact, if he hadn'ta had his empire around him, my mother and three kids, he woulda ended up in the loony bin. But he had the kind of insanity that only in my later years I've come to understand. It was one of the good things I got. He was a monster. He beat the shit out of me from the day I was born, and my brother, my sister.

"Alone with all his sickness, all his craziness, and total paranoia, where the walls were coming in on him, he'd get up in the middle of the night, decide that the kids were his enemies, and come in and beat the crap outta us."

My daddy died when I was twenty months old and mama married my daddy's brother. Until I was almost seven years old, I never knew he was not my real daddy. I know how strange that sounds, but I don't remember ever knowing. He was daddy, and I called him daddy and loved him as daddy in spite of the fact that he was drunk going in and coming out, and incredible in his violence, with the scars of a perfect set of somebody's teeth in his cheek under his left eye. Every night I lay in bed trembling, thinking, this time he's gonna kill mama. Her screaming and begging ripped and shook through the house as he beat her and beat her, usually stopping only when he got too tired to go on.

I came back to Blake long enough to hear him say: "He wound up a wreck of a person," and I was instantly standing beside daddy the day I saw him for the first time in fifteen years. I had not seen him once since mama found the courage to divorce him. I had just got out of the Marine Corps and decided to find him. He was wearing an old overcoat, split in the back, and sipping thin soup with his ruined mouth, sitting alone in the back of the cold little greasy room where he lived. I wanted to call him daddy but couldn't. He wouldn't look at me. He didn't want to talk. I left with the impossible wish that he would suddenly turn and say: "I love you."

Something beautiful and dreadful and mysterious had been happening all day. I felt it every time Blake spoke directly to me, but I had no name for what it was, did not then, do not now. I kept thinking that what Blake was saying, I'd said before. That what he had done, I'd done, too. And it all went as deep and intimate and mortal as blood and bone.

From this distance, sitting here on my porch writing this at three o'clock in the morning, the whole thing—the sense of knowing I knew what he knew before he told me, the dreadful thought that your own skin might not wholly belong to you, the unthinkable possibility that you might someday exchange it with another human being—the whole thing sounds at best like a silly fabrication. Or maybe crazy. But while it was happening, it was as real as breathing. And worse, there were times before it was over when I wasn't sure whether I was getting his story or my own. Or if the distinction between the two was a distinction at all, or only a puff of breath. A word. But somewhere I knew there was a mirror image. A face looking out of the green depths in warped glass. And I no longer thought it possible to find out if the face was his or mine.

In an act of near desperation, trying to get outside my own head, I asked if he saw his brother and sister much.

"My brother is two and a half years older'n me and lives in New York. I haven't seen him in twenty years. My mother lives in the East someplace. I haven't seen her in ten years." He paused and looked at the burning end of his cigarette. "An my father croaked in 1955 I think it was."

I had to get off that subject for a while. "Besides doing good work in things like *Pork Chop Hill* and *Tell Them Willie Boy Is Here* and creating the great role of the gimpy aspirin freak in *In Cold Blood,* the country now knows you as Baretta. Does it ever bother you that you might get stuck in this thing, this Baretta?"

"I *ain't* gonna get stuck in this thing, an you can take dat to the bank. You get used to the dressing room, the cars, and pretty soon the studio becomes your home. They want one more year and one more year and pretty soon you're imitating yourself in front of that box and you don't even know it. And then finally, after seven or eight years, you wind up out on the street. That is the fear I have. People say, 'Whatever happened to Doug McClure? Or this one or that one?'

"Nobody, I don't give a damn if it is John Garfield, if he was doing Baretta, he could burn out. There's no way in the world it can happen different. Eventually the audience doesn't care anymore because you're doing the same thing, and the other thing is, you can't do it well anymore."

He pointed to a new book of mine called *A Feast of Snakes* that I had brought him. "You can only write that book once. And you can write a version of it a second time, but trust me it'll be shit. No matter how hard you try, you gotta move on to other things or accept the fact that that's as far as you're going with your life. Put it in the bank, I *will* be out of *Baretta.*"

"Do you know when, how much longer it'll take?"

"I know exactly. But I can't tell you."

"That's a lock, cool. I know you just spent six months in court. You want to say anything about that, what it dealt with?"

"With *Baretta* and with me and with what's best for the show and my career. I had to go to the mat, and it worked out fine."

"Good, man. I'm glad. I'm glad it's by God working for *somebody.*"

Then, in my inimitable fashion as an interviewer—and for reasons I no longer remember—I was suddenly off into long, rambling praise of my son Byron, who is thirteen and who is such a goddamn good buddy of mine, when I happened to remember that I didn't even know if Blake had any children.

"You got any kids?"

"Two," he said. "Boy and a girl."

"Would you care if they became actors?"

"I don't give a shit. With my kids I found the secret is to not teach'm but to learn from'm. They're born with everything. And what most people do is squash it and take it away from them. If you can just lay back and trust whatever God there is in this universe that made them kids, made'm to work, that someplace there's more good in us than bad or we'da never made it outta the trees in the first place, we woulda killed each other in the caves. *There's no such thing as a kid who needs fixing.*"

He leans up off the couch now, leans toward me, and that energy that's always in him really starts pumping. "I went into therapy. I had to have a head man because I was all screwed up. I was lucky; I found a good one. It's a young science, and ninety percent of them guys are fulla shit. But there's a philosophy there someplace that works. I get a lot of mail from a lot of people about therapy. How do you help yourself, whether it's by reading books on therapy or by going to a doctor or going to a priest, how do you help yourself?

"And the thing I learned is this: I am what I am. I'm crazy, I'm hostile, I got a lot of drive, I got a lot of hate, a lot of fear. For most of my life I tried to put that away and be like other people, and therapy didn't change me. But what I learned is and what I want to tell other people whether they're kids or grownups or whatever they are: if you can get to the place where you can take whatever you are and use it out there in the world, not try to put it away and say I'm not angry, I'm a good boy, I'm not scared of the dark anymore . . . whatever your problem is . . . instead of going into the corner like a dog and chewing on your own feet. If you can take that . . . that *whatever is in you,* and turn it up and say that's what the hell I am, an I gotta find a way to make that work, then you'll be OK."

I was sitting in a tiny room at the typewriter trying not to wake up my eight-year-old son. Beside me in boxes were manuscripts. All rejected. Rejected because they were no good. I'd written five novels and hundreds and hundreds of short stories. I'd written ten years, and not a word had seen print. The room was filled with a palpable despair. I was young then and I could consistently miss three nights of sleep every week and survive fairly well. But beside the typewriter lately I'd begun keeping a jar of speed. I popped pills all day long like M & M's. It was the only way I could work every day to support my family and write at night to keep alive what I knew was true: I was a writer. A fiction writer. And a goddamn good one. It was in me somewhere, but something had gone horribly wrong. And it had pretty much driven me crazy. There were times when I was absolutely nuts. That night I was on the bitter end of a five-day run. It was Friday and I hadn't been on a bed since Sunday. I turned and looked at all that worthless work stacked against the wall. Why was it all so god-damn bad? Because by then I knew the work I had done, and was doing, was no good. I had worked just hard enough and learned just enough to know that I wasn't neglected or overlooked by several thousand dumb publishers of one kind or another. No, I was a twenty-four-karat fake; that was the trouble.

When that thought of being a *fake* formed in my speed-splat-tered brain, a brain that must have been carrying a blood pres-sure approaching stroke country, I had what I think of as the only revelation of my life. It was all utterly clear.

For many and complicated reasons, circumstances had col-laborated to make me ashamed that I was a tenant farmer's son. As weak and warped as it is, and as difficult as it is even now to admit it, I was so humiliated by the fact that I was from the edge of the Okefenokee Swamp in the worst hookworm and rickets part of Georgia I could not bear to think of it, and worse to believe it. Everything I had written had been out of a fear and loathing for what I was and who I was. It was all out of an effort to pretend otherwise. I believe to this day, and will always believe, that in that moment I literally saved my life, because the next thought—and it was more than a thought, it was dead-solid con-viction—was that all I had going for me in the world or would ever have was that swamp, all those goddamn mules, all those screwworms that I'd dug out of pigs and all the other beautiful and dreadful and sorry circumstances that had made me the Grit I am and will always be. Once I realized that the way I saw the world and man's condition in it would always be exactly and in-evitably shaped by everything which up to that moment had only shamed me, once I realized that, I was home free. Since that time I have found myself perpetually fascinating. It wasn't many weeks before I loved myself endlessly and profoundly. I have found no other such love anywhere in the world, nor do I expect to.

Somebody knocks on the door and says they'll be ready to go in about ten minutes. Blake has to make a change, and he shucks down right there. I know the reason he's got a photographic double is because his wheels are messed up, bad knees and ankles. Blake's been talking into my tape recorder while I've been riding the stoned and happy high he's given me, and I'm still riding it as I wonder if he could possibly be a bike freak, too.

Knowing absolutely what's about to come down, I begin to tell him of my addiction to motorcycles, about how I once left Florida and rode a Triumph to Wyoming and up into Canada and out to California and back across the Rockies to Colorado Springs and then south across Raton Pass into New Mexico and down into the Mexican desert and from there to New Orleans.

"I was gone a year and a half," I said. "One of the best things I ever did for myself. Kept a journal. Called it *There's Something About Being Straddle of a Thing.*"

The moment he looked up and our eyes met I knew how it was going to be. I felt like I could even have helped him tell whatever his bike story was, although I'd not yet heard it.

He said: "That's a great title. You got that right on the tee. *There's Something About Being Straddle of a Thing.* Motorcycles. I *love*'m. I got fucked-up legs from bikes. I was up on Mulholland Drive and went right off the mother. And the last thing I remember was thinking I gotta get away from the bike before we land or it's gonna get me. When I woke up, there was something hot dripping on my forehead. I had come about fifty or sixty feet down and the bike was above me hung in a tree. And the hot oil was dripping on my forehead. And it was like the Lord was saying: 'Next time I'll let the bastard drop.' It woulda come right on top of me and it woulda been all over."

He hadn't even stopped telling the story before I was already half lost in the foggy Christmas morning of 1958, just a little before daylight, when I laid a motorcycle down and went under one side of a semi—an eighteen-wheeler carrying U.S. mail—went under one side and came out the other. I don't know how fast the truck was going, but I was over the speed limit, whatever it might have been. I always was in those days. There was no way I could not have been killed. It was a totally impossible accident to have survived. But all it did to me was finish the job on the same knee that another bike had started the year before.

Back on the set between takes I was curious about how much time he managed to get off doing a series. Actually, I wasn't curious about much of anything by now. I was content just to stand there with a guy I felt like I'd known my whole life—which, of course, I had.

"This past summer I got outta here by myself with nobody, without my family, not even my dog, in my four-wheel van, and I disappeared for six weeks. That's the first time I've done that in years and years. I spend all my time off working on this shit. Trying to bring lousy scripts to life, trying to bring mannequins with suits on to life. On the show I work off a lot of hate. I got a lot of hate in me."

"You're just going to get in trouble again," said Charné as she was putting me on a plane in Florida earlier this year. Charné is a lady I've written a lot about for many reasons; one of the reasons is she takes really good care of me when she can. Sometimes she can't. Sometimes nobody can. "What the hell's eating you this time?" she said.

"I don't know."

"If you could see your face, you'd go back home and go to bed."

She was right, of course. I was in a boiling, seething, sourceless rage. I thought I was on my way to Tulsa, Oklahoma, and I meant to go. Where I was actually on my way to was a jail cell in Grapevine, Texas. Nothing serious. Just your run-of-the-mill hate that had surfaced during the night from wherever it keeps itself and it had to be worked out. The cops let me walk the next morning. Someday I'd like to write a thing called *Jails I Have Known.* One thing I'll be damn sure to include is how the cops in Grapevine handcuff you. If you'll just reach over your right shoulder with your right hand, and then take your left hand and put it on your left kidney and go on up with it until your fingers touch between your shoulder blades, you'll have it. I'd never been fitted to a pair that way before, and it hurt like hell. But them good ole boys in Grapevine know what they're doing. The pain from the cuffs and lying cold all night on a naked cement floor cooled my fever like Vicks poultice from the soothing hand of my dear old mama.

I knew that Blake's wife, Sondra (whom I met later, a gracious and gentle lady with the smooth and supple body of a dancer, which she was and is), had been an actress and had given up her career, only recently to begin it again. How did that come about?

"When both our kids came along, one right after another, we made the decision—I made the decision and then talked her into it—that the only way we could keep our kids from winding up junkies and crazy like most of the kids in Hollywood was to at least give them a home, let'm know who their mother was, for better or worse, not have maids around raising them.

"She quit working entirely, and I didn't make no location jobs or nothing like that. And we put in our time. She paid her dues and then went back to work, and I'm so fucking happy. Because she's doing great. She was dynamite in *Helter Skelter.* She's in *The Woody Guthrie Story,* she's in the Jimmy Caan-Burt Young movie that Sam Peckinpah directed. Her career is doing great. All the chicks she was working with when she quit have all burned out. Because television eats up people like a garbage disposal. One year a girl does a lead in every show—she's hot—and the next year she's history. The studios don't give a damn. They don't listen and they don't care as long as they can make a buck off your ass. The day you're burned out, you can't get'm on the phone.

"I used to think I was gonna find somebody or something and that was gonna save me. Like Brando found Kazan, Bogart found Huston, and they made great movies together. I thought I'd have my family like that and live happily ever after. That's bullshit. That's a jack-off dream I threw out. Today you gotta do it for yourself."

I said: "You see much of your own work?"

"None."

"Go to the movies much?"

"Hardly at all. You go sometimes and you see the guys in the trenches and it breaks your heart a little bit. They're down there in the trenches and they've been there a long time and it ain't working for'm." He shrugged his shoulders in a way that clearly meant he acknowledged the way the world works, that fairness was not a thing you could count on. "But that's all right, too. I played the hand I got. That's all you can do."

"You got any favorite actors?"

"Yeah. But most of'm are dead and in the grave. But even in the grave they're more alive than most of us walking around. John Garfield, Paul Muni, Charles Laughton, Claude Rains, Robert Ryan. In the Pepsi generation we've forgotten what real class is. I think there was a time, even with writers, when it was a better environment. When Clifford Odets was writing great plays and there was a fever for greatness. At the time Paul Muni was cooking, he wasn't alone. There were other giants around. People inspired each other. What's around you today is a bunch of mannequins. I can get more out of reading Jack London before I go in front of the camera than I can sitting and talking to other creative people, cause they just ain't that creative.

"Can you imagine being on the set where there was a director like Lewis Milestone? And when you could turn to Claude Rains and Paul Muni and those kind of people? I mean, they tried to get the best outta you at all times, not the worst. Everything now goes toward getting shit out of you. Give us the minimum, and even that's too much." He paused a moment. "What's the guy who writes the cop stuff?"

"Wambaugh?"

"Yeah. Now if you compare that to Harold Robbins, it ain't bad. It's pretty good. It ain't worth a shit if you compare it to Jack London. Paul Newman is OK, if you don't mention Paul Muni."

"What's the best work you think you ever did? Picture? Maybe just a scene?"

"The best work I think I ever did was the death-house scene by the window in *In Cold Blood*. That's the one where I think I got the closest to where I wanted to go."

Later we were back in the trailer, me smoking, him sucking on a little snuff. And we got to talking about our children and from that to parents.

He said: "You need them parents. They have the instinct to try to be bigger for their children in certain ways. I try to give my children things I know they ain't ever gonna get from anybody else. They make me want to be strong for'm. Make me want to do right for'm. I never had that. And when I went out in the world and found a friend or a director or sometimes even a situation, I expected a parental response from it. And for years, people always let me down. I thought people were no good. What I was looking for were parents. People ain't like that, and so I formed the conclusion that people were crap and the world was crap and I'd stick a lousy needle in my arm.

"I finally realized that the demands I was making were too big. Too big for the world. And that the world was not at fault, just one of those things. I was looking for that kind of love and that kind of dedication and that kind of respect that you can only get from parents.

"When I first went into therapy thirteen, fourteen years ago, I never had any kind of physical contact with people. My house —what a cold and rigid place that was. About the only time my mother touched me was when she had to swab my throat. Or put a Vicks hot pack on my chest. Or hang a piece of garlic around my neck. And when I went into therapy, I was in there about three years. And I was tight. Tense, man. I wasn't gonna lay on no couch, talk no garbage, but something was happening underneath.

"One day—this is how shrewd this doctor was and most of'm ain't—he understood to wait his turn. One day he got up when I left and walked out of his office onto this little dirt area. Said: 'I'll see ya tomorrow.' It was the first time he ever walked me out. And I started panicking. He said: 'I'll see ya tomorrow.' And he put his arm around my shoulders, and I cried and I cried and I cried. I cried for about half an hour, man. I got snot all over the front of his jacket. I came totally apart.

"Because if he would have said to me, Johnny, your problem is that nobody ever caressed you, your mother never hugged you, *that's all words.* The real secret of a great doctor or a great anybody is to make it happen emotionally. That's what this guy did. For the first time I understood emotionally how removed from the world I was. I got in my car and drove up on Mulholland, up and down Mulholland all day and into the night, and all this shit was coming back, all the times I wanted my mother to touch me, how when she was swabbing out my ear I wanted to press my head against her belly and hold her. It all came back on a gut level."

We sat for a moment looking at each other across the little

distance between the chairs. I felt good. I thought there was noplace else he could take me. But I was wrong. He had been quiet a long time when he looked up and, in a voice that was flatter and more laconic than I had heard from him before, said: "I have a dream, and I bet I have it once a week." He is bemused. It is almost as though he is talking of himself to himself. "Wherever I am, whatever I'm doing, I'm naked. And I can't get no clothes on. Sometimes I'm at the airport and sometimes I'm at school in a hallway. Can't get no door open. To get inside. To get away. Sometimes I even try to crawl into a locker. I can't get my hands on no clothes, and everybody else is dressed. And it's always in a public place; sometimes I'm running through a park. I think if I run fast enough and far enough, I'll get someplace I can get some clothes on.

"The essence of that dream is what we been talking about. That wherever you are, you don't belong. That everybody else has got it, but you ain't got it. Everybody else has the equipment. But they can see what you are, they can see because you're fucking naked. Your belly ain't right, or your dick ain't circumcised, or whatever it is. THEY CAN SEE IT!"

By now I'm on my feet holding my head. "Jesus, Jesus," I'm saying. I show him my arm. "Look, I got goose bumps." I put my hand on his shoulder. "I swear on my eyes I have the same goddamn dream. Over and over, I have that goddamn dream."

He said: "Yeah, yeah, man." And as he said it, he gave me that brief sweet hug that country people give their blood kin.

In the taxi awhile later, going back up the hill to the hotel, I watched the endless trams of tourists pour into the biggest studio in the world, into the land of fantasy and endless happiness where all dreams come true.

The Wonderful World
of Winnebagos

Charné, a lady who is great company in the woods or anywhere else for that matter, and I had taken our packs off and were lying behind a low stone wall looking out into the deep mist-shrouded valley below. Behind us some people were feeding a raccoon in the little paved area where cars could pull off the highway. The coon was a great fat thing, bigger than any coon I'd ever seen. Three families of tourists were stuffing it with tourist food, Fritos, Cracker Jacks, marshmallows, and pouring little saucers of Coca-Cola, which the coon seemed to love. They soon tired of feeding the coon, though, and got into their campers and roared off up the Skyline Drive which goes through Shenandoah National Park in Virginia. The coon made no move to leave. Now and then he would look off down the road and seem to sigh.

We were lying in the grass and he didn't see us. Neither did the folks in the Winnebago who pulled into the empty lot and stopped. The coon got up, stretched, and ambled over to the camper. A door swung open. But nobody got out. Then a couple of little fluffs that looked like popcorn came sailing through the door and landed in front of the coon. He ate them. The little beast's appetite was insatiable. Another piece of the stuff was dropped down just by the door. I saw a very white arm and hand. Pudge. Looked feminine. The coon had lived too long without his instincts. He walked over to the Winnebago and looked right up into the door as if he was considering buying the rig or something. At that moment a net—it looked like the kind used to catch butterflies, only bigger, stronger—slammed down over the coon, and he was drawn, kicking and hissing, into the Winnebago, which then roared away down the Skyline Drive.

"Did you see that bastard rip off that coon?" I said.

Charné said: "Wouldn't surprise me if he had a deer and a couple of bear cubs in there, too."

Earlier in the week we'd come down a steep incline to Byrd's Nest Number Two (one of the burdens of hiking in Shenandoah National Park is the names of the campsites. They all sound as if they were thought up by a stoned PR man in Los Angeles) and found fifteen young Japanese students surrounding a shelter. There was a bear on the roof, a bear that must have weighed 200 pounds. The Japanese all had Nikon cameras to their faces. They were screaming. The bear was terrified. We'd heard them screaming a half mile away and speculated on what they might be doing. But it never occurred to us that they might have treed a bear.

As we stood in the trail and watched, the animal—a light froth hanging from its mouth and breathing like a bellows—suddenly leaped off the shelter and spread the young Japanese like a covey of quail. The bear, when it hit the ground, made a sound like a bull alligator, but that didn't intimidate the students. They quickly regrouped and chased the bear into the woods, their little cameras pressed against their faces.

Charné said, "It would serve them right if they caught it."

"Take more than a Japanese with a Nikon to catch a bear," I said. "They're quick, bears are."

The coon had been gone for about an hour and we were still in Crescent Rock Overlook near Hawksbill Mountain getting a little sun and resting when I heard a tourist parent say to a tourist child: "Get the clubs, son. I've got the balls here in my pocket."

We turned very slowly and watched a kid of about fifteen come bouncing out of a Winnebago. He had golf clubs in his hands. Drivers. He walked over to his dad and gave him one. They both took ventilated nylon soft-billed golf caps out of their back pockets and carefully adjusted the caps on their heads. They were both wearing golf shoes. Their double-knit cuffless trousers and Ban-Lon shirts were color-coordinated. They took a couple of practice swings, professional as hell: head down, follow-through, locked left arm. Just then a thin lady wearing a candy-striped pantssuit popped out of the camper.

"You boys hurry now," she said. "I'm going to warm up Suzy."

Suzy was apparently the name of the Winnebago, because the lady went up front and got under the steering wheel. A sweet little puff of blue smoke shot out of Suzy's tail pipe.

"Who went first on the last one?" said the man.

"I did, dad," said the boy, flexing his knees.

"OK, son," he said. "All right then."

The man whipped out a red tee from his back pocket, approached the little stone fence we were now sitting on, and worked the tee into a crack on top of the fence. He put his golf ball on top of the tee and then leaped up beside it. He looked out onto the imaginary fairway which, in this case, stretched west twenty miles to the South Fork of the Shenandoah River and on beyond that to Massanutten Mountain. He set his feet and took a couple of those little swings that miss the ball, the way all golfers do. The third time, the club came way round behind his head, his body twisted in a tight corkscrew, hips firm, and he really unloaded on the ball.

It was the scariest sight I ever expect to see. Hair rose on the back of my neck. My hands got sweaty. And into my nose came the smell of a room where somebody has died. All the while the little white golf ball kept rising, gently rising, then interminably hanging out there on the hazing, blue horizon, framed against the remote forests of Massanutten. Finally, it began to drop, and drop, and drop, and we all sat following its descent into the deep valley below.

"What do you make it, son?" said the man.

The boy had come over to stand beside him. His face was flushed. They were both breathing rapidly. "Well," said the boy, "we're at four thousand and ten feet."

"Fantastic," said the dad. He took out a little spiral notebook from his back pocket. He did some quick figures with a pencil. "I'd say it was at least a two-thousand-yard drive."

"At least," said the boy. They beamed upon one another.

I couldn't stand it. I went over to where they were. "What are you doing?" I said.

The man turned his glowing face on me. "See that shot?" he said. "Fantastic shot. You a golfer?"

"No," I said.

His face perceptibly dimmed. "Oh," he said. "You couldn't have appreciated that shot if you're not a golfer."

"What are you doing?" I said.

He hopped down off the wall. "My boy and I are hitting a golf ball, one each, off every overlook in the park." He turned to his son. "OK, Billy, let's see the old slammer."

The boy, more agile than his father, was instantly on the wall, and instantly the little white ball was hanging again in the air between us and Massanutten Mountain.

"Sweet baby Jesus," breathed the father, "you really caught that one."

"What are you doing?" It seemed the only response I could make.

The Winnebago roared up behind us. The thin lady was hanging out of the window. "All right, you boys," she said. "Suzy's hot to trot."

The man turned to me. He had started to frown slightly when I kept asking my question. "You ought to take up golf," he said. "Great game." He and the boy went through the door of the camper. The door slammed. He leaned out the window at me. He was beaming again. "One ball at each overlook," he said. "It's a great feeling knowing they're out there." Suzy roared away with the man and the boy waving.

Charné came over and stood beside me. "Why'd he say he was doing it?"

"I don't think he said."

She said: "We more than likely just saw a record."

"You think so?"

"I feel sure of it," she said. "If that wasn't a record, it'll do till one comes along."

I suppose I should have been grateful to the tourists for the entertainment they provided. Those Winnebagos are stuffed with *children.* This was a surprise to me because I thought only old folk would be crazy enough to own those goddamn campers that clog the nation's highways. I figured only men and women stunned and driven half-mad by retirement and the horror of their golden years would drive aimlessly around getting in everybody's way, befouling the air, and nesting in little groups beside the road. But no. They're full of children and dogs. God knows what sort of familial perversities are performed nightly under the prefabricated roofs of Mr. and Mrs. American's Winnebagos. Whatever goes on, though, it obviously encourages them to breed.

At the Loft Mountain campground, children ran in packs like dogs. I'll never forget a deer that was damn near captured by the vicious Winnebago children. Charné and I were lying in a ditch drinking beer (one of the great things about Shenandoah National Park is that you can buy beer all over the place) when some deer came walking by. They almost stepped on us. Magnificent creatures. They were wandering in and among the picnic tables, protected, at their ease.

From a small grove of trees burst a gang of screaming children. They knew exactly what they were about. First, they cut out the smallest deer, a doe, and managed to chase her into the very grove of trees in which they had been hiding. Next, they circled her and joined hands, all the while screaming like banshees. There must have been twenty-five of the little devils. Their leader was a cross-eyed terror, about eighty pounds with beige-colored hair, who would someday grow up to take his rightful place on some used-car lot, but for now he wanted that deer. He screamed at his troops and whipped them into shape, staying always outside the circle himself, holding nobody's hand but rather threatening, kicking ass, encouraging, and generally keeping everybody fired up.

I knew what was going to happen. They would gradually tighten the circle and finally fall upon the doe. They'd skin her with their bloody baby's teeth and eat her heart.

They would have, too, if a ranger had not happened along. He charged the circle and sprung the deer free. Then he had a fit.

"You goddamn kids leave these animals alone," he screamed. You could just tell by the way he got so suddenly apoplectic that he'd caught children chasing the animals before. "If you harass these animals anymore and *I* see you, *I* will personally throw you and your parents out of the park. Do you understand? Do you?"

The children did not answer, and they did not look the least bit contrite. What they did look was dangerous. They glared back at the ranger, and while he was screaming, they actually moved in on him a little, circling as they went. Charné saw the same thing.

"That ranger better watch his ass," she said.

They did look cunning enough to take him unawares. I was prepared to see them circle and fall upon him with their teeth as I had been sure they were about to do with the deer. But they didn't. And the ranger was smart enough not to press the issue. He got the hell out of there, and we watched the children come back together and hike off into the little woods, no doubt to lay in wait for another deer. Or who knows? Maybe it was the ranger they were plotting for now.

Carny

I woke up screaming and kicking, catching the ride boy in the ribs with the toe of my boot (which I had not bothered to take off), and when the toe of the boot struck him just below the armpit, he screamed, too, and that caused the lot lady he was rolled in the blanket with to scream—and there the three of us were, thrashing about in my Dodge van, driven stark raving mad on a crash from Biphetamine 20's (a wonderfully deadly little capsule that, taken in sufficient quantities, will make you bigger than anybody you know for at least ninety-six hours running) and driven mad, too, by the screaming siren that woke us up to start with. It was the middle of the night—or, more accurately, the middle of the morning, about 4 A.M.—and the electronic system set to catch burglars and tire thieves had tripped, but I—addled and nine-tenths stunned from too long on the road with a gambler, chasing carnivals across half a dozen states—I didn't know it was my siren or that I was in my van or who I was with or why I was where I was.

But as soon as I opened the side door and saw the black Ferris wheel and the tents standing outlined against the sky, I calmed down enough to get the keys out of my pocket. I couldn't find the right key to turn off the alarm, though, and all the while the siren was screaming and the ride boy, who was about fifty years old, had come out of the van naked from the waist down with his lot lady, who looked like she might have been fifteen, hanging on his back.

"What the hell?" the ride boy kept shouting at me. "What the hell?"

"Alarm!" I kept shouting back. "Alarm." It was all I could get my mouth to say as I fought with the keys.

Lights were coming on in trailers all around us, and out of the corner of my eye I saw the Fat Lady from the ten-in-one show standing beside the little wheeled box that her manager used to haul her from carnival to carnival behind his old Studebaker. She was so big that her back was at least a foot deep in fat. By the time I got the key in the switch and turned the alarm off the Midget had appeared, along with several men who had apparently been gambling in the G-top. Unfortunately, the sheriff's deputy, red-faced and pissed off, had arrived, too. He pushed his flat-brimmed hat back on his head and looked at the van and then at the freaks from the ten-in-one show and then at me.

"You want to take your driver's license out of your billfold and show it to me?" he said.

"My what?"

"You want to git on back in there and put your britches on?" he said to the ride boy. The ride boy didn't move, but the lot lady, who was a local and in some danger, maybe, of being recognized by the cop, turned and got into the van.

He had a flashlight on my license now, and without looking up, he said, "You want to tell me how come you got that siren?"

"Look," I said, pointing. "There's a goddamn air jack." The sight of that jack slipped under the front end of my van made me mad enough to eat a rock.

But the deputy sheriff refused to look. He said, "Only your fire, law-enforcement, and your rescue veehicles allowed to have a siren."

The carny people had closed in around us now. The cop flashed his light once at them, but when the light fell upon the illustrated face of the Tattooed Man, he looked immediately back at the license.

"You want to—"

But I cut him off and said that two months earlier some malevolent sonofabitch had jacked up my van and taken the wheels. I'd come out of the house one morning and found it up on concrete blocks. So I had the doors and hood wired and had a mercury tilt switch rigged to the chassis. If anyone tried to jack it up, a siren went off. While I talked about the tilt switch and the rigged hood and doors, his face drew together on itself. He had never heard of such a thing, and it obviously upset him.

"You want to come on down to the station with me?" he said.

"But what for?" I was getting a little hysterical now. "What about the jack? What about the fucking jack?"

He glanced briefly at Big Bertha where she loomed enormous in the slanting light from a trailer. "You want to watch you language in front of—"

"Hello, Jackson."

We all turned, and there was Charlie Luck, sometimes called Chuck and sometimes Luck and sometimes Chuckaluck and sometimes many other things.

"This man here's got a sireen, Charlie. I think it might be illegal."

Charlie bit his lip and shook his head in disgust. "Has he still got that? I told you, boy, to git rid of that goddamn sireen." He had, of course, told me no such thing.

Charlie was beautiful in a brown suit and soft brown cap and square-toed brown shoes. There was no flash to him at all. Everything he was wearing was very muted and very expensive. He came over and put his arm on the cop's shoulder. "Officer Jackson," he said in just about the most pleasant voice you've ever heard, "could I talk to you over here for a moment?"

They turned away from us, and immediately Big Bertha was struggling up the steps into her little wheeled box. The ride boy got back into the van with his lot lady, mooning us all as he went. The trouble was over. Everybody knew everything was fine, now that Charlie Luck was here. I stood watching, admiring the earnest, head-to-head talk he was having with Officer Jackson, who was nodding now, agreeing for all he was worth with whatever Charlie Luck was saying.

My feeling for Charlie Luck went far beyond admiration. I loved him. He was a hero. Some people have only one or two heroes; I have hundreds. Sometimes I meet six or seven heroes in a single day. Charlie Luck was a great man who just happened to be a gambler, in the same way that Bear Bryant is a great man who just happens to be a football coach. Bryant could have stumbled into a brokerage house when he was twenty and owned Wall

Street by now. Instead, he happened into football. Same with Charlie Luck. Somebody showed him a game when he was sixteen and he never got over it. He became perfect of his kind. The perfect carny. The perfect hustler.

Charlie Luck was never registered for the draft. He's never paid any income tax. Officially, he does not exist. Or, said another way, he exists in so many different forms, with so many different faces, that there is no way to contain him. He knows a place in Mississippi where he can mail away for an automobile tag that is not registered. If somebody takes his number, it can't be traced. And even if it could be traced, it would be traced to an alias.

To my knowledge, Charlie Luck has six identities, complete with phony Social Security cards and driver's licenses, even passports. He has six, and he's contemplating more. He's very imaginative with his life. With his past. Sometimes he's from Texas. Other days, from Maine. I sometimes wonder if he knows where he's from or who he is. He's probably forgotten.

The sheriff's deputy turned and, without looking at me once, walked to his car. Charlie Luck came over to where I was. He watched me for a moment, a little half smile showing broken teeth.

"A siren?" he said. "Well, what do you know about that? I heard the thing over in the G-top. Thought it was a fire truck. Thought maybe something was burning up."

"What did you say to the cop?"

He shrugged. "One thing and another. I told him I'd shut you down, take your siren away."

"You wouldn't do that."

"Of course not." He pointed to the open door, where the ride boy was locked with the lot lady. His mouth suddenly looked as though he tasted something rotten. "I told you about letting those things use your van."

"She came up and he didn't have anyplace. I couldn't think of a way to turn him down."

"You better start finding a way or you'll queer everything." He started to walk away but then stopped. "Hang onto that jack. We'll send it into town sometime and sell it."

I got back into the van and listened to the snores of the ride

boy and the cotton-candy wind breakings of the lot lady. Charlie
Luck was disappointed in me for letting the ride boy sleep in my
van, because the workers, the guys who up-and-down the rides
and operate them, are at the very bottom of a well-defined carny
social structure. A lot lady is a carnival groupie. She is given to
indiscriminately balling the greasy wired men and boys who
spend their lives half-buried in machinery. It was definitely un-
cool of me to associate with them. And inasmuch as I was traveling as Charlie Luck's brother, it was even worse.

Charlie had been reluctant—very reluctant—to let me in with
him to start with. But he owed me. Back in November, I had
managed to persuade a cowboy down in a place near Yeehaw
Junction, Florida, which is great cattle country and where they
have one of the last great cowboy bars, not to clean out one of
Charlie Luck's ears with the heel of his boot. Charlie had been
grateful ever since. That day in Florida, he bought me a beer after
the cowboy left, and we went to a back booth, where he watched
me drink it and I watched him bleed.

"Name's Floyd Titler," he said. "Friends—and you definitely
a friend—friends call me Short Arm."

"Harry Crews is mine." We shook hands across the table.

"Sonofabitch nearly killed me," he said, dabbing at an eye that
was rapidly closing with a handkerchief he'd just soaked in draft.

"I never saw anybody do that," I said, pointing to the handkerchief.

"You just have to be careful none of the alcohol gets in your
eyes. Otherwise, it's great for the swelling."

I finally got around to asking what he was doing in Florida,
because nobody is *from* Florida, and he said he wintered down
there and worked games in a carnival up North in the summer.

"You work hanky-panks or alibis or flats?" I said.

He stopped with the handkerchief. "You with it?" he said.

"A sort of first-of-May," I said. "I ran with a carnival a little
about twenty years ago."

To a carny, you are said to be "with it" if you have been on the
road with a carnival for years and run your particular hustle well
enough to be successful at it. They call anyone who's been with
a carnival for only a short time a first-of-May. I wanted to talk to

him about his game. He didn't want to talk. Not about that. But it was easy enough to find out that he ran a flat joint, also called a flat store or sometimes a grind store or simply a flat.

"I've seen most of them," I said.

"Good," he said. "That's good." He went back to working on his eye.

The more I talked with him, the more I wanted to get back with a carnival. I thought if I did it right, I might get him to let me travel with him some the following summer. But I made the mistake of telling him I was a writer. I suppose I would have had to tell him sooner or later, anyway.

"That'd burn down my proposition," he said.

Nobody has a job in a carnival; he has a proposition.

"I've never blown anybody's cover. Never."

"It'd be dull, anyway," he said.

"No such thing as a dull subject. Only dull writers. Think about it, will you?"

"I'll think about it."

I figured I might as well remind him he owed me. That's the way I am. "You could still be over there on the floor with that cowboy walking around on your face."

It took a little doing, but he finally let me go with him for a while. I particularly wanted to see the gamblers one more time on the circuit, and I knew I had to do it soon or they would be gone forever. Twenty years ago practically every carnival had flat stores. But the flats are not welcome in very many carnivals today. Of the more than 800 carnivals that work this country, probably fewer than 50 still have flat joints. Ten years from now I don't believe there will be any at all.

They are condemned because of the heat they generate. If a flat is allowed, as the carnies say, to work strong, there will be fistfights, stabbings, and maybe even a shooting or two in a season, all direct results of the flat-store operation. Every carnival has a patch, who does just what the word says. He patches up things. He is the fixer, making right whatever beefs come down. Generally, flats keep the patch very busy.

Perhaps unique in the history of carnivals, Charlie Luck—a flattie himself—was also the patch. He was able to operate as the patch only because he usually did not actively run a joint. Rather, he had two agents who worked for him in flat stores he independently booked with the owner of the carnival. So far I'd traveled 600 miles with him and I'd seen no real violence in his flats— some very pissed-off people but no violence. And now, this was to be the last weekend before I went back to Florida. We'd just made a circus jump—tearing down and moving and setting up in less than a single day. It took me a long time to get back to sleep, because the ride boy had dropped another capsule, strapped on the lot lady, and was noisily working out at the other end of the van.

They did, however, finally rock me to sleep, and I didn't wake up until late afternoon. The carnival Charlie Luck was with worked nothing but still dates, which is to say it never joined any fairs where they have contests for the best bull or the best cooking or the biggest pumpkin. Fair dates work all day. Still dates never have much business until late afternoon and night. I changed my clothes in the van and went out onto the midway.

The music on the Ferris wheel and at the Octopus had already cranked up. The smell of popcorn and cotton candy and caramel apples was heavy on the air. A few marks from the town had showed up with their kids. Several fat, clucking mothers were herding a group of retarded children down the midway like so many ducks. I didn't know where Charlie was. He had a trailer, but he usually slept in a motel. I walked over to get a corn dog, and while I was waiting for it, I listened to two ride boys, both of them in their early twenties, talk about shooting up. They were as dirty as they could get, and as they talked, their teeth showed broken and yellow in their mouths. All the workers on carnivals have European teeth. Anybody with all his teeth is suspect. Several locals were standing about eating corn dogs, but the two ride boys went right ahead discussing needles and the downers they had melted and shot up. They were speaking Carny, a language I can speak imperfectly if I do it very slowly. When I hear it spoken rapidly, I can understand it just well enough to know what the subject of discussion is without knowing exactly what is being said.

The marks stared at the two boys babbling on in this strange language full of z's and s's. God knows what the marks thought they were speaking. In Carny, the word *beer* becomes bee-a-zeer and the sentence *"Beer is good* becomes Bee-a-zeer ee-a-zay gee-a-zood. It is not too difficult as long as you are speaking in monosyllables. But when you use a polysyllabic word, each syllable becomes a kind of word in itself. The word *mention* would be spoken mee-a-zen shee-a-zun.

It is a language unique to carnivals, with no roots anywhere else, so far as I know. And it does what it is supposed to do very effectively by creating a barrier between carnies and outsiders. Above everything else, the carny world is a self-contained society with its own social order and its own taboos and morality. At the heart of that morality is the imperative against telling outsiders the secrets of the carnival. Actually, it goes beyond that. There is an imperative against telling outsiders the truth about anything. That was what made being there with Charlie Luck as risky as it was. Either one of us could have been severely spoken to if what we were doing had got out.

I ate my corn dog as I walked down past the Octopus and the Zipper and the Sky Wheel and past the House of Mirrors. I was on my way for a quick look at the ten-in-one, which I had seen every day I'd traveled with Charlie Luck. Ten-in-one is the carny name for a freak show, possibly because there are often ten attractions under one tent. This was a good one but not a great one.

I was especially fond of the Fat Lady and her friends there under the tent. I think I know why, and I know I know when I started loving freaks.

Almost twenty years ago, when I had just gotten out of the Marine Corps, I woke up one day in an Airstream trailer in Atlanta, Georgia. The trailer was owned by a man and his wife. They were freaks. I was a caller for the show. My call was not particularly good, but it was good enough to get the job and to keep it. And that was all it was to me, a job, something to do. The second week I had the job, I was able to rent a place to sleep in the Airstream from the freak man and his freak wife. I woke up that morning in Atlanta looking at both of them where they stood at the other end of the trailer in the kitchen. They stood perfectly still in the dim, yellow light, their backs to each other. I could not see their faces, but I was close enough to hear them clearly when they spoke.

"What's for supper, darling?" he said.

"Franks and beans, with a nice little salad," she said.

"I'll try to be in early," he said.

And then they turned to each other under the yellow light. The lady had a beard not quite as thick as my own but three inches long and very black. The man's face had a harelip. His face, not his mouth. His face was divided so that the top of his nose forked. His eyes were positioned almost on the sides of his head and in the middle was a third eye that was not really an eye at all but a kind of false lid over a round indentation that saw nothing. It was enough, though, to make you taste bile in your throat and cause a cold fear to start in your heart.

They kissed. Their lips brushed briefly and I heard them murmur to each other and he was gone through the door. And I, lying at the back of the trailer, was never the same again.

I have never stopped remembering that, as wondrous and special as those two people were, they were only talking about and looking forward to and needing precisely what all of the rest of us talk about and look forward to and need. He might have been any husband going to any job anywhere. He just happened to have that divided face. That is not a very startling revelation, I know, but it is one most of us resist because we have that word *normal* and we can say we are normal because a psychological, sexual, or even spiritual abnormality can—with a little luck—be safely hidden from the rest of the world. But if you are less than three feet tall, you have to deal with that fact every second of every day of your life. And everyone witnesses your effort. You go into a bar and you can't get up onto a stool. You whistle down a taxi and you can't open the door. If you're a lady with a beard, every face you meet is a mirror to give you back the disgust and horror and unreasonableness of your predicament. No matter which corner you turn on which street in which city of the world, you can expect to meet that mirror.

And I suppose I have never been able to forgive myself the

grotesqueries and aberrations I am able to hide with such impunity in my own life.

Inside the tent, the Fat Lady was already up on her platform, ready for the day's business. She had a pasteboard box under her chair. The box was filled with cinnamon buns that her manager bought for her. She could get through about ten pounds of cinnamon buns a day. Her manager said he'd owned her—that was his phrase, owned her—for three years and in that time he had never seen her eat any meat. She stuck, he said, pretty much to pastries.

"How is it today, Bertha?"

She nodded to me, put the last of a cinnamon bun into her mouth and reached for another one. Her little eyes deep in her face were very bright and quick as a bird's.

"You see Charlie Luck?" I said. I wasn't really looking for him. I just wanted to talk a little to Bertha.

"He was here with one-eyed Petey," she said. "You want one of these?"

"Thanks, but I just had a corn dog."

"Luck's probably back in the G-top, cutting up jackpots."

"Probably," I said.

Cutting up jackpots is what carnies call it when they get together and tell one another about their experiences, mostly lies. The Tattooed Man came in with the Midget and the Midget's mother. The Midget's mother was nearly as tall as I was and very thin. She always looked inexpressibly sad. During the show, she wandered among the marks, selling postcards with a picture of her tiny son on them for a quarter apiece. The Tattooed Man had intricate designs in his ears. Little flowers grew on his nose and disappeared right up his nostrils. He was a miracle of color.

"I surely do admire your illustrations," I said.

"How come I got'm," he said. He was from Mississippi and had a good Grit voice.

"How many dollars' worth you reckon you got?"

"Wouldn't start to know. For years all I'd do was put every nickel I could lay hand to for pictures."

He had eyelashes and an eyelid tattooed around his asshole. It looked just like a kind of bloodshot eye and he could make it wink. For \$2 over and above the regular price of admission to the ten-in-one show, you could go behind a little curtain and he'd do it for you. Carnies have nothing but a deep, abiding contempt for marks and what they think of as the straight world, and nowhere is that contempt more vividly expressed than in the Tattooed Man's response when I asked him why he had the eye put in there.

"Making them bastards pay two dollars to look up my asshole gives me more real pleasure than anything else I've ever done."

Charlie Luck came in looking for me and handed me \$5. "I sent the jack into town. That's your half."

"Charlie, that was a fifty-dollar jack."

"The guy took it said he got ten."

"And you believed him?"

He took another five out of his pocket and handed it to me. "What the hell, take it all. He was probably lying, and besides, it was your van. You oughtta have it all."

Charlie dearly loved a hustle, any hustle, on anybody. "Come on out here; I want to see you a minute."

As we were leaving, Bertha called around a mouthful of cinnamon bun, "That's a wonderful siren; I liked it a lot."

"Thank you, Bertha," I said. "That's sweet of you to say."

Out on the midway, Charlie Luck said, "You thought any more about what I asked you?"

"Charlie," I said, "I told you already."

"Look what I'm doing for you and you can't even do this little thing for me."

"It's not a little thing. I'm liable to get my head handed to me."

"You not working the show, you just traveling with me. You don't know anybody on this show. It'll be all right. Nobody's going to mind."

"You don't know that."

"I'm telling you I do know that. It'll be all right. You're leaving tomorrow, anyway. And I gotta know. I gotta have a firsthand, detailed report."

"Report, for Christ's sake!"

"I gotta know."

Charlie Luck's problem was this. He was nailing this lady named Rose who worked in the girlie show. Like the Tattooed

Man, Rose had a specialty act that the marks could see by paying extra. Rose also had a husband. A large, mean, greasy husband who worked on the Ferris wheel. Charlie Luck wanted to know what she did in her specialty act. She wouldn't tell him. He couldn't go see for himself, because one of the strongest taboos in the carnival world is against carnies going to the girlie show. Most of the girls have carnies for husbands, and the feeling is that it is all right to show your wife to the marks but fundamentally wrong to show her to another carny, one of your own world.

"Hey, come in here and let me get my fortune told," I said.

We were passing a gypsy fortune-teller, and I was reminded of the gypsies and their wagons passing through Georgia when I was a boy. But mostly I was just trying to get Charlie Luck to stop thinking about Rose and her specialty act.

"You let that raghead touch your hand and you never come on to my game again."

"I just wanted my fortune—"

"Ragheads can't tell time, much less fortunes."

Carnies are not the most liberal people in the world. A few blacks are tolerated as laborers, and maybe an occasional gypsy to run a mitt camp, or fortune-telling booth, but not too long ago, it wasn't unusual to see advertisements in *Amusement Business,* the weekly newspaper devoted in part to carnivals, that said plainly: "NO RAGHEADS."

"Look," said Charlie Luck. "You think you seen my proposition. But you haven't seen me take any real money off anybody. Go bring this thing back for me and I'll run the game tonight. I'll run it strong."

"You don't have to run it strong," I said.

"I will, though, if you'll do this thing."

Charlie got bent bad over women. I found out later that the cowboy was on him in the bar in Yeehaw Junction over a woman, although I never found out precisely what it was about. But Charlie was, to use the kindest word, kinky when it came to ladies. Everybody I talked to said the same thing about him. I don't know why this was true, or how long it had been true of him, and I didn't try to find out. It wasn't any of my business, unless he wanted to tell me, and he didn't seem to. The girlie show had only joined us at the date preceding the circus jump. I was with Charlie Luck the first time he saw Rose in the G-top. He had known her now a total of four days, but he reminded me of the way I'd been when I fell totally and deeply in love the first time, at the age of thirteen. He'd honed for Rose from the first second he saw her and had managed to nail her two hours later in my van. He'd asked me for the van because he was afraid to take her to his trailer.

She came out of the van first and left. Then he came out—face radiant under this soft brown cap—and kept saying to me, "Did you see her? Did you?"

"I saw her, Charlie."

"Was she beautiful? God, I practically almost never seen anything like her in the world."

"Right," I said.

She looked about forty-eight years old, thick in thigh and hip, but had slender, almost skinny calves. The left calf was badly varicosed. Her face was a buttery mask of makeup. I couldn't figure what the hell she had done in there to him to string him out so bad. When I finally got into the van to drive to town, it smelled as though most of the salmon of the world had been slowly tortured to death all over my red-and-black carpeting.

"All right," I said finally, as we walked down the midway. "I'll catch Rose's bit for you, if you want me to. But I want you to remember one thing. Afterward I don't want any conversation about it. You know, they used to cut off the heads of the guys who brought bad news to the king."

"Now, what the hell's that supposed to mean?"

"Nothing," I said. "It means nothing."

"I'll catch you after the eight o'clock show," he said. "I gotta go settle a beef about a fifty-cent piece of slum. The shit I put up with."

Slum is what carnies call the cheap merchandise they give out in the little booths that line the midway. For that reason, hanky-panks and alibis are also called slum joints. Hanky-panks are simple games of skill such as throwing darts at balloons. Alibis are games in which the agent is continually making alibis about why you did not win. Also, alibis—unlike hanky-panks—are liable to be gaffed, or rigged, and they are also liable to have a stick who is said to work the gaff. A stick is a guy who pretends to be a mark and by his presence induces the townspeople to play.

I strolled down the midway and watched it all come down. A stick who was working the gaff at a game called six cat was winning tons of slum. Six cat is an alibi in which the object is to knock down two cats at once with a ball. The stick quit playing as soon as he had attracted half a dozen marks. The agent was singing his song, alibiing his ass off: "He, woweee! Look at that! That was just a little too high! A hair! No more'n a hair an you woulda won! Too much left. Bring it down, bring it down, and win it for the lady."

I watched the mark finally get thrown a piece of plush, in this case a small, slightly soiled cloth giraffe. The poor bastard had paid only $12 for something he could have bought for two and a quarter out in the city. The six cat was gaffed and the agent had done what's called cooling the mark by rewarding him with a prize after he had taken as much money as he thought he could get away with.

Eighty-five million people or thereabouts go to carnivals every year in this country, and I do not want to leave the impression that all of them are cheated. Most of them are not. But the particular carnival Charlie Luck was running with is called a rag bag, and it means that everything is pretty run-down, greasy, and suspect. The man who books the dates and organizes the lot in such an operation will allow anything to come down he thinks the locals will stand for. Few people realize that one person or family almost never owns a carnival. One person will put together a tour —a combination of dates in specific locations—and then invite independent concessionaries to join him. If you look in the publication I mentioned earlier, *Amusement Business,* a sweet little paper you can subscribe to for $20 a year, you will find such notices as these: "Now booking Bear Pitches, Traveling Duck, can also use Gorilla Show." "Will book two nice Grind Shows. Must be flashy."

The independent concessionaries pay what is known as privilege to work these dates. The privilege is paid to the man responsible for lining up the dates, organizing and dispensing necessary graft, and arranging for a patch. It is interesting to notice that the farther south a show goes, the rougher it becomes. There may not be a single girlie show or flat in Pennsylvania, but flatties and girlies both may be playing wide open and woolly in Georgia. Whether it is true or not, it is the consensus among carnies that you can get away with a hell of a lot more in the South than you can in the North.

Carnies can conveniently be divided into front-end people and back-end people. Front-enders are carnies who work games, food, and other concessions. The back-enders are concerned with shows: freak shows, gorilla shows, walking-zombie shows, and—where I was going now—girlie shows.

The guy out front was making his call, but it wasn't a very good call. His voice was more than tired, it was dead. He rarely looked at the marks who were crowding in front of the raised platform now, and once he stopped in mid-sentence and picked his nose.

"Come on in, folks. See it all for fifty cents, one half a dollar."

Four middle-aged ladies in spangled briefs and tasseled halters —all of it a little dirty—were working to a fifties phonograph record about young love. The ladies were very active, jumping about in a sprightly fashion, their eyes glittering from Bipheta-mine 20's, the speeder far and away the favorite with carnies. From Thursday to Tuesday whole carny families—men, women, and children—ate them like jelly beans. Rose looked right at me but either didn't see me or didn't give a damn, for which I was grateful. I didn't want her paying any attention to me, because I kept thinking of her huge greasy husband out on the Ferris wheel right now splicing cable with his broken teeth.

I paid my half dollar, went inside feeling like a fool, and saw the same ladies doing pretty much what they had been doing out front and doing it, if you can believe it, to the same goddamn phonograph record. But before they began, the semicomatose caller pointed out that there would be a second show right after this one to which no one who was female or under eighteen would be admitted. Those who were admitted would have to pay $3 a head. That threw several good ole boys into a fit of leg slapping and howling and hot-damning. They were randy and ready and seemed to know something I did not know. Rose even permitted herself a small smile and a couple of winks to the boys who apparently knew who she was, had maybe seen her show before, and were digging hell out of the whole thing.

After the first show was over and they had made us lighter by $3, things happened quickly. Peeling the eggs took the longest. But first they added a drummer to the act. Really, a drummer. The ladies had retired behind a rat-colored curtain, and out onto the little platform came an old man dressed in an ancient blue suit with a blue cap that at first I thought belonged to the Salvation Army. And it may have. Ligaments stood in his scrawny neck like wire. He sat on a chair and put his bass drum between his legs. The caller started the record we had already heard twice, which, incidentally, was by Frankie Valli, and the old man started pounding on his drum. His false teeth bulged in his old mouth every time he struck it. Never once during the performance did he look up. I know he did not see Rose. I was fascinated that he would not look at her when she came out onto the stage. She was naked except for a halter. I swear. She had her tits clinched up, but there was her old naked beaver and strong, over-the-hill ass. She was carrying six eggs in a little bowl. She carried it just the way a whore would have carried a bowl, except she had eggs in it instead of soap and water. She squatted in front of us—taking us all the way to pink—while she peeled the eggs. When they were peeled, she placed them one by one in her mouth, slobbered on them good, and returned them to the dish. Then, still squatting, with Frankie Valli squealing for all he was worth and the old man single-mindedly beating his drum and several of the good ole boys hugging each other, she popped all of the eggs into her pussy and started dancing. She did six high kicks in her dance and each time she kicked, she fired an egg with considerable velocity out into the audience. On a bet with his buddies, a young apprentice madman caught and ate the last two.

I left the tent disappointed, though. I'd seen the act before. Once, many years ago, I knew a lady in New Orleans who could do a dozen. Not a dozen of your grade A extra-large, to be sure. They were smalls, but a dozen nonetheless.

I found Charlie Luck down in the G-top. A G-top is a tent set up at the back of the lot exclusively for carnival people to socialize with one another. Marks are not allowed there, and the carnies' socializing usually comes in the form of gambling games of one kind or another. It is not unusual for a carny to walk into the G-top at the end of the May-to-October season with $20,000 in his pocket and walk out the next morning wondering how he's going to get a dime to call his old mother for a ticket home on the Trailways. Some very heavy cheese changes hands in that tent, and I was amazed that the other carnies would sit down to a table with Charlie Luck. He had exceedingly quick hands, and more than once he showed me his short-change proposition. You could open your hand flat and he would count out ninety cents into it. You could watch him do it, but when he finished and you counted your change, you'd be a quarter short. He would press a nickel into your palm and at the same instant take out a quarter he'd just put down. He could count nine $1 bills or a five and four ones into your hand and inevitably he would take back over half of it. It's called, among other things, laying the note, and it's a scam usually run off in a department store or a supermarket.

"Down where I come from," I'd said to him once, "we don't sit down to seven card with folks who have fingers like you do."

He looked me dead in the eye and said, "These guys know I would never cheat them in the G-top. When we do a little craps or cards back there, they know that's my leisure, my pleasure. Cheating is business. The only place, and I mean the *only* place, I ever steal is when I'm working the joint right out there on the midway. I'd be ashamed of myself to do it anywhere else."

Charlie Luck saw me from across the G-top and immediately got up from the table and came to meet me. We walked back out onto the midway. It was dark now, and the lot, laid out in a U shape, was jammed with men and women and their children, laughing and eating, their arms loaded with slum. Screaming shouts of pleasure and terror floated down out of the night from the high rides, glittering and spinning there above us.

"Did you see it?" he finally said after we'd walked for a while. "Did you see her do it?"

"Yeah, I saw her do it."

"The specialty act, too?"

"I told you I'd go."

"Then lay it out for me."

I laid it out.

"Eggs? Hard-boiled fucking eggs?"

"Right."

"And she'd kick and fire?" He took out two capsules. "You want one of these?"

"You know I'm a natural wire," I said. "What I need is a drink to calm me down. Let's go by the van before we go to the game."

He swallowed both capsules and made a face, but the face was not from the dope. "Goddamn eggs and goddamn drummer. I'd need a drink, too. I may even have one."

By the time we got to the van he'd worked himself into a pretty good state over Rose and her specialty act.

"I don't put my dick where hard-boiled eggs've been," he kept saying. "Jesus, a pervert. I'm tainted."

"You ain't tainted, man," I said. "You just like you were before. I wish to God somebody could guarantee me my dick wouldn't go nowhere worse than a few boiled eggs. Besides, I don't know what you expected, taking her out of a girlie show."

"How was I to know? I never been in a girlie show once, not once," he said. "Over half my life I'm with a carnival. Never once did I go near a girlie show."

"Didn't you talk to her?" I said. "You should have asked if she ever put anything up in there."

Charlie Luck jerked his cap lower on his ears and stared straight ahead. "You don't ask a lady a thing like that," he said.

He poured a little straight vodka on top of the speed, and we walked over to his proposition. The flat was near a punk ride between a glass pitch and a grab joint. The grab joint sold dogs and burgers and a fruit punch called flukum. Charlie Luck let the kid off for the rest of the night, and we got behind the counter. Charlie banged things around, positioning his marbles and his board and muttering to himself. He finally quit and stared balefully out at the passing crowd. He made no attempt to draw anybody in. Nobody so much as looked at us.

"You taking it in tomorrow?" he asked.

"I told you," I said. "I got to get back. There's only so much of this that'll do me any good, anyway."

"Maybe I'll go in, too," he said. "There's not but a little more than a week left on the season."

"I've enjoyed it," I said. "We'll cross again. Maybe we can sit down and have a beer with the cowboys."

He smiled. "Maybe." He sighed deeply. Then: "You don't gamble with cripples or ladies or children. I keep them out of my proposition. You beat one of them and you got heat, bad heat. Gamble with a fat guy who looks like he can afford it. The thing you like is if he's dressed up real good, too."

"One thing, Charlie," I said. "I been meaning to say this to you, but I didn't yet. Maybe I shouldn't now. But you don't gamble. You're not a gambler. No offense, Charlie, but you're a thief is what you are."

"Actually," he said, "I'm a gambler who doesn't lose. That's what I like to think I am. I just took the risk out of it."

"No risk, no gamble. No gamble, no gambler. You're a thief."

"Well, sort of. The word doesn't bother me. I only do what they let me do."

The thing you have to know right off is you can't win from a carny gambler unless he wants you to. And he doesn't want you to. Of course, like any other hustler, he may give you a *little* something so he can take away a *lot* of something. But that's a long way from winning.

The carny's success in flat joints depends upon having a good call and expert knowledge of just how far he can push a mark and the certainty that there is larceny in all of us. A good call simply means someone is passing on the midway and you are able to "call" him to you and get him involved with your hustle. A call itself is a hustle. The agent plays the mark off against the clothes he's wearing, or the woman he's with, or his youth, or his old age —in fact, anything that will make him rise to the challenge, which doesn't appear to be much of a challenge to start with. Many times an agent will walk out onto the midway, calling as he goes, and literally grab a mark, take hold of him, and lead him over to the proposition. I've known agents who could consistently operate like that and get away with it. Others can't. The moment I touch a guy, he swings on me. He thinks he's being attacked.

Beside me in the store, Charlie Luck had dropped another

Biphetamine 20. His eyes were wet as quicksilver, and he was mumbling constantly about Rose. Finally, he said to me, "Lay it out for me again. How it was, what she did, the crowd. Six, you said, half a dozen, and none of'm mashed she fired'm out at the marks?"

I laid it out for him again, just as straightforward and with as much detail as I could, even to the smells in the tent, saving nothing.

When I finished, he seemed to think about it for a moment. "All right," he said.

"Don't you think we ought to try to take a little money now, Charlie?"

"OK. Yeah." He turned to watch a middle-aged couple approaching down the midway. He looked back at me. "One thing. Don't call me Charlie Luck anymore."

"What should I call you?"

"Tuna," he said.

"Tuna?"

"Like in fish. Tommy Tuna. A name I always liked. Brings me good things."

"I got it," I said. "OK."

"You got to be careful with names," he said. "Names can be bad for you. Or names can be good for you. You know?"

I didn't know, so I didn't say anything.

"A name can get dirty. Start to rot. Bring you nothing but trouble." He sucked his teeth and sighed. The middle-aged couple had stopped and were looking at us. The lady carried two little pieces of slum, a ceramic duck and a small cloth snake. "I don't think I'll be Charlie Luck anymore."

"You mean for a little while."

"I mean ever."

I loved him for that. He just willed himself to be someone else, submerged as Charlie Luck and came up Tommy Tuna. I know how easily I did the same thing. My fix is other people's lives. It always has been. As I stood there watching the well-dressed couple, secure in their middle age and permanent in their home, a fantasy started in me, a living thing. I felt my teeth go rotten and broken, my arms fill with badly done, homemade tattoos. I was from some remote place like Alpine, Texas, and I'd joined the carnival when I was fourteen and ever since been rootless, no home except the back of a semi carrying a disassembled Octopus, and I lived off people—marks—those two there smiling at me. I suddenly smiled back. They had no way of knowing my secret and utter contempt.

"Tuna," I said quietly, "let me take this."

"Take what?"

"These two here. Let me do it."

"Do it."

"All right, here we go," I called. "Hey! Lookahere! *Your* game. Yeah! You. Come here. Come *here.* In here and let me show you the little game. I can tell by the look on your face, big fella. This is your game! A quarter. Nothing but twenty-five cents. Win the little lady this right here. Big panda. Come here! Come on!"

They smile uncertainly at each other. The lady blushes. The guy looks away.

"Hey, you just married? I can see it. I can see how in love you are, how you want this right here for the little lady, right? *Come over here."*

They've turned now and they're mine. I had thought they might walk on, and in spite of the fact that I've never been a caller who could actually grab anybody, I was ready to vault the counter and take the guy by the arm. The rule is that the mark gets deeper into your hustle with every move he makes toward you. He looks at you. He moves a little nearer. He lets you explain your game. He bets. If you can get him to do that much and don't take everything he's got, or as much of it as you want, you ought to find another business.

"See that bear? See that bear right here? You want it for the lady?" Tommy Tuna keeps his bear nice. An enormous panda under clear cellophane. The bear must be worth $20. "Look, she wants it! Look at her face! A quarter, it's yours for a quarter! OK? Can I show the game to you?"

The lady is blushing and squeezing the guy's arm and pressing into him. And he's already got his quarter out.

"Look, I got marbles and I got a board." I whip the board out and show it to him. The board has little indentations on it. On the bottom of each indentation is a number: a one or a two or a three on up through nine. There's a little chute that leads down to the board. "You need a hundred points to win this game. Right? One hundred points to win that bear. Cost you a quarter. You roll the marbles down the chute, we add up the total. Each total gives a number toward the hundred points you need. Right?"

He's still got his quarter in his hand. Both of them are leaning over the board. He wants to give me the quarter so bad it's hurting him and he's not even heard the game. He just knows he's risking only twenty-five cents.

"Right? Each total gives a number toward the hundred points you need." I look him in the eye and smile. I take him by the wrist and pull him a little closer. "Here's the kicker. You keep rolling till you get the hundred points you need to win. *Without paying another penny.*" I pause again. He's smiling. She's smiling. I'm smiling. Tommy Tuna's smiling. "Unless . . . unless the total you roll is thirty. If you roll a thirty, the cost of the game doubles, but you *keep* the points you've earned toward the hundred and roll again."

The lady says, "Do it, honey. Oh, do it."

And here is where much of the carnies' contempt for the mark starts. The guy walks up to *my* game. He doesn't know the game, has never seen it. He sure as hell doesn't know me. He doesn't see or doesn't care that on the board there are not an equal number of ones, twos, threes, and so on. If he cared to check the board or think about it, he'd see the odds are overwhelming that he'll roll the losing number nearly every time. And each time you roll a 30, though you keep the points you already have, you don't get to count the 30.

He rolls the marbles. As soon as they stop in the slots, I'm taking them out again as fast as I can, palm partially obscuring the board, adding aloud in a stunned, unbelieving voice, "Two and nine, eleven, and six is seventeen and, wow, oh golly! Nine and nine and nine . . . twenty-seven to the seventeen and . . . that's forty-four *big* points, almost half of what you need to win that bear for the little lady. This must be your lucky night!"

He had, of course, rolled a 30. He takes the marbles again, and

I quick-count him to 52. "Hey, this bear's gone tonight. It looks like your night." He's flushed. You'd think he had $5000 on the line. He whips down the marbles, and guess what? He rolled that 30. But he's got fifty cents out almost before I can count the losing number for him. We go again and I take him up to 65. He rolls and loses. The bet's $1. Before he knows what's happened, he's looking at an $8 bet and he needs only 22 points to win.

I was just about to give him the marbles and made the mistake of looking at the lady. You'd have thought the guy was losing the mortgage on the house. She was nearly in tears. I hand him the marbles. He rolls a 30, but I count him into 105. Pandemonium squeals. Hurrahs. Down comes the bear and off they go. Tommy Tuna took me by the arm and led me to the back of the booth.

"You sonofabitch," he said.

"Yeah, I guess. But don't come down on me too hard. I'll pay you for the bear."

"Not the point. You had the gaff so deep into that fucker, you coulda made him bet his wife."

"It was the lady. Hadn't been for the lady, I could've done it."

"It's all right. You done good, anyway." He smiled toward the front of the booth, where four marks—all men, well fed, well dressed and apparently at the carnival together—were yelling to come on and play the game. They had been drawn to the booth by my loud counting, and they'd stayed to see the man easily win the bear.

Tommy Tuna went over to the four marks. He shrugged, looked sadly at his board. "Maybe I'm crazy," he said, "but I feel like a little action." He leaned closer to the marks. "Fuck the bears. Let's bet some money." He went into his pocket and came out with the biggest roll of bills I've ever seen. He showed the roll to the marks. I saw nothing but hundreds. "I'll play you no limit. Just like with the fucking bear, it takes a hundred points to win. The first bet'll cost you a buck. The bets double after that. I'll pay ten to one. Did you get that? Ten to one I'm paying. If you're betting a hundred dollars when you reach the hundred points to win, I'll pay you a thousand."

He said it quickly, in a flat, unemotional voice. They were into it immediately, and Tuna quick-counted them to 37 points.

There seemed to be no way to lose. All four guys were pooling their money with the intention of splitting the take. But by the time they had accumulated 82 points, they'd lost $255. The next bet was gonna cost them $256. The whole thing had taken about five minutes, but Tuna pointed out they needed only 18 more points to win, and after all, he *was* giving ten-to-one odds.

"Sumpin might goddamn funny goin on here," said the biggest and meanest-looking of the four.

"Gee," said Tommy Tuna in a quiet, sad voice. "You fellas do seem to be having a real bad run of luck. I can hardly believe it myself."

They withdrew a few steps to consult and then came back and went for the bet. They rolled a 30. Tommy Tuna scooped up the money. All four of them howled simultaneously as if they'd been stung by wasps. They'd been cleaned out. The big, mean one moved to come over the counter when, as if by magic, Officer Jackson appeared on the midway, only a few feet away.

He came over and said, "You want to tell me why you hollering like this?"

The big one said, "This bastard's running a crooked game, that's why."

"You want to tell me what kind of game?"

He told Officer Jackson what kind of game. He also told him they'd been taken for over $500 in less than ten minutes.

"Gambling?" Officer Jackson could hardly believe it. "That's against the law. It's against the law for everbody here. If it's true, I'll have to lock you up. *All* of you." Then he turned to the four guys and actually said: "And if I do, and if it's true, he's got your money to bail hisself out with." He paused and looked at each of the four in turn. "You want to tell me what you want to do?"

After the four guys had left, Officer Jackson and Tommy Tuna went over to the corner and had a short, earnest conversation, which I did not hear. Then Officer Jackson left.

Tommy watched the cop disappear down the midway and said in a wondering voice, "You know, I once took twelve thousand dollars off a oilman in Oklahoma. He never said a word about it. A real fine sport."

I said, "Some days chicken salad. Some days chickenshit."

Running Fox

"I known from the start I didn't have no show, but I sure woulda liked to feed in her lilies," Buck said.

It was almost midnight, and we were sitting on my porch on the edge of Lake Swan. We'd been sitting there for a long time with a little whiskey, watching the light from a full moon running across half a mile of water, running in a line arrow straight in the windless night right up to where we sat rocking in wicker chairs, the whiskey on the floor between us.

"Well," I said, "well, what the hell."

I'd already made all the other responses I could think of, and none of them had helped. It didn't look as if anything was going to help.

Buck said: "Moon like that makes a man just naturally git to wanting to feed in somebody's lilies. But I didn't have no show." He took a pull at his whiskey. "Didn't matter, though. I sure woulda liked to feed in her lilies."

In one form or another, I'd heard Buck say that dozens of times over the last twenty-four hours, the notion had settled in him solid as bone, and it had made him a little nuts. But that didn't mean I could just abandon him, either. He'd been my friend almost longer than I could remember. Besides, I'd been around that block myself. A man honing for a woman he didn't get and is never going to get has resulted in various maimings, murders, and suicides, even the collapse of governments.

The night before, I had driven halfway across the state to Stucky's Saloon just off Memorial Boulevard in Lakeland,

Florida, to hear the greatest banjo picker in the world, Paul Champion, work out with Jim Ballew on guitar, backed up by Ed Bradford on bass. I'd drive anywhere to hear Paul Champion pick, but besides that, Stucky's Saloon is my kind of place, a roadhouse out on the edge of town with a parking lot full of pickup trucks where you can buy a lot of trouble real cheap. Consequently, there is seldom any real trouble, just a lot of foot stomping and beer drinking and good ole boys telling each other Friday-night lies, their elbows propped on damp tables, their sweating faces half hidden in smoke so thick you could cut it up and make work shirts out of it.

When I came in, I saw Buck sitting in a far corner with a lady. He was leaning across the table, but she was tilted back in her chair, looking not at him but at the ceiling. I sat down and for two hours listened to Champion picking "Earl's Breakdown" and other down-home things that broke my heart, playing rough, playing smooth, playing bitter and sweet, sometimes all in the same moment.

The last call had come for drinks when Buck sat down at my table. He was nearly two ax handles broad at the shoulder, with a belly that had cost him several thousand dollars' worth of beer. That was when he told me of his dying hunger for lilies and that the lady who owned them had just left. He didn't have to tell me anything. I knew it all by the time he settled in his chair and I got a good look at his face. Lilies were growing all over it. You don't know a guy as long as I've known Buck without being able to see things like that. Some men's madness is alcohol or dope or gambling; Buck's is lilies. And when the madness is on him, it is not a very pretty thing to see, could in fact be scary in its violence. It had to run its course, sometimes an hour or two, at times a lot longer. We sat there at the table, and I said all the meaningless things you say to a friend who is hurt and you don't know how to help, for whom there is no help except to do what you can while he rides it to the end, wears it out.

"I don't want to go home," he finally said.

"Then don't."

"It's noplace to go."

"Why don't you drive up to Swan with me?"

He'd been up there before; he knew how far it was. "Could I do that?"

"You ask any more questions like that, I'll get four or five other guys and beat the shit out of you."

"How'd I get back?"

"I'd make you walk," I said.

He put as much of a smile on his face as was possible for him at the time. "It'd be a long walk."

"Try to quit acting like trash," I said. "How did you think? I'll bring you back."

"All the way back down here?"

"Got nothing better to do." Which was the truth. "I'm between things. I'm bored. But the mood you're in'll more than likely probably bore me even more."

He got a real smile then. "Try me."

We left Stucky's Saloon at two o'clock and didn't get to Putnam Hall until eleven, a drive that would ordinarily have taken less than three hours. But Buck knows every place in Florida where you can get what he calls "an after-dinner drink," by which he means a drink after all the bars have legally closed. What you're apt to run into in places like that, though, is a whole gang of Bucks. Guys already drunk and carrying something mean and dangerous on their backs.

The only real trouble we had was in a little place about halfway home. I was standing at the bar feeling good about taking care, or trying to, of somebody I loved, and feeling lousy about love making such things necessary, when a chair broke against a wall and Buck had some poor unfortunate jacked up, slapping him in an offhand, almost good-natured way. But since Buck stands six feet four inches, offhand and good-natured can be pretty brutal. I got over to where they were as best I could and pulled Buck away from the guy. The boy, who was good-sized himself, didn't even look back; he made for the door. Buck threw me over a table as if I'd been a puppy and staggered after the boy.

When we got outside, the boy was sitting in a sports car of some kind grinding away at the starter, but the engine wouldn't take hold and Buck was coming down fast. When he saw he wasn't going to make it, the guy jumped out of the sports car and ran off into the night, leaving Buck howling for him to come back. He went around and slammed at the aerial, one of those long, steel whiplash kind of things that people use on CB radios. I think it surprised Buck as much as it did me when it came off in his hand. He held the aerial, whipping it around over his head, still screaming.

Then he suddenly quieted and looked at the long aerial. "You come on back here, sumbitch!" he shouted. "You don't, I'm gone whip your car."

"Buck," I said, "Buck, wait. . . ."

"I'm gone whip you or your car one," he howled.

And without even pausing, he spun and brought the aerial down across the windshield. While I watched, he gave the little car a severe beating. Everywhere he hit it, the hood, the doors, over the top, it left the long scarred imprint of the aerial. He had worked himself into a rage, but by the time he had satisfaction his shirt was sweated through, his flushed face had calmed, and he was breathing easier. I couldn't bear to look at the car.

"Don't you reckon," I said, "we better git the hell out of here?"

"I reckon," he said.

Back in my van, he cracked a Budweiser tallboy. "I feel a little better somehow," he said. Then he gave a long sigh. "But I sure woulda loved to feed in them lilies."

We stopped in Putnam Hall, a little place with two stores, one of them Lonnie's Tavern, where I always shoot pool. We stopped and ran a few racks of eight ball. Buck was calm now, but it was a calm with an edge on it. He was still depressed and spent most of the time grinding his teeth occasionally during a long monologue full of lilies and hunger. Then we drove the five miles on to my place. We had some food and spent the rest of the day in a one-sided conversation about why a man had to make such a fool out of himself over women.

But he still wasn't to the end of it, and I sat there in the rocking chair watching the moon shift the path of light over the water, trying to think of what I could do to help him find the relief he needed.

Finally, I said: "Let's go git Pete and run the dogs."

"I'd like to run them dogs," he said. "But we cain't do that."

Buck was thinking of Pete's wife, a kind and gracious lady who didn't take kindly to having her husband dragged out at two o'clock in the morning.

I said: "I'll take care of it."

"If you think you can," he said.

"I think I can."

What I meant was that I thought I'd better, because Buck was getting lower and lower, and I knew we'd end up somewhere else. And this time it might not be a car that got hurt. It could very easily be me, and if it's one thing I hate, it's getting hurt. Besides, as much as I loved Buck, I was exhausted by the whole thing. Love or no love, there are few things more boring than another man's grief.

Actually, I handled it easily enough by parking in front of the house and blowing my horn until Pete leaned out of the door, spitting and cursing. When he saw the van, he came out to us wearing only his drawers. I could hear his wife in the house where lights were coming on. I hoped I hadn't woke up the children, but these were desperate times.

"Want to go run a fox," I said.

He leaned in my window, squinting. "That you in there, Buck?"

"It's me all right, boy, but don't tell your wife it was me come with this crazy sumbitch."

"Tell 'er I'll make it up to her," I said. "Tell her anything, but git the damn dogs and let's go git in the woods."

Pete hustled his balls, spit twice, looked up at the full moon still blazing out of the sky, and said: "I wouldn't mind running them dogs a little tonight."

I had known that all along. Pete'd rather listen to hounds cut a scent in the woods under a full moon than drink when he was thirsty, and he was thirsty most of the time.

We left my van at his house and got into Pete's pickup, five hounds caged behind us, yelping and baying, already knowing they were about to be worked. On the drive up toward Quincy, Pete cracked a bottle of Jim Beam and we told him about being in Lakeland to hear Champion and Ballew pick, and about the sports car, and then we all told each other several interesting lies before we finally stopped in a little clearing deep in the woods.

"We gone have a good run here," Pete said. "It's an old fox uses this head of woods I musta run fifty times. He's smarter'n all of us put together."

It occurred to me that that wouldn't necessarily make him very smart. But I didn't say anything, and we got out and built a fire. Pete took a pot out of the back of the truck, where the dogs were going crazy now, and we made some sawmill coffee. Poured some water out of a gallon milk jug into the pot, which was smoked and solid black, and dumped in nearly a half cup of Maxwell House. It was already boiling before Pete let the dogs out. We pulled a log up by the fire, and when the rank coffee was ready, we cut it a tad with a fine dollop of Jim Beam. Then we sat on the ground, leaning against the log, and listened to the dogs.

"I bet you ten bucks that bitch dog of mine, Ponder, will cut his track first."

Both of us had been with him and his dogs before, and neither of us answered. We sat listening to the echoing sound of the dogs —half bark, half yelp—a sound filled with anxiety and longing as they crossed and recrossed the woods, searching for the scent they'd come to find. Then out of the random yelping and barking came a high, lilting howl that can only be compared to a bugle.

"That's Ponder and she's cut fox," said Pete.

"She's got the best mouth I ever heard on a hound."

"Been a woman, I'da married her," Pete said.

"She's the only one got the scent," I said. "Them other dogs are just trailing her."

"Them othern of mine ain't got much nose," said Pete. "Never have had much nose, them other dogs."

But they finally got the scent, too, and the woods came alive with a bugling that no man who has ever heard it will ever forget. It wasn't long until daylight, and we spent the time listening to the fox do what he did best, confound hounds. Once he actually got *behind* the dogs, but Ponder didn't take long to find out she'd been made a fool of and the pack soon turned and was dead on the scent again.

Occasionally a fox is brought to bay in a half-blown-over tree, but the object of this kind of hunt is not to kill the fox. The object is to listen to the music of the dogs and argue endlessly over the quality of their noses, over which dog is leading and which trailing, over which one is confused and which one running with plumb-line certainty. As the light came up, I could sense that Buck had ridden it to the end, had worn his hunger out, and that there would be no more talk of lilies.

Once it got broad daylight, we saw a tent set up not far away. Or rather we didn't see it until a boy and a girl got out of it and came toward us. It was not unusual to see backpackers in these woods, and I guessed they were students from the University of Florida, but I never asked, didn't want to know. They came over to where we were sitting around the coals of the fire. They told us they'd heard the dogs last night and that these were great woods to hike in. I guess we seemed impolite, but stunned from a night of sipping Jim Beam, none of us answered. The boy, who said his name was George, said they hadn't been rained on once, but it wouldn't bother him if it flooded.

The girl, who I was appalled to find was named Georgette, said: "That's why we're out here in the woods, so nothing will bother him."

The boy rambled on some more without any prompting from us about camping, and just from his manner I knew immediately, or thought I knew, that her name had not always been Georgette and that it had been his idea to change it.

"See," said Georgette, "he's very nervous."

"We're all nervous," I said, not wanting to hear about it.

"I fall into a fit of anger over practically nothing," said George.

"I got a uncle has fits," Pete said through a Jim Beam smile.

"I don't have *fits,*" said George, the color rising in his face. "I can't control my temper. About anything."

"Frankly," said Georgette, "he just goes nuts."

"Goddamm it, Georgette," said George. his face going redder, his thin eyebrows bunching.

"Easy, feller," Buck said.

The boy took several deep breaths and said: "I brought James Fenimore Cooper out here with me. I read in the evenings. Relax, don't lose my temper. Don't let *anything* bother me."

Pete held up a curved cow horn. "We got to go call up them dogs."

"Well," said George, "nice talking to you. Have a nice day."

We'd put dirt over the fire and were about to get into the truck when we heard George scream that he couldn't get the goddamn bow saw to work. The hysteria in his voice made us turn and watch where they were apparently trying to make a fire in front of their tent.

We watched while George kicked an aluminum pot into the air, knocked down their tent, and jumped up and down on it. Georgette stood with her hands caught against her breast as he wrecked their camp. Finally, he snatched up what I could only assume was his James Fenimore Cooper book and began to tear pages out of it and throw them over his head.

That was when Georgette could stand it no longer. The moment she touched his arm, he dropped the book, set his feet, and caught her on the point of the chin with a wicked right hook. She dropped like she'd been shot. The entire thing had been played out with the ritual of Japanese theater, and I knew it was not the first time he had coldcocked old Georgette.

"Think we ought to go over there and see if we can help her?" I said.

"I wouldn't git into that on a bet," Buck said.

"I don't know what you guys gone do, but I got dogs to call. Don't, Ponder'll be run clean in the next county."

In the pickup, driving away from the clearing, Buck smiled his old good smile and said: "Damned if I don't feel like somebody just told me I didn't have cancer."

Leaving Pasadena—Resume Safe Speed

When I picked up the phone and said hello, he didn't say terrific, so I knew it was not another PR man returning one of my calls. He just said hello and told me he was the one who'd been trying to find me to buy a movie option on one of my novels. I recalled his letter catching up with me just before I left Atlanta.

"I've been traveling in Georgia," I said. "It sometimes makes me hard to find."

He asked why didn't I get a cab over to Encino, and we'd talk about it.

"God, yes," I said. "Where are you and where am I?"

"What?" he said.

But without waiting for me to decode, he gave me directions and a street number. "You're only about forty minutes away. How soon will you leave?"

"When I put the phone down."

"Terrific."

A favorite word in the greater Los Angeles area, *terrific* is, and as infectious as swine flu. I came back with a bad case of it in my own mouth. With good reason. I'd been locked up for a whole day in a Holiday Inn, calling and returning calls to PR men, trying in my innocent fashion to confirm an appointment that had been confirmed two weeks earlier. The PR man said "terrific" a lot, and inside of thirty minutes two of them said: "You're where?"

"Pasadena," I said.

"You know what *we* say out here when we're offered a bad deal, one we just can't stand to hear? We say Pasadena. *Pas-e-deen-aaa.*"

If all this sounds silly and absurd, it's only because it was. But I wanted to finish the job and get back home to my work, and I was driven a little crazy with it all by late afternoon. I would have gone anywhere to see anybody without anything just to get out of Pasadena.

The guy who wanted the option met me at the door. Through the window I could see his pool out back. Between me and the window was a lovely blond lady who said she'd read my book and was glad I could come by. I said I was glad she was glad. I did, I actually said: "I'm glad you're glad." Sometimes I get off one line after another like that in the presence of lovely blond ladies.

The moviemaker took me out back and showed me his guest-house, and then on back and showed me the tennis courts and on back to the stables, where horses ambled about at their leisure in a small pasture. Then he took me inside the house and offered to take a six-month option on my novel for less money than it would cost to shoe the horses in his pasture there in the middle of the city. I didn't say yes or no but just kept sucking on the beer the lovely blond lady had given me.

"What do you think?" he said.

I said: "It's hard to imagine anybody reading my book in Rome." That, of course, was no answer at all, but for the moment he acted as though it was.

"I called Vic after I talked to you this afternoon," the man said. "He's coming by. He'll tell you himself."

It's hard for me to imagine anybody anywhere reading a novel. I know more people writing novels than reading them. But apparently Vic Morrow had found the book, read it, and brought it here to Encino. Slouching, surly, mean-as-a-mad-dog Morrow. At least on the screen, which was the only way I knew him.

"I was in Rome and it was a screaming bummer," said Vic Morrow. "I picked up your book and took it back to the room. Saved my life."

"Jesus," I said. "Now you got me in your hip pocket forever."

I liked him the moment I saw him through the glass wall of the house. Slouching he was; surly he was not. He had a fine, ruined face that had obviously been around a lot of blocks. It was not

a face you'd want to get on the wrong side of. He was extraor-
dinarily well read, and he was able to talk about what he had read
without being either pompous or boring. A neat trick almost
nobody can work.

Some other guys had come in and an argument had started.
There was a great deal of shouting about "artistic control." They
were talking about the book on which they still did not have an
option, but I didn't listen much. At some point I went back to
make another drink. Coming out, I went by a room where the
blond lady was lying in a bed big enough to play soccer on. She
was reading *Helter Skelter*. I went in and sat on the far side of the
bed from her. She smiled at me and put the book down. Through
the wall I could hear them shouting about artistic control.

"This is a good place to read that," I said. "A lot of light and
friendly voices." She only smiled and didn't say anything. I was
bored to the point of tears and violence, but I didn't want her to
know that. I knew I should be back in Pasadena stroking PR men
over the telephone in the name of duty.

I nodded toward the shouting beyond the wall. "I don't think
they're going to be able to do business," I said.

"Oh, sure," she said brightly. "They always shout like that. It
doesn't mean a thing."

"Nothing?" I said.

"Nothing," she said.

I went back out into the room where the men were shouting.
They stopped momentarily when I came in, so I said: "Listen, if
Vic'll send a picture to my boy Byron—a picture with his name
on it—I'll just sign the thing the way it is with the terms from the
letter and we won't have to shout anymore. But he has got to send
his friggin picture or the deal is off."

Vic Morrow said: "Now you got me in your hip pocket."

Morrow had graciously offered to drive me back to Pasadena,
even though he lived in the opposite direction. And I had ac-
cepted his offer because I could think of nothing more devastat-
ing than a Holiday Inn room after a long ride in a taxi. We were
on the freeway but had somehow worked it so that we were lost.
Fortunately, neither of us seemed to care much. I was trying out

various handles and twenties and other things I know nothing about on his CB radio while he told me a story about a great and dear friend of his who is a black dwarf.

"You ever know a black dwarf?" he said.

"Yeah."

"Dwarf, not a midget," he said.

"Dwarf, not midget," I said.

"That's unusual," he said. "Anyway, my man is out on the Strip. It's the middle of the night and he's going home. A girl pulls to the curb in an enormous car and calls him over. 'You want to go to Vegas?' she says. 'Sure,' he says, and climbs in. Well, they go to Vegas, check in, get it on. Everything's great. My man goes to sleep. The next morning he wakes up and she's gone. And she's taken everything. *Everything.* His clothes are gone, wallet, even his shoes and socks. He's naked and alone in a Vegas hotel room. He sent out a one-word telegram: 'HELP.' Can you believe that?"

I'd quit fooling with the CB radio, taken as I was with his story, and particularly with the line *naked and alone in a Vegas hotel room.*

After a while I said, "Yeah, I believe that. I believe it all. I'm the world's champion believer."

The bartender said we must have gone right through Pasadena to get where we were, which was the next town over, called Arcadia, I think. I had switched to whiskey sours, explaining to Morrow that it had just occurred to me that I had not eaten in several days and when that happened I always switched from vodka to whiskey sours because the sugar and the orange slice and the cherry are great sources of energy.

By the time the bar closed I was as confused as a ten-dick dog, but it had nothing to do with the small grove of oranges and cherries I'd eaten my way through. I was turned around because of the story Vic Morrow had been telling me there in the bar, a long story of ultimate possibilities out of a screenplay he had written.

Inasmuch as it's Vic Morrow's story, I won't go into it here. Enough to say that it is bizarre, at times almost surreal but not surreal at all, and altogether human. There is an image that once it was told to me there in the bar, I could never get out of my head. The image is this: during orgasm a flower blooms out of a woman's mouth.

We went out into the night and into his car to find Pasadena while all manner of flowers bloomed out of all manner of mouths every time I blinked.

We got back on the freeway and found Pasadena, but we couldn't find the Holiday Inn. I was still looping inside Morrow's story and I didn't much care if I never found it.

"I want to walk," I said when we stopped for a light. "The thing's around here somewhere. I'll find it."

"You sure you want to walk?"

"I think so," I said. "I'll catch you later, before I go back. Take care."

I don't remember anything after that until I was turning into what I thought was a street. By the time I knew it was a dead-end alley I also knew there were two guys behind me. Before I had time to be afraid, I went down in a great explosion of flowers and mouths. I remember thinking how nice it was of them to take only the money and leave my wallet there on the pavement beside me.

I went under and played a bit part in Vic Morrow's movie. I came to saying: "Do it again. Do it again."

And the voice above me said: "Shit, no, I ain't hittin' him again. Some kind of pervert. He *likes* it."

I, of course, had been talking about the flower blooming again. I only wanted to see it come unfolding out of her mouth one more time.

The Trucker Militant

I wanted to talk to an independent trucker, and that was why I was sitting in the enormous truck stop not far from where I live, just off Interstate 10, which joins Jacksonville and Tallahassee, Florida. I'd been sitting for about two hours, watching the drivers come in for coffee and a cigarette, sometimes for eggs and a steak, watching them walk their slow, cramped walks from the big rigs to the place where they eased themselves carefully onto a stool in the section of the restaurant that was roped off and marked with a sign: "FOR TRUCKERS ONLY."

I knew the man I wanted when I saw him get down from a twin-stacked Peterbilt and head for the rest room before finally coming into the restaurant, limping a little, as though his slightly bowed legs hurt him. After he had himself settled and made his order with the waitress, I got up from where I was sitting with the tourists and walked over to where he was. I'd already eaten one breakfast, but I ordered another and sat picking at the eggs, waiting for him to get through three cups of coffee. I got him started talking by mentioning the way tourists drive once they get into Florida.

He glanced at me and said: "It's a sumbitch out there, all right." I thought maybe I'd picked the wrong man, that he was not going to be very talkative, but then he put down his fork and went into a long, easy monologue about drivers generally, about how he was probably as guilty as anybody else once he got out of his rig and into his car, which he didn't get to do very often because he was usually out somewhere pushing a load. "Hell, it ain't nothing but human nature."

195

We talked awhile about nothing, and then I said, nodding my head toward a rack of *Overdrive* magazines that stood beside the cash register: "That Mike Parkhurst."

I made my voice as neutral as I could, just dropping the statement into the middle of the talk.

He looked at the magazines and then back at me. "You independent?"

"About as much as you can get," I said. "Free-lance." I didn't want to tell him that I was a writer because most people know how sorry and unreliable writers are and usually refuse to talk with them. But he kept looking at me, so I said: "I'm a writer."

He nodded his head slowly. "Had a cousin was a rider. Rodeoed all over this country till he ruint his leg. Bull that done it. You ride mostly horses or mostly bull?"

"Mostly bull," I said. "I will git on a horse now and then, but I mostly do bull."

"We all got to do something," he said.

"But I hauled produce more'n a little out of Bean City, down by Okeechobee," I said, feeling good that I'd managed not to have to look the man in the eye and tell him an outright lie, and then feeling even better when he started talking about Parkhurst and his magazine.

"I got this month's *Overdrive* out on the seat right now. They broke the mold when they made Mike Parkhurst. He's done more for us drivers than we'll ever do for him." He chewed thoughtfully on a piece of bread. "Wonder somebody ain't already killed the sumbitch. Somebody still might."

Somebody might. But he'll take some killing, Mike Parkhurst will. You don't have to be with him long before you know he's a man who has spent his life covering his own ass and doing it well. His offices occupy the second floor of a small, unimpressive building in Hollywood, California. The morning I went to see him I was an hour late because somebody had boosted my tape recorder out of the room where I was staying in what was called a motel but was actually a whorehouse, and I was wet because it had been raining for two days in Los Angeles, where it never rains, and I'd had trouble getting a ride because the largest cab company in town was not operating. Everything was running with such a predictable rightness—at least predictable for my life—that I knew everything was going to be fine.

Still, it stopped a little when I walked in off the street and saw the stairs blocked by double-locked, electrified, iron-grille doors. A lady sat off to the left in a glassed-in booth. I told her Mr. Parkhurst was expecting me, and presently he came down the stairs, smiling, a big man in slacks and a tieless sport shirt that hung loosely over his belt.

We went up to his office, and I fumbled with the recorder I'd bought that morning from a company whose merchandise I've never trusted. While I tried to get the thing cranked up, I told him what had happened.

"You should've just come on and used one of mine," he said. "Why don't you let me get you one? You don't have to use that."

"Hell, I bought the thing," I said. "We might as well see if it works."

When I finally got the thing's little batteries humming, it served me better than I had any reason to expect. I'd heard that Parkhurst lived behind German shepherds and bodyguards, and since the iron doors downstairs were still on my mind, I asked him about it.

He shrugged. It was not something he was interested in talking about, but he did anyway. Without saying if he'd ever actually kept bodyguards, he said: "They get in the way. Besides, what good would it do? If they can kill the President, they can kill me. I can take care of what I need to take care of."

As he talked, I looked around his office, paneled in what looked like pecky cypress, with a reel-to-reel tape machine and a TV in the wall behind him. In front of his desk was a couch long enough for a very big man to sleep very comfortably on. Directly across from me was a high series of shelves of the sort you might find in somebody's den, filled with mementos and plaques of various sorts. He saw me looking at the shelves.

"That's what I call my violence center," he said, smiling.

"Violence?"

"Come over here."

The first thing that caught my eye when we got to the wall was a long shelf of books. He had Mailer's *Of a Fire on the Moon* and Dan Jenkins' *Semi-Tough, Body Language,* a book by Mencken and . . . and there on the glass shelf was a handful of .38 caliber slugs. I picked one of them up, half expecting to see a notched cross on its soft lead nose. When I raised my eyes, Parkhurst was unholstering a long-barreled .38 revolver, one of the truly mean-looking handguns of the world.

"How'd you come by that?" I asked.

"In 1962, as a joke, I rode a horse from California to Texas. Took about two months, and I carried this thing because I was camping out at night by the side of the road. It was to protest, among other things, the rip-off of unfair speed laws and to publicize the fact that we're living in the nineteenth century with twentieth-century thinking. It wasn't really to call attention to the magazine. I would, though, when I met a trucker somewhere, talk about *Overdrive,* explain that it was meant to be a national forum for the independent truckers and for the problems that they encounter."

The owner/operator is a trucker, in contradistinction to all those others who are simply truck drivers. The independent trucker owns the rig he's sitting in, and it usually represents not only his livelihood but his life.

It is probably impossible to overstate the difficulties that face an independent trucker, difficulties that come from big government, big unionism, big business, and, finally, difficulties that come from the fact that independent truckers have historically resisted national organizations, resisted national representatives of any kind. The very thing in his character that made him an independent trucker to start with made him determined to go it alone, made him resist banding together with his own kind for his own good.

But in 1962, Parkhurst got the independent truckers to do precisely what they had never done before—band together in a national organization big enough to carry political and economic clout. He was an independent trucker himself, and in 1961 he started the magazine *Overdrive* because he was tired of being jerked around by what he felt to be unfair laws regulating the trucking industry and even more tired of being jerked around by meaningless promises from Congress about the prospect of relief through legislation. The Independent Truckers Association grew directly out of the pages of *Overdrive,* the first issue of which was printed with the money Parkhurst got by selling his own eighteen-wheeler and the $300 he was able to borrow from Household Finance. From the beginning he has been the driving force behind not only the magazine but also the association. And it is an association, not a union, a distinction he is always quick to make.

"Some people called our shutdown in '74 a strike," Parkhurst said, speaking of the nationwide truckers' protest against high fuel prices and the fifty-five mph speed limit. "We can't strike because we're not a union. I've never used the word *strike.* I've been quoted as using it, but when that's happened, it was always a misquote."

"But," I said, "whether you call it a strike or a shutdown, you. . . ."

"It was a shutdown."

"But you were hardly a neutral observer, were you?"

For an answer he showed me a block of wood with four roofing nails attached to the top of it, points up. An engraved brass plaque on the side read: "GENERAL MIKE PARKHURST, OVERDRIVE ARMY, SHUTDOWN 1974, BATTLE OF BREEZEWOOD, BY PRIVATES BILL AND GRACE SCHEFFER."

"It's just a homemade thing that was given to me, but I'm kind of proud of it. Very handy for giving flat tires."

Next, he showed me a belt, the buckle of which could be released by a tiny catch, and when the buckle came away from the leather, it unsheathed a triangular dagger. "Survival knife," Parkhurst explained.

We stayed at the violence center a long time because there was a lot to look at, including a nickel-plated London Twist double-barreled shotgun. It had been the most prized possession of a trucker, but he'd given it to Parkhurst after the shutdown of 1974. The stock is engraved with the legend: "TO MIKE PARKHURST, THE ORIGINAL FREE MUSKETEER. FROM THE MIDDLETOWN TRUCKERS."

Overdrive and the people connected with it know something

about violence. A truck-stop owner had acid thrown on some of his merchandise for selling the magazine. It was displayed in an Ohio garage and the place was blown up. Gunmen shot up a place in Indiana and threatened to return unless the magazine rack was taken out.

For thirteen years Parkhurst employed a full-time investigative reporter, Jim Drinkhall, who knows more about the misuse of money in the teamsters' enormous (about $1.4 billion) Central States pension fund than anybody else in the country, and he claims he has never investigated a pension-fund loan that was a straight business deal and absolutely legitimate. Drinkhall has worked for the *Wall Street Journal* since February 1977 but still contributes to *Overdrive*.

Drinkhall was the one who caused a series of federal investigations in 1973 by writing that almost $1.5 million had not gone to a company in New Mexico but that part of it had appeared in Chicago in the hands of a wiretap expert with syndicate ties.

Is it any wonder that Parkhurst has about $25 million worth of libel suits pending against him at any given time? This only enhances the reputation of the man and his magazine, though, because he has never lost such a suit. But he has won his share, libel and otherwise. It makes it all the more strange that in the first sixteen years *Overdrive* has been published, not one trucking publication in the country has had a single word of praise for its accomplishments.

Parkhurst and I finally moved from the violence center back across the room to his desk.

"What kind of circulation do you have?" I asked.

"About sixty thousand. We started in September of '61, had to shut down for a couple of months, but we've been monthly since February of '63. The first issue cost ten cents, but we didn't collect any money on it. We told the truck stops to keep the money and send in their next order until we could prove there was a need for the magazine. They did, and it sold well. Before long we went to a quarter and then to fifty cents. Long before *Playboy* went to a dollar a copy, we were already there. Today the magazine sells for two-fifty, about forty thousand copies at truck stops and the rest by subscription."

Though *Overdrive* has prospered, Mike Parkhurst lives mod-
estly, even frugally, with his wife in a rented house. Whatever the
journal nets in revenue is put back into the Independent Truckers Association for legislating, lobbying, and other causes. From
all evidence, Parkhurst is that rarest of beings, an altruistic cru-
sader. Fully one-fourth of his twenty-four staff members make
more money than he does, and this seems to bother him not at
all.

Sometimes Parkhurst's methods cost him money. Every adver-
tiser is warned that his product will be tested by the staff and
criticized in the magazine if it is found defective. White Motor
Corporation pulled advertising because of *Overdrive*'s criticism of
one of its products. But Parkhurst doesn't mind enemies, not
even powerful enemies like Frank Fitzsimmons, president of the
International Brotherhood of Teamsters. Fitzsimmons followed
Parkhurst on NBC's *Tomorrow Show,* hosted by Tom Snyder, on
August 12, 1976. Parkhurst had claimed that a man named Glick
had borrowed $162 million from the pension fund; that Glick was
worth only a quarter of a million; that he was thirty-two years old;
that his past track record as an investor was a series of failures.

SNYDER: Did he get that money . . . a man named Glick . . . a
  hundred and sixty-two million? And if so, my question is why?
FITZSIMMONS: I don't think Mr. Glick borrowed one hundred and
  forty million dollars as far as the pension fund is concerned.
SNYDER: A hundred and sixty-two [million] was the figure Mr.
  Parkhurst used.
FITZSIMMONS: I think Mr. Parkhurst again is another frustrated
  individual which publishes a magazine and which could be
  another real investigation for people to find out . . . where
  Parkhurst gets his financing. His magazine shows that he keeps
  condemning the Teamsters all the time. The magazine itself
  definitely can't support itself. He has heavily advertisements
  from truck manufacturers [Parkhurst has one ad salesman], as
  well as large employers, union and nonunion, and also from
  truck stops. I've been told this—I don't know this for sure—
  that when he goes out and solicits an ad for his magazine, if
  things are not right, then the next issue carries the degree of

unpleasantness on the particular truck stop or individual [that] doesn't subscribe. I'm also told, and I can't say that I know this for a certainty . . . that Mr. Parkhurst's magazine is . . . has been financed by *Reader's Digest,* and he does maintain, as I've been told, an arrangement with the Ku Klux Klan, as well as the Communist party.

SNYDER: Who told you this?

FITZSIMMONS: Oh, I get this from a source.

SNYDER: Your own "Deep Throat"?

FITZSIMMONS: No, I've been told this, but I'm not going to divulge the source like the newspaper and the news media.

"Would you," I asked Parkhurst, "talk about the differences you have with the teamsters union, about practices, reforms?"

"That would take too long and tell you more than you really want to know. But if I could reform the teamsters union, I'd start by making it a multicandidate system, with the national president elected by popular vote. Right now it's a one-candidate system and the presidents of the local unions elect the national president. A popular vote is no good if only one guy is on the ballot."

I said: "Isn't the president of a local responsive to the members he represents?"

"It depends on the man. There are some good, honest, hardworking local presidents. But they are generally yes-men when it comes to national policy. All you have to do is remember that Fitzsimmons got elected last June in Vegas by unanimous acclamation. Can you imagine Jimmy Carter being elected unanimously?"

"What next?"

"I want competition, open and fair competition. I want unregulated trucking. The teamsters union doesn't. The teamsters support the stranglehold the ICC has on the trucking industry. The companies who have ICC licenses can do pretty much whatever they want to do, and what they want to do most is force the independent truckers to give them kickbacks, undeserved kickbacks for nothing, for no service whatsoever. *Overdrive* was started as a way to fight for a little justice for the independent trucker. The Independent Truckers Association was formed for just that reason, nothing more, nothing less.

"It is going to be an uphill fight all the way because Jimmy Carter was elected President," he said. "I was not a great Ford admirer, but for the independent truckers he was a lot better than Jimmy Carter will ever be. Carter is Mr. Railroad. His whole orientation toward the problem of transporting goods favors railroads. All the efforts that I made to try to get Jimmy Carter to come out and do something specific on behalf of the independent truckers he dodged. On the other hand, Ford endorsed just such legislation. When the Motor Carrier Reform Act was first laid on Ford's desk in late 1975, he asked those present in the room what the teamsters union thought about it. When he was told the teamsters opposed it, he said, 'It must be a pretty damn good bill, then,' But since Carter cares more about the railroads than he does about justice for the little man; he's not at all concerned that we're losing trucking companies at the rate of one every two and a half days. He doesn't care that they are being swallowed by bigger companies, with no end in sight."

I'd been watching him as much as listening to him. He had driven a truck for ten years before he became a publisher and editor, and those ten years had marked him forever. His gestures seemed calibrated to certain tolerances, and it was just the way he moved that made you know he was a trucker still. Never mind that he had sold his rig sixteen years before. It might as well have been parked down at the curb, the motor running, waiting for him to get through with me so he could head for the other side of the country. Truckers are different from you and me. And that difference shows in everything they do.

As a way of life, a trucker never wakes up many days in a row in the same room or on the same street or even in the same city. He looks out of his moving window in the morning at a mountain and that afternoon upon a desert. One night he could freeze a custard on his hood when he's running full bore; the next night he could cook a minute steak in the same place.

Sure, he may have a wife and children and a mortgage somewhere, complete with all the domestic trivia that every real man is supposed to carry on his back with such humiliating eagerness, but by God, when he fires up that diesel, he becomes a sudden and beautiful *wheel,* rolling beyond the reach of bill collectors and beyond even the sweet, necessary love of a good woman.

He is alone most of the time, and he likes it that way. He is, as much as anyone can ever be, a loner. His world reeks of it. He often spends hours on his CB radio, talking in a strange sort of nonlanguage to men with strange kinds of nonnames like Alabama Spitter or Squirrel Hair. Some of them are men he may have known for five, six, or ten years, sometimes longer. He may know how many children they have, where they're from, and how much they still owe on the rig they're pushing. He may know practically everything there is to know about them—except what they look like.

Almost everything about the trucker is special. The best bed and the best restaurant and the best barbershop and the best shower and the best whorehouse I was ever in were all in truck stops. Most of the truckers I knew back in the fifties were convinced J. Edgar had put his agents on long-distance rigs to stop the interstate traffic in whores. I don't know if he did nor not. Either way, it would not have surprised me. What could a man whose passion was small dogs and racehorses know of the loneliness of the long-distance truckers?

But I know. I know partly because I have gone to some conscious trouble to know and partly because my own life has caused me to have an almost blood-kin feeling for the trucker. Or at least a certain kind of trucker: the independent, over-the-road owner/operator. He is the sharecropper of today's highways.

But that was Parkhurst's word, *sharecropper* was. I'd never thought of it that way or used the word *sharecropper* in connection with trucking. When Parkhurst hit on the word, though, it seemed the only right and true word to describe the conditions under which independent truckers must operate. We'd been walking around the offices on the second floor of the little building and had stopped in front of a machine that was giving a printout of the money owed *Overdrive* by truck stops across the country for sales of the magazine. Parkhurst's eyes as he watched the type race off the machine were contained, bemused even, but his voice was the voice of outrage. "Forty-five years ago there were about two hundred thousand truck lines in the United States. Today there are maybe fifteen thousand lines that hold certificates of authority from the Interstate Commerce Commission. These are *regulated* lines, or so they are called. If an independent trucker wants to haul regulated goods—and that means just about anything—he is forced to give up to fifty percent of the gross revenue to a company that may not even own one truck. All the company may own is the ICC certificate, and that gives them the license to continue the system that makes the independent trucker a sharecropper. That's all he is today, a sharecropper."

"I'm not sure whether I follow all of that or not," I said, "but I sure as hell understand sharecropping."

"Nobody understands sharecropping," he said, "like an independent trucker."

"I understand sharecropping," I said, "as well as anything else in the world. But being a trucker is another thing. Suppose I bought a truck and intended to be independent, what is the first thing I would have to do?"

"First, if you intended to travel nationwide, you'd have to fill out one pound nine and three-quarter ounces of forms."

I could only stare.

"I weighed them once," he said, "and that's what they come to."

"Then what?" I said.

"Then you'd be in business, but you couldn't haul anything legally that has been processed in any way. About all that leaves you is produce. Apples, oranges, grapefruit, that kind of thing. If it's been processed, though—put in a can—you can't haul it. The only people who can haul anything that has been processed are people who have an ICC license, and you can't get an ICC license."

"Why can't I apply for one?" I asked.

"You can apply," he said, "apply all you want to. But it is just about impossible for anybody today to get the right to haul goods from the Interstate Commerce Commission."

"Doesn't that make some sort of monopoly?" I said.

"It's exactly what it makes. The fifteen thousand or so lines that have certificates of authority are quick to talk about free enterprise and competition. There's competition all right, but it's rotten to the core. That's why twenty-five percent of all produce haulers who were in business two years ago have disappeared completely."

"Get back to that truck I bought," I said. "I filled out the forms and I'm ready to go. I'm independent, own my own truck, no ICC license."

"Let's say that you decide, 'I don't want to lease my truck; I just want to haul produce.' Let's say you go down to get some potatoes. You start hauling them in April, when they start coming out of Florida, to Boise, Idaho. Now you're twenty-two hundred miles away from home. What do you get in Boise, Idaho? There aren't many things you can legally haul out of Boise, Idaho, and if you can't find a load of something like apples or potatoes, you can't go. Or you have to go empty—haul postholes. There might be an air-conditioning manufacturer in Boise who has a load of air conditioners going back to Florida. You can't haul them. Even though they want you to, even though they say, 'Harry, we want you to put these on your truck.' If they put those air conditioners on your truck and you agree to haul them for a thousand dollars, you're breaking the law. You have to lease your truck to a company that's not in the business of hauling anything. They just own the license. They'll say, 'We'll let you haul the air conditioners, but you have to give us thirty percent for the privilege of hauling them.' "

"I don't think many people know something like that goes on, and once they hear it, they won't believe it."

"We have letters in our files from multimillion-dollar companies who want to put their products on your truck and they're frustrated because they can't. It's the middleman, these trucking companies who are helping to keep the trucking industry locked up. Say it's canned peas you want to haul. Canned peas can literally last for years. As long as they don't freeze from California to New York, you can haul them in any kind of truck. You can haul them in a wheelbarrow. You're going to get thirty-seven hundred dollars to haul that from California to New York. But you, you got a good rig, a better truck, a refrigerated unit, inches of insulation, so you gotta go out in a strawberry field and load the most perishable goods there are and haul them back to New York in three days. For that, you're gonna get two thousand dollars. And Consolidated Freightways is going to get almost double that for hauling canned peas. Cause they have the license. So to get some of what they're getting, you've got to be a sharecropper, because you have to lease your truck to them. You know Mayflower, North American, all those big companies? Those tractors are owned by the guys who are driving them. Because they have to lease their tractors back to the companies and the companies in turn take thirty to fifty percent off the top."

In the restaurant where we'd been talking for almost an hour, the trucker sopped up the last of his breakfast with a piece of bread and stood up.

"What you hauling?" I asked.

He looked at me and for the first time his face went sour. "Air," he said. "I've drove all the way back from Texas cause I couldn't git a load. But I'd die and go to hell before I'd lease my rig to one of them thiefs."

"You may have to die and go to hell then, the way things are," I said.

"Might," he said. Then his face went light with a mean and beautiful smile. "Some others might have to go with me, though."

I sat watching him walk out to his rig, and thought that he was probably right. Sharecropping can make a good man dangerous.

Climbing the Tower

I was on the University of Texas campus in Austin, back in the state where I had sworn never to go again—having flown from Gainesville, Florida, to Atlanta, to Dallas, to Austin—and I was shaking and scared, feeling very tenuous, as though I had somehow become a shapeless floating fog without substance or identity.

There are some days when I feel my own mortality stick in my throat, when I can't swallow it or spit it up. The feeling first started when I was a child, and it always came on Sunday. An evangelist named Harvey Springer saved my soul when I was twelve years old, but before he saved me, he made me smell the sulfur and feel the brimstone of hellfire and know for sure that I was corrupted beyond even the mercy of God. So on Sunday I would feel my mortality—though at that time I did not know the word—plugging my throat like a lump of half-cooked dough filled with finely ground bits of razor blade.

We all, of course, know we are going to die, but none of us, of course, *believes* he is going to die. Like having a deformed child, it is something that always happens to somebody else. But on the ride in the taxicab from the airport to the University of Texas campus, I not only believed in my death, I could also smell the open grave I would someday be lowered into and could even read the little name cards attached to the funeral wreaths sent by friends and relatives. I took a newspaper clipping out of my pocket for perhaps the tenth time in the last two hours and read that in Capetown, South Africa, my last novel had been banned by the Directorate of Publications. Anyone who owned or imported or distributed *A Feast of Snakes* was, the newspaper clipping said, "in violation of the law and subject to heavy penalties." I read it again because it made me feel more substantial to know that somewhere in Africa somebody had actually read my work and reacted to it so violently that he listed me among those the government looked upon with disfavor.

But even that did not help enough, so when I got out of the taxi, before I went over to the office of the man who invited me to the university, I rushed to the library and looked myself up in the card catalogue. And yes, there I was. I left the university library still feeling diaphanous, still feeling the morning terrors and black twirlies, a burden I carry better at some times than at others. I was softly mumbling to myself as I went into the office of the professor who'd invited me to the university to play writer. God only knows why writers do such things, go hundreds, sometimes thousands, of miles to read out of their work the very things that the people in the audience could read just as easily for themselves. If I let myself think about it too much, that alone is enough to give me a bad case of the black twirlies.

The professor greeted me cordially. We left his office immediately because before I gave the reading that night, I was supposed to have a seminar, if you can believe it, in Southern fiction. I was a little late and we had to step lively going across the campus. As we were walking down a long, gentle, sloping hill, the professor turned to me and said casually: "It was right back there where he started shooting."

I looked over my shoulder, and there it was behind me, the Texas Tower, where one Monday morning in 1966 Charles Whitman had shot dead twelve people and wounded at least thirty-three others, after having killed his mother and wife the night before. That mindless slaughter was suddenly alive and real for me, as though it were happening again, and it was all I could do to keep from running for cover. I wanted to tell the professor that I didn't want to hear about it, that I couldn't hear it, but I didn't know how to tell him without sounding a little nuts.

As we walked, he spoke casually, glancing now and again over his shoulder at the tower. "When they first started dropping," he said, "they couldn't tell where the fire was coming from. They started dropping here." He pointed at his feet. "And then they started dropping over in the street and then on the other side."

By now I was concentrated, screwed down about as tight as I ever get, but I managed to continue walking and not to do anything unseemly.

"They've closed off the tower now," he said. "Students started committing suicide off the top of it—jumping."

I tried not to listen. I tried to think of the newspaper clipping and the anonymous whatever in South Africa who had banned my book and tried to remember the little square cards neatly on iron cylinders in the card catalogue.

"But it didn't do a lot of good," he said. He pointed off to the left toward a high stadium wall. "They've started jumping off the stadium now. It does just as well."

In the classroom I rambled on about various novelists and short story writers from the South and elsewhere, saying that I didn't know any storytellers who wanted an adjective— Southern or gothic or ethnic—in front of the word *novelist.* I told them that I was a novelist from the South and that I had no alternative but to write out of the manners of my people. A student raised her hand and asked the question that writers learn to invent convenient lies about: "Mr. Crews, where do you get your ideas?" I began my standard reply, which, of course, is a lie that I won't repeat here. But as I spoke, I saw quite clearly the teenage Charles Whitman, dressed in his eagle scout uniform, standing in the Catholic church where he served the priest as altar boy. And from the other side of the room I saw the same Whitman, now twenty-five years old, with a Marine Corps footlocker full of weapons: a 6-millimeter Remington Magnum rifle with a four-power scope, a .35 caliber Remington pump rifle, a .30 caliber reconditioned Army carbine, a 12-gauge sawed-off shotgun, a 357 Magnum pistol, and a 9-millimeter Luger. It was Monday morning, August 1, 1966, and he was pulling the footlocker across the administration office on his way to the top of the tower where he would become one of the biggest mass murderers in the history of this country. The night before, on Sunday, sometime between

10 P.M. and daylight, he had killed his mother and his wife.

I saw Charles Whitman as a little boy and later at the age of twenty-five after the killings; I saw him there in the seminar room and knew that I was not remembering something or conjuring something, but that I actually saw him. At the same time I knew that he was not there, that he was safely and securely buried in the ground that waits for all of us. I did not feel any contradiction in what I saw and knew. The two mutually exclusive perceptions rested comfortably side by side in my head.

Late that night, when the party was over, the obligatory party at which I obliged my hosts by getting very drunk, I went alone back out to the Texas Tower. I sat in the grass and looked up at it, 307 feet high, and all manner of things ran through my mind. One of the first was Goethe's statement "There is no crime of which I cannot conceive myself guilty." And I thought about the fact that Charles Whitman had told the university psychiatrist that there were days, many days, when he wanted to climb the tower with a deer rifle and start shooting people. How long must he have resisted the temptation? What battles must he have fought in himself before he finally lost it all forever? It excuses nothing and resolves nothing, and this is no defense for him. But sitting there in the grass, I could imagine myself on the perch high above the campus where the streets looked like diagrams laid out for a housing development; I could imagine myself perched there with my Marine Corps footlocker full of death.

As sentimental, romantic, and grotesquely obscene as it may sound, we all know that there are people throughout the world resisting with all their might and will climbing the tower, because once the tower is climbed there is no turning back, no way out of it, no way down except death. It is probably a good thing that the University of Texas officials had closed off the tower because I know that I would have tried to find access to the building, as late as it was, climbed to that perch almost at the top where Whitman calmly and with incredible accuracy shot mothers and husbands and children, shot them dead because it was in him to do it, because his life and everything that made it had taken him there.

Sometime toward morning I got up from where I was sitting

in the grass and walked back to my room. When I got back to the room, I dived to the bottom of a vodka bottle and didn't come up.

As it turned out, the vodka didn't help very much because that night I dreamed the circumstances of what I had known and been morbidly fascinated with for years. I'm not proud of saying that I am morbidly fascinated with such a thing, but again, it is only the truth. That night I dreamed of how, less than three weeks before Charles Whitman climbed the tower, Richard Speck had systematically slaughtered student nurses in their Chicago residence, taking them one by one apart from the others and killing them.

When I awoke, I knew that this day was to be worse than the day that preceded it and that I could not hope to get down from where I was until I was safely home with my books and my type-writer and all the crippled and ruined manuscripts lying about on the desk. I wanted to get back to the place where I had resisted so many things, and failed at so many things, back to the place where even when I succeeded I failed because it was never good enough.

Graham Greene said: "The artist is doomed to live in an atmo-sphere of perpetual failure." I am very nervous about the word *artist,* not as I have used it, but the way it has been used by so many people who have no right to bring the word into their mouths in the first place. But I know what it means to live in an atmosphere of perpetual failure. I would not presume to think this makes me in any way unique. All of us whose senses are not entirely dead realize the imperfection of what we do, and to the extent that we are hard on ourselves, that imperfection translates itself into failure. Inevitably, it is out of a base of failure that we try to rise again to do another thing.

Finally, with myself more or less intact, I was able to leave Austin and make my way back to Gainesville, Florida. But going home was soured by the realization that I had to go again through Dallas, Texas, that city of doom. I seem to be unable to go into Dallas without getting into some sort of trouble, without having some hostile hand put upon me and some hostile voice accuse me of something which I never have the courage to deny. In that city

I always want to throw up my hands and say: "Whatever the charge, I plead guilty." In Dallas, Texas, I *am* guilty.

I did not leave Charles Whitman in Austin. I will never leave him. The autopsy, after he was slaughtered by an off-duty policeman by the name of Martinez, showed that he had a tumor the size of a pecan growing in his brain stem near the thalamus. It was surmised by various psychiatrists that the tumor could possibly have caused Charles Whitman to climb the tower. Although almost all modification of behavior is associated with the frontal lobe of the brain, it is obvious that since it is housed fairly tightly in a bony box, pressure in the brain stem might translate itself through the brain to the frontal lobe. So, conceivably, it could have caused what happened that Monday morning in 1966. How comforting to think that it might be so. But I do not believe that what happened at the University of Texas at Austin was caused by a tumor.

What I know is that all over the surface of the earth where humankind exists men and women are resisting climbing the tower. All of us have our towers to climb. Some are worse than others, but to deny that you have your tower to climb and that you must resist it or succumb to the temptation to do it, to deny that is done at the peril of your heart and mind.

All the way home to Gainesville, I felt that same tenuous diaphanous quality in the way I walked and what I did and what I said. Someone at that moment was climbing his tower, and I could only hope that he would not look down on me. But worse, much worse, I hoped that I would be spared being on the tower myself, because if I believe anything, I believe that the tower is waiting out there. I have no answers as to why it is out there, or even speculations about it, but out there somewhere, around some corner, or in some green meadow, or in some busy street it is. Waiting.